IMMORTALS: THE RECKONING

"The eighth and final book in this sexy paranormal series, *Immortals: The Reckoning*, joins all three multi-talented authors Jennifer Ashley, Joy Nash and Robin T. Popp for three riveting stories of super hot heroes and heroines."

—A Romance Review

IMMORTALS: THE REDEEMING

"Tain's story is powerful, sensual and extremely exciting. The magical paranormal world created with the Immortal series is phenomenal. Absolutely fabulous!"

—Fresh Fiction

IMMORTALS: THE GATHERING

"With excellent style and passion, she gathers the plot threads and weaves them into a spellbinding climax."

—RT Book Reviews

IMMORTALS: THE CALLING

"Deftly mixing dangerous adventure, dark magic, and a surfeit of scorching chemistry between her hero and heroine, Ashley creates an addictively readable romance, the first in a marvelously original new paranormal series that is bound to cast its own bewitching spell over readers."

—*Booklist*

JENNIFER ASHLEY

PRIDE MATES

LEISURE BOOKS NEW YORK CITY

A LEISURE BOOK®

February 2010

Published by

Dorchester Publishing Co., Inc.
200 Madison Avenue
New York, NY 10016

ISBN 10: 0-8439-6005-1
ISBN 13: 978-0-8439-6005-1
E-ISBN: 978-1-4285-0803-3

Visit us online at www.dorchesterpub.com.

ACKNOWLEDGMENTS

Special thanks go to Theresa A. and Kerrie D., two defense attorneys extraordinaire who answered my many questions in minute detail. They helped me understand how a defense attorney spends her days and what kinds of challenges a female in the field might experience. I am extremely grateful to them for their time and knowledge; any errors in the book are mine. Also many thanks to my editor, Leah, who once again didn't flinch when I presented her with my idea for a brand-new world. Working with her is always the greatest pleasure.

PRIDE MATES

Chapter One

A girl walks into a bar . . .

No. A human girl walks into a Shifter bar . . .

The bar was empty, not yet open to customers. It looked normal—windowless walls painted black, rows of glass bottles, the smell of beer and stale air. But it wasn't normal, standing on the edge of Shiftertown as it did.

"You the lawyer?" a man washing glasses asked. He was human, not Shifter. No strange, slitted pupils, no Collar to control his aggression, no air of menace. Well, relatively no air of menace. This was a crappy part of town, and menace was its stock-in-trade.

Kim told herself she had nothing to be afraid of. *They're tamed. Collared. They can't hurt you.*

When she nodded, the man gestured with his cloth to a door at the end of the bar. "Knock him dead, sweetheart."

"I'll try to keep him alive." Kim pivoted and stalked away on her four-inch heels, feeling his gaze on her back all the way.

She knocked on the door marked "Private," and a man on the other side growled, "Come."

I just need to talk to him. Then I'm done, on my way home. A trickle of moisture rolled between Kim's shoulder blades as she made herself open the door and walk inside.

A man leaned back in a chair behind a messy desk, a sheaf of papers in his hands. His booted feet were propped on the desk, his long legs a feast of blue jeans over muscle. He was a Shifter all right—thin black and silver Collar against his throat; hard, honed body; midnight black hair; definite air of menace. When Kim entered, he stood, setting the papers aside.

Damn. He rose to a height of well over six feet and gazed at Kim with eyes blue like the morning sky. His body wasn't only honed; it was hot—big chest, wide shoulders, tight abs, firm biceps against a form-fitting black T-shirt.

"Kim Fraser?"

"That's me."

With old-fashioned courtesy, he placed a chair in front of the desk and motioned her to it. Kim felt the heat of his hand near the small of her back as she seated herself, smelled the scent of soap and male musk.

"You're Mr. Morrissey?"

The Shifter sat back down, returned his motorcycle boots to the top of the desk, and laced his hands behind his head. "Call me Liam."

The lilt in his voice was unmistakable. Kim put that with his black hair, impossibly blue eyes, and exotic name. "You're Irish."

He smiled a smile that could melt a woman at ten paces. "And who else would be running a pub?"

"But you don't own it."

Kim could have bitten out her tongue as soon as she said it. Of course he didn't own it. He was a Shifter.

His voice went frosty, the crinkles at the corners of his eyes smoothing out. "I'm afraid I can't help you much on the Brian Smith case. I don't know Brian well, and I don't know anything about what happened the night his girlfriend was murdered. It's a long time ago, now."

Disappointment bit her, but Kim had learned not to

let discouragement stop her when she needed to get a job done. "Brian called you the 'go-to' guy. As in, when Shifters are in trouble, Liam Morrissey helps them out."

Liam shrugged, muscles moving the bar's logo on his T-shirt. "True. But Brian never came to me. He got into his troubles all by himself."

"I know that. I'm trying to get him *out* of trouble."

Liam's eyes narrowed, pupils flicking to slits as he retreated to the predator within him. Shifters liked to do that when assessing a situation, Brian had told her. Guess who was the prey?

Brian had done the predator-prey thing with Kim at first. He'd stopped when he began to trust her, but Kim didn't think she'd ever get used to it. Brian was her first Shifter client, the first Shifter, in fact, she'd ever seen outside a television news story. Twenty years Shifters had been acknowledged to exist, but Kim had never met one.

It was well known that they lived in their enclave on the east side of Austin, near the old airport, but she'd never gone over to check them out. Some human women did, strolling the streets just outside Shiftertown, hoping for glimpses—and more—of the Shifter men who were reputed to be strong, gorgeous, and well endowed. Kim had once heard two women in a restaurant murmuring about their encounter with a Shifter male the night before. The phrase "Oh, my God," had been used repeatedly. Kim was as curious about them as anyone else, but she'd never summoned the courage to go near Shiftertown herself.

Then suddenly she had been assigned the case of the Shifter accused of murdering his human girlfriend ten months ago. This was the first time in twenty years

Shifters had caused trouble, the first time one had been put on trial. The public, outraged by the killing, wanted Shifters punished, pointed fingers at those who'd claimed the Shifters were tamed.

However, after Kim had met Brian, she'd determined that she wouldn't do a token defense. She believed in his innocence, and she wanted to win. There wasn't much case law on Shifters because there'd never been any trials, at least none on record. This was to be a well-publicized trial, Kim's opportunity to make a mark, to set precedent.

Liam's eyes stayed on her, pupils still slitted. "You're a brave one, aren't you? To defend a Shifter?"

"Brave, that's me." Kim crossed her legs, pretending to relax. They picked up on your nervousness, people said. *They know when you're scared, and they use your fear.* "I don't mind telling you, this case has been a pain in the ass from the get-go."

"Humans think anything involving Shifters is a pain in the ass."

Kim shook her head. "I mean, it's been a pain in the ass because of the way it's been handled. The cops nearly had Brian signing a confession before I could get to the interrogation. At least I put a stop to that, but I couldn't get bail for him, and I've been blocked by the prosecutors right and left every time I want to review the evidence. Talking to you is a long shot, but I'm getting desperate. So if you don't want to see a Shifter go down for this crime, Mr. Morrissey, a little cooperation would be appreciated."

The way he pinned her with his eyes, never blinking, made her want to fold in on herself. Or run. That was what prey did—ran. And then predators chased them, cornered them.

What did this man do when he cornered his prey? He wore the Collar; he could do nothing. Right?

Kim imagined herself against a wall, his hands on either side of her, his hard body hemming her in . . . Heat curled down her spine.

Liam took his feet down and leaned forward, arms on the desk. "I haven't said I won't help you, lass." His gaze flicked to her blouse, whose buttons had slipped out of their top holes during her journey through Austin traffic and July heat. "Is Brian happy with you defending him? You like Shifters that much?"

Kim resisted reaching for the buttons. She could almost feel his fingers on them, undoing each one, and her heart beat faster.

"It's nothing to do with who I like. I was assigned to him, but I happen to think Brian's innocent. He shouldn't go down for something he didn't do." Kim liked her anger, because it covered up how edgy this man made her. "Besides, Brian's the only Shifter I've ever met, so I don't know whether I like them, do I?"

Liam smiled again. His eyes returned to normal, and now he looked like any other gorgeous, hard-bodied, blue-eyed Irishman. "You, love, are—"

"Feisty. Yeah, I've heard that one. Also spitfire, little go-getter, and a host of other condescending terms. But let me tell you, Mr. Morrissey, I'm a damn good lawyer. Brian's not guilty, and I'm going to save his ass."

"I was going to say *unusual*. For a human."

"Because I'm willing to believe he's innocent?"

"Because you came here, to the outskirts of Shiftertown, to see me. Alone."

The predator was back.

Why was it that when Brian looked at her like this, it didn't worry her? Brian was in jail, angry, accused of heinous crimes. A killer, according to the police. But Brian's stare didn't send shivers down her spine like Liam Morrissey's did.

"Any reason I shouldn't have come alone?" she asked, keeping her voice light. "I'm trying to prove that Shifters in general, and my client in particular, can't harm humans. I'd do a poor job of it if I was afraid to come and talk to his friends."

Liam wanted to laugh at the little—spitfire—but he kept his stare cool. She had no idea what she was walking into; Fergus, the clan leader, expected Liam to make sure it stayed that way.

Damn it all, Liam wasn't supposed to *like* her. He'd expected the usual human woman, sticks-up-their-asses, all of them, but there was something different about Kim Fraser. It wasn't just that she was small and compact, while Shifter women were tall and willowy. He liked the way her dark blue eyes regarded him without fear, liked the riot of black curls that beckoned his fingers. She'd had the sense to leave her hair alone, not force it into some unnatural shape.

On the other hand, she tried to hide her sweetly curvaceous body under a stiff gray business suit, although her body had other ideas. Her breasts wanted to burst out of the button-up blouse, and the stiletto heels only enhanced wickedly sexy legs.

No Shifter woman would dress as she did. Shifter women wore loose clothes they could quickly shed if they needed to change forms. Shorts and T-shirts were popular. So were gypsy skirts and sarongs in the summer.

Liam imagined this lady in a sarong. Her melon-firm breasts would fill out the top, and the skirt would bare her smooth thighs.

She'd be even prettier in a bikini, lolling around some

rich man's pool, sipping a complicated drink. She was a lawyer—there was probably a boss in her firm who had already made her his. Or perhaps she was using said boss to climb the success ladder. Humans did that all the time. Either the bastard would break her heart, or she'd walk away happy with what she'd got out of it.

That's why we stay the hell away from humans. Brian Smith had taken up with a human woman, and look where he was now.

So why did this female raise Liam's protective instincts? Why did she make him want to move closer, inside the radius of her body heat? She wouldn't like that; humans tried to stay a few feet apart from each other unless they couldn't help it. Even lovers might do nothing more than hold hands in public.

Liam had no business thinking about passion and this woman in the same heartbeat. Fergus's instructions had been to listen to Kim, sway her, then send her home. Not that Liam was in the habit of blindly obeying Fergus.

"So why do you want to help him, love?" he asked. "You're only defending him because you drew the short straw, am I right?"

"I'm the junior in the firm, so it was handed to me, yes. But the prosecutor's office and the police have done a shitty job with this case. Rights violations all over the place, but the courts won't dismiss it, no matter how much I argue. Everyone wants a Shifter to go down, innocent or guilty."

"And why do you believe Brian didn't do it?"

"Why do you think?" Kim tapped her throat. "Because of these."

Liam resisted touching the strand of black and silver metal fused to his own neck, a small Celtic knot at the base of his throat. The Collars contained tiny programmed chips enhanced by powerful Fae magic to keep Shifters in check, though the humans didn't want to acknowledge the magic part. The Collar shot an electric charge into a Shifter when his violent tendencies rose to the surface. If the Shifter persisted, the next dose was one of debilitating pain. A Shifter couldn't attack anyone if he was rolling around on the ground, writhing in agony.

Liam wasn't sure entirely how the Collars worked; he only knew that each became bonded to its wearer's skin and adapted to their animal form when they shifted. All Shifters living in human communities were required to wear Collars, which were irremovable once put on. Refusing the Collar meant execution. If the Shifter tried to escape, he or she was hunted down and killed.

"You know Brian couldn't have committed a violent crime," Kim was saying. "His Collar would have stopped him."

"Let me guess. Your police claim the Collar malfunctioned?"

"Yep. When I suggest having it tested, I'm greeted with all kinds of reasons it can't be. The Collar can't be removed, and anyway it would be too dangerous to have Brian Collarless if he could be. Also too dangerous to provoke him to violence and see if the Collar stops him. Brian's been calm since he was brought in. Like he's given up." She looked glum. "I hate to see someone give up like that."

"You like the underdog?"

She grinned at him with red lips. "You could say that, Mr. Morrissey. Me and the underdog go back a long way."

Liam liked her mouth. He liked imagining it on his body, on certain parts of his anatomy in particular. He had no business thinking that, but the thoughts triggered a physical reaction below the belt.

Weird. He'd never even considered having sex with a human before. He didn't find human women attractive; Liam preferred to be in his big cat form for sex. He found sex that way much more satisfying. With Kim, he'd have to remain human.

His gaze strayed to her unbuttoned collar. Of course, it might not be so bad to be human with her . . .

What the hell am I thinking? Fergus's instructions had been clear, and Liam agreeing to them had been the only way Fergus had allowed Kim to come to Shiftertown at all. Fergus wasn't keen on a human woman being in charge of Brian's case, not that they had any choice. Fergus had been pissed about Brian's arrest from the beginning and thought the Shifters should back off and stay out of it. Almost as though he believed Brian was guilty.

But Fergus lived down on the other side of San Antonio, and what he didn't know wouldn't hurt him. Liam would handle this his own way.

"So what do you expect from me, love?" he asked Kim. "Want to test *my* Collar?"

"No, I want to know more about Brian, about Shifters and the Shifter community. Who Brian's people are, how he grew up, what it's like to live in a Shifter enclave." She smiled again. "Finding six independent witnesses who swear he was nowhere near the victim at the time in question wouldn't hurt either."

"Oh, is that all? Bloody miracles is what you want, darling."

She wrapped a dark curl around her finger. "Brian said that you're the Shifter people talk to most. Shifters and humans alike."

It was true that Shifters came to Liam with their troubles. His father, Dylan Morrissey, was master of this Shiftertown, second in power in the whole clan.

Humans knew little about the careful hierarchy of

the Shifter clans and prides—packs for Lupines—and still less about how informally but efficiently everything got done. Dylan was the Morrissey pride leader and the leader of this Shiftertown, and Fergus was the clan leader for the Felines of South Texas, but Shifters with a problem sought out Liam or his brother Sean for a chat. They'd meet in the bar or at the coffee shop around the corner. *So, Liam, can you ask your father to look into it for me?*

No one would petition Dylan or Fergus directly. That wasn't done. But chatting about things to Liam over coffee, that was fine and didn't draw attention to the fact that the person in question had troubles.

Everyone would know anyway, of course. Life in a Shiftertown reminded Liam very much of life in the Irish village he'd lived near until they'd come to Texas twenty years ago. Everyone knew everything about everyone, and news traveled, lightning-swift, from one side of the village to the other.

"Brian never came to me," he said. "I never knew anything about this human girl until suddenly the police swoop in here and arrest him. His mother struggled out of bed to watch her son be dragged away. She didn't even know why for days."

Kim watched Liam's blue eyes harden. The Shifters were angry about Brian's arrest, that was certain. Citizens of Austin had tensely waited for the Shifters to make trouble after the arrest, to break free and try to retaliate with violence, but Shiftertown remained quiet. Kim wondered why, but she wasn't about to ask right now and risk angering the one person who might help her.

"Exactly my point," she said. "This case has been handled badly from start to finish. If you help me, I can spring Brian and make a point at the same time. You don't mess with people's rights, not even Shifters'."

Liam's eyes grew harder, if that were possible. It was like looking at living sapphire. "I don't give a damn about making a point. I give a damn about Brian's family."

All right, so she'd miscalculated about what would motivate him. "In that case, Brian's family will be happier with him outside prison, not inside."

"He won't go to prison, love. He'll be executed, and you know it. No waiting twenty years on death row, either. They'll kill him, and they'll kill him fast."

That was true. The prosecutor, the county sheriff, the attorney general, and even the governor wanted an example made of Brian. There hadn't been a Shifter attack in twenty years, and the Texas government wanted to assure the world that they weren't going to allow one now.

"So are you going to help me save him?" Kim asked. If he wanted to be direct and to the point, fine. So could she. "Or let him die?"

Anger flickered through Liam's eyes again, then sorrow and frustration. Shifters were emotional people from what she'd seen in Brian, not bothering to hide what they felt. Brian had lashed out at Kim many times before he'd grudgingly acknowledged that she was on his side.

If Liam decided to stonewall her, Brian had said, Kim had no hope of getting cooperation from the other Shifters. Even Brian's own mother would take her cue from Liam.

Liam had the look of a man who didn't take shit from anyone. A man used to giving the orders himself, but so far he hadn't seemed brutal. He could make his voice soft and lilting, reassuring, friendly. He was a defender, she guessed. A protector of his people.

Was he deciding whether to protect Brian or turn his back?

Liam's gaze flicked past her to the door, every line of his body coming alert. Kim's nerves made her jump. "What is it?"

Liam got out of his chair and started around the desk at the same time the door scraped open and another man—another Shifter—walked in.

Liam's expression changed. "Sean." He clasped the other Shifter's arms and pulled him into a hug.

More than a hug. Kim watched, open-mouthed, as Liam wrapped his arms around the other man, gathered him close, and nuzzled his cheek.

Chapter Two

Kim made herself close her gaping mouth and turn away. None of her business if Liam Morrissey was gay. Seriously disappointing, but none of her business.

The second man held Liam in a tight hug, then with a thump of fists on backs, they released each other. Liam smiled—man, how gorgeous was he when he smiled? He had his arm around the second man's shoulders.

"Sean, this is Kim," Liam said. "She wants me to help her with Brian."

Sean had dark hair and blue eyes like Liam, and a body as honed, but his face was harder, his look sterner. He had a stillness in him that wasn't in Liam, as though something had happened to him that he'd never quite gotten over.

"Does she now?" Sean was saying. "And what did you tell her?"

"I was about to explain when you barged in without warning me. What if I'd thought you were a Lupine? I'd have taken your head off."

"Your sense of smell's that bad, Liam, that you'd mistake your own brother for a wolfman?"

"He's your brother?" Kim asked in a shaky voice.

"My brother, Sean Morrissey."

Kim's face heated. "Oh."

Liam still had his arm firmly around the other man. "Why? Who'd you think he was?"

Kim tried to control her embarrassment. "I thought you were a couple."

Liam burst out laughing, a warm sound. Sean smiled slightly. "Are all humans this crazy?" he asked Liam.

"They're all that ignorant," Liam said. "I've decided to let her talk to Brian's mum."

Sean's smile faded, and he and Liam exchanged a look that held caution, warning. Because they didn't trust humans? Or something more?

Both men focused on Kim again. No one could look at someone like a Shifter. They saw everything, missed nothing. She found that having two equally good-looking men give her the once-over wasn't bad, even if they were Shifters, potentially dangerous and potentially deadly.

"Sounds good," she made herself say. "Here's my card. Call me when you've set something up with her."

"I meant I'd take you around now," Liam said. "No time like the present."

"Right now? Without warning? Not always a good idea."

"She'll know we're coming."

Kim shrugged, pretending to share their nonchalance. Her years as a lawyer had made her anal—make appointments, keep detailed records, cover your ass on everything. Their casualness unnerved her.

And yet she sensed these men weren't relaxed at all. Liam and Sean shared another look, an unspoken warning, as if they were communicating something she couldn't hear.

But whatever. Kim had a job to do, and Brian had said that getting Liam's help was key.

She walked out the door Liam held open, her head up, trying not to melt when she passed between the two men's extraordinary heat.

* * *

They walked to Brian's house. Kim had been preparing to share the close space of her car with two Shifters, but found herself walking slightly behind Liam, with Sean behind her.

The house wasn't far. A couple of blocks, that was all, Liam assured her. *He* wasn't the one in the four-inch heels, she wanted to growl. Kim's shiny black pumps were great for office meetings, bad for hiking.

It wasn't a hardship following Liam, though. The man had a fine ass cupped by snug jeans, and he walked easily in the heat. No wonder people came to Liam with their problems—he looked like a man who'd invite you to rest your head on his shoulder while he made everything bad go away. His brother had the same height and build, the same strength, the same blue eyes, but Kim would gravitate to Liam if she had to choose. Sean had a wariness, a pulling back that she didn't sense in Liam.

The first block had a convenience store with a littered parking lot on one corner; another bar, closed, on the opposite end; and a boarded-up store and two bungalows left over from better times crammed in the middle. No one but the three of them walked here, and any street traffic sped through to newer and more prosperous parts of town.

Liam led Kim around the corner behind the derelict buildings. They passed through a wide-open gate in a chain-link fence and crossed a field. Kim winced and watched where she stepped, knowing her legs and feet would be open season for Texas chiggers.

When they reached the other end of the field, Kim stopped so quickly that Sean almost ran into her.

"*This* is Shiftertown?"

Liam grinned. "Not what you expected, eh, love?"

Kim had thought Shiftertown would be a slum, a ghetto of people not wanted in other parts of town. The houses were small and old, yes. The street itself was cracked and potholed because the city deemed repairs there a low priority. But Kim looked down the street at what appeared to be a beautiful and comfortable suburb. Every yard was green, with gardens or flower boxes running riot with summer flowers. The buildings were painted and in good repair, and most houses had deep porches filled with plants and furniture.

There were no fences anywhere. Kids played in yards and ran between houses without fear. One front yard sported a plastic wading pool filled with kids and a couple of dogs, while two moms watched from the porch steps. They were young women, casual in shorts and baggy T-shirts, legs stretched to the sun while the kids played. Everyone in the yard and on the porch, including the dogs, wore collars.

One of the women looked up and waved. "Good day to you, Liam," she called. "Hello, Sean." The other woman raised her hand in greeting but didn't speak. Kim felt the gazes of both Shifter women on her dark gray suit and stupidly high heels.

Liam and Sean gave them a casual wave back. The kids jumped up and down, and one sent a big splash of water over the edge of the pool.

"Look, Liam, I've got my own swimming pool."

"It's grand, Michael. You look after your brother now."

Michael turned to the littlest child in the pool, who was splashing happily. "I will," the older boy said seriously.

They moved on. The Shifters didn't hide in their houses, the way residents did in Kim's neighborhood.

They roamed outside in the hot weather, working in the yard, looking after kids, talking to their neighbors. Everyone they passed waved or smiled at Liam and Sean, some greeting them, "Now then, Liam. How's your dad?"

By the time they reached the end of the block, Kim understood how Brian's mother would know they were on their way without Liam calling ahead. Every Shifter they passed noted Liam and Sean, every Shifter recognized Kim for the human stranger she was. Someone would be on the phone or running through the back-yards to alert Brian's mother.

Brian had been living with his mother, Sandra Smith, at 445B Marble Lane, Kim knew from her files. She'd assumed the address meant an apartment or duplex, but it turned out to be a house set behind another house. A driveway ran past 445A and stopped at the garage of 445B.

Both houses had the look of the 1920s or '30s, low-roofed bungalows with brick-pillared porches, dormer windows, and separate garages. The front screen door opened as they approached, and a slender woman leaned against the doorframe.

"You've brought her then," she said.

Kim had never met Sandra Smith. When Kim first started putting together the case, she had requested that Sandra come to Kim's office and talk to her. Sandra had refused, and after a while had stopped answering the phone when Kim called. That was part of the reason Kim wanted to talk to Liam, to find *someone* who could help her build a solid defense for Brian.

"I hope you don't mind the intrusion, Mrs. Smith," Kim began as they approached the porch.

Sandra abruptly turned and went inside, the screen

door banging behind her. Kim winced. This interview was not going to be easy.

Liam and Sean pushed past Kim to enter the house, no human custom of standing back to let a lady through a door first. Brian had explained the apparent rudeness to her. To a Shifter, letting a female enter a room or building ahead of a male was ludicrous. You couldn't be sure what danger lurked on the other side. The male checked it out and then gave the all clear for the female to enter. How could you protect your mate otherwise?

Kim followed them inside and stopped in surprise. Sean had taken Sandra into his arms, letting her lean against him while he rubbed his cheek on her hair. Liam moved to stand behind Sandra. *Very* close behind Sandra. He rested his chest on her back and both he and Sean murmured to her.

This was crazy. The way Liam had greeted his brother had made Kim think the two of them had something going on. Now she swore the brothers and Sandra were in a threesome.

Liam and Sean stepped away from Sandra, and Sandra wiped her eyes. Kim was struck by how young the woman looked, too young to have a twenty-five-year-old son. Sandra could be thirty, though her eyes spoke of a woman who'd seen far more of the world than Kim had.

"Can I get you coffee, Ms. Fraser?" Sandra asked, her voice shaky.

"No, no," Kim said. "Don't go to any trouble."

Sean smiled at Sandra. "I think a big pot would be grand, Sandra. I'll help you, shall I?"

Sandra softened under his look, and she and Sean walked to the back of the house to the kitchen. Sean went in first, then ushered Sandra in with his hand on the small of her back.

"What was *that* about?" Kim asked Liam.

"Sit down, Kim. You look all out."

She hadn't really expected him to answer. Kim collapsed to the sofa with a grimace and laid her briefcase on the coffee table. Her feet were killing her. She ran her finger inside her shoes, but it didn't do much good.

"Are you hurting?" Liam sat down next to her—right next to her, inside her personal space. "Let me see your feet."

Kim blinked. "Sorry?"

"I saw you limping. Get those ridiculous shoes off and swing your feet up here."

His eyes were so damn blue. Why did she suddenly long to feel his warm hands on her feet, on her ankles, up her legs under her skirt to where her stockings ended at bare thigh . . . ?

He was a *Shifter*. This wasn't right.

"I can't do that."

"You mean you won't."

"How do you think that would that look? For the mother of the man I'm defending to come back in and find you giving me a foot massage?"

"She'd think it was the first sensible thing you did. You hide behind those clothes like they're a suit of armor. She'll not open up to you if you do that."

"But she will if I play footsie with you?"

Liam smiled a heart-thumping smile. "Get your damn shoes off, woman."

Oh, to hell with it. When in Rome . . . or Shiftertown.

Kim couldn't stop her groan of relief as she eased the heels from her feet. Liam patted his lap. Kim leaned into the corner of the couch and plopped her ankles on Liam's thigh.

"Is everything in Shiftertown backward?" she asked.

"Backward?"

"Men enter a room first, it's better to kick off your shoes on a stranger's couch than be businesslike, and you say hello by rubbing yourselves all over each other." Kim sagged in pleasure as he moved strong hands over her feet. "Ooh, that's good."

Liam's thumb traveled over her arch to her heel, his touch warm. Did the man know how to loosen tension, or what?

Another groan escaped her. "This is better than any day spa I've been to. You could make money doing this."

"Shifters aren't allowed in any profession where they touch humans." His voice went soft. "We might bite."

Kim didn't think she'd mind being nibbled on by him. Her nervousness about Shifters hadn't quite drifted away, but Liam was dissolving her fears little by little, at least about him. "I think I'd make an exception for you."

"Pheromones."

Her eyes popped open. "Sorry?"

"Sean and I felt Sandra's distress, and we calmed her down. She needed our touch. Like you need me rubbing your feet."

Kim thought about their caressing, group hug. "She must have been *very* distressed."

"She is. Why wouldn't she be?"

"Was Sean distressed when he came in your office? You hugged him too."

"Of course I hugged him. He's my brother. Don't you hug your brother or your sisters?"

"I don't have a family," Kim said. She couldn't keep the sorrow out of her voice. "Not anymore."

Liam gave her a look of open pity. "No wonder you're so tense. What happened to them?"

"I don't like to talk about it."

"Talk about it anyway."

Kim had always thought it best not to open up, but Liam's blue eyes and gentle voice pried something loose. "It's no big secret. My brother Mark died when I was ten. He was twelve. He was hit by a car while he was walking down to a corner store with his friends—a hit and run. My parents passed away a few years ago, within months of each other. Old age, is all. They had their kids late in life. So now it's just me."

The story was simple, easy to relate. Her grief had burned away to emptiness long ago. She lived in the big house she'd inherited from her parents, and it was—so quiet. She tried to cheer it up with weekend parties or office mixers, but the warmth never lasted. Her parents' neighborhood was one of standoffish elegance; no kids would dare splash in plastic pools in any front yard on her street.

Liam gently squeezed her feet. "I'm sorry for you, Kim Fraser. It's the hardest thing, losing a brother. It's like losing a part of yourself."

He was too right. Kim's next words came reluctantly. "When Mark was killed, I blamed myself. I know that's stupid. I was at a friend's house miles away, and I was ten years old—what could I have done? But I kept thinking that if I'd been there, I could have warned him, pulled him out of the way, kept him home altogether. *Something.*"

Liam's warm, relaxing fingers slid beneath each of her toes. "Sean and me, we had a brother. Kenny. We lost him about ten years ago. You always wonder, if you'd persuaded him to do something different that day, would he still be alive?"

"Exactly." After seventeen years, Kim had never

found anyone who really understood, not friends or colleagues or the child counselor she'd been hauled off to. Now a Shifter she'd met an hour ago wrung the truth from her heart. "I'm sorry, Liam. About your brother."

He acknowledged the sympathy with a nod. "Did they ever get the bastard who hit Mark?"

Kim shook her head. "The police picked up a guy, but it turned out he didn't do it. Everyone wanted him to be guilty, wanted someone to blame, but I knew he hadn't done it when I saw him. He was so scared, and his wife was crying, and I said it wasn't him—but of course, how could I know? I was a kid and hadn't even been there. In the end, evidence came to light that cleared him. But everyone was pissed that he was innocent. They couldn't catch the real guy, so they wanted a substitute."

His hands slowed. "Is that when you decided to become a defense attorney?"

"No, I wanted to be a doctor." She grinned. "Or a dancer, I couldn't decide. I was ten. But I wanted the right guy to pay. I knew that if the wrong person went to prison, then whoever really did hit my brother would have hurt that many more people, you know?"

"Well reasoned for a ten-year-old."

"I thought about it. A lot. For a while, I couldn't think about anything else." Hence the child counselor.

"I know." He looked grim again.

Kim wanted to ask how his brother had died, but at that moment Sandra and Sean returned with the coffee. Kim tried to jerk her feet from Liam's lap, but he closed his hands around her ankles and held them fast. She glared, and he smiled back, showing her nice white teeth.

Sean set a tray on the table. It held the whole works:

cups, a pot, cream, and sugar. No artificial sweetener. Kim wondered whether that was because Sandra didn't like artificial sweetener or whether Shifters never had to worry about their weight.

Sandra didn't look surprised or shocked that Kim had her stockinged feet in Liam's lap. She poured out a cup of coffee and handed it to Kim without comment.

"So, tell us, Kim," Sean said, as he sat down and took his cup, "is there any chance for Brian?"

Kim couldn't lie to them. "Brian's DNA was on the victim, Michelle, and in her bedroom, and now that everyone watches *CSI*, they figure DNA is the magic truth. But Brian says he'd been dating Michelle and had gone to her house, so of course his DNA would be there and on her too."

"Then what can we do?" Sandra asked, angry. "If this DNA has already convicted him?"

"We can prove he was nowhere near the scene of the crime that night," Kim said. "Which is why I'm here. Neither the private investigator I hired nor my journalist friend who's been following the case can find any information on his whereabouts that night. I mean, no information at all. Like he'd vanished for twenty-four hours. But I can't believe *no one* saw Brian or knew where he was going."

Hell, everyone on this street had known within minutes that Liam and Sean were taking the human lawyer to Brian's house. They probably knew Kim's full name and her favorite color by now. "I'm having the investigator look into Michelle's side of things—see if she had a jealous ex or an abusive father, or even a normally nice friend upset that Michelle was dating a Shifter. I'm trying to find any evidence the police overlooked in their zeal to arrest a Shifter."

"Your investigator came around and asked me questions." Sandra sounded pissed about it. "But Brian didn't tell me himself he was walking out with this girl, so how could I know?"

"But you might know something that can help," Kim said. "I'm sorry, I know this is painful for you, but Brian's clammed up about Michelle, so I have to poke and pry. I think getting him released is more important than keeping his personal secrets, don't you?"

"Is it?" Sandra had a bit of the same Irish lilt as Sean and Liam, but Brian didn't. He'd told Kim that his father came from a different clan, she guessed not an Irish one. Either that or his clan had lost their accent after living in Texas awhile.

Kim didn't really understand how the Shifter clans worked, though Brian had tried to explain a little. She knew that each immediate family belonged to a larger, extended family group called a pride, and *they* belonged to an even more extended group called a clan. Shifters never married within the pride, and tried to marry outside the clan. When a female married, she joined her husband's clan and pride, leaving her own. Kim had thought clans were based on what kind of animal the Shifter turned into, but Brian said it was more complicated than that. This Shiftertown was home to several clans, as well as several species of Shifters, and there was another Shiftertown with more clans on the northeast edge of Austin.

Liam's father, Dylan Morrissey, was more or less the official head of the Austin branch of his entire clan, but also the unofficial head of this Shiftertown, even over the other clans. But no, Kim couldn't talk directly to Dylan, Brian told her. He was off-limits to non-Shifters. She could petition him through Liam and Liam only.

Why not Sean? Kim wondered, glancing at Liam's brother. What position did he hold in the clan hierarchy? Officially and unofficially?

Sean helped himself to coffee and exchanged a glance with Liam. "So you need to find someone who was with Brian at the time in question?" Sean asked.

Kim could have sworn that Liam had nodded ever so slightly, as though letting Sean know it was all right to say this. Nonverbal cues were flowing thick and fast.

"An independent witness would be terrific," Kim said. "Someone without a grudge against Shifters. And preferably not a Shifter him- or herself."

"Tall order," Sean said.

"The girl is human," Sandra snapped. "What human will come forward and say my son didn't do it?"

She had a point. Kim knew that locating a witness was a long shot, but it would be a nice change to find something concrete. *Innocent until proven guilty* was not working in Brian's case. The fact that he was Shifter had already condemned him in most people's eyes. Kim had to exonerate him or he didn't stand a chance.

Liam started massaging the tops of Kim's feet, which made her tense limbs start to droop.

"I might be able to find out where Brian really was," Liam said. "You should have come to me about this right away, love."

"I didn't know that, did I? Like I said, Brian is the first Shifter I've ever met, and to get him to tell me that you, Liam, even existed was an amazing feat." Brian hadn't bothered to mention Sean.

"We don't like talking about ourselves," Sean said.

"I don't see why not. Shifters exposed themselves years ago, and everyone knows all about you. There's nothing to hide anymore."

She felt the three exchange another wordless communication, and it irritated her. It reminded her of being eight years old and watching her two best friends whispering and giving her gleeful looks, not letting her in on the secret.

A cell phone vibrated on Liam's belt. He looked at the readout, and without a word gently lowered Kim's feet to the floor. He stood and walked to the kitchen, closing the door, shutting them out.

Kim felt cold without his warmth beside her, even in the July heat. "Anything you can tell me might help," she said to Sean and Sandra. "Right now I can only win this case by tearing holes in the prosecution, and there aren't many holes. I need something that will stick a fork in the case and shred it."

Sandra drank her coffee, her gaze moving from Kim to the windows. Kim caught a glimpse of her sadness as she looked away, her near despair.

She's resigning herself to losing her son, Kim realized. Sandra thought there was no hope. She'd already started grieving for him.

Sean was watching Kim with an assessing look. She still wasn't sure about him, or where the haunted feeling she got from him came from.

"I don't like to lose, Sandra," Kim said briskly. "I want to see Brian walk free and the real person pay for his crime. I won't let you down."

Sandra didn't answer. Sean nodded at Kim. "I'm sure you won't."

Liam strode back into the room. Kim realized that the other two had said very little while Liam had been gone. Had he signaled them not to? And why?

Liam took up his coffee cup without sitting down and took a long swallow. He looked over the rim at Sean, who came alert.

"Everything all right?" Kim asked. "Did you get bad news?"

Liam clicked his mug to the tray. "No, an errand Sean and I need to run. I appreciate you coming all the way out to Shiftertown, Kim Fraser, but now it's time for you to go."

Chapter Three

"What's going on?" Kim demanded as she strode down the driveway with Liam. "I just get you talking, and suddenly you're throwing me out."

Liam looked down at the fuming woman next to him. Sunlight danced on her black hair, the afternoon warmth making her smell good.

He was finding her enticing, even when she was mad as hell. When he'd announced the interview was over, she'd jammed her shoes on her feet, said a sweet good-bye to Sandra, and stalked out. Now as they walked back down the driveway, she glared at him.

"Sandra was uncomfortable," he offered. "She's not easy around humans."

"And you? Are you comfortable around us?"

"Not really. But more than she and Sean are."

"Is that why you work at a bar?"

Liam shrugged. "Humans like to see Shifters in bars. It brings in business." She didn't need to know the real reason he worked there.

They'd reached the sidewalk in front of 445A. Kim swung to face him with hands planted on hips. "I'm trying to *help*. Why does Sandra believe Brian has no chance? *I'm* on the case."

Liam hid a smile. She was like a fox terrier determined to bring down a lion. He admired her balls, first in believing Brian's innocence, and second, for coming down to meet big, dangerous Shifters like him and Sean.

She didn't realize *how* dangerous her pilgrimage was, and Liam wasn't going to tell her.

"And you on the case should be good enough?"

"I'm good, Mr. Morrissey. Michelle and her family will only get closure if the right guy goes down."

Liam lifted his hands. "I agree with you, love. It's not me you have to convince."

"Then why won't you tell me anything?" She regarded him with suspicion. "Something's going on. You and Sean know it. Sandra knows it. Hell, Brian knows it. I'm the only one in the dark. Help me out here."

Liam put his hands on her shoulders, and her blue eyes flickered with discomfort. Why did humans worry so much about touching? "We're grateful to you. You're the first human we've met who cares about Shifters. But you have to let me handle it from here."

If she didn't, Kim could die. Liam had already broken Fergus's rules by not placating her and sending her away at once, but Fergus could stuff it.

He couldn't tell Kim that he didn't know all that was going on, either. Sandra was hiding something, even from Liam, and it annoyed Liam that he didn't know what.

"You don't get it, do you?" Kim asked him. "I shouldn't have even come to talk to you, but I'm desperate. I have to be very careful about every point I have, so whatever you come up with will have to be checked and double-checked. It's not that I don't trust you, it's that I can't."

Liam circled his thumbs on her shoulders. "Well, you will have to trust me, sweetheart."

A shiver went through her body. She wanted to be touched; he could feel it. She needed it. But she fought it. *Humans.*

She glanced at his hands. "Has anyone ever told you that you're not PC?"

"Why, because I enjoy touching your soft skin and call you sweetheart? Or because I won't let you have it your own way?"

"What was the phone call you took about?"

"Oh, now you're prying into *my* business, are you? It was personal. Do you have a boyfriend?"

She blinked. "Talk about personal."

"Do you?" Liam repeated. "Someone special in your life?"

Kim pursed her lips as though she had to think about it. "Yes, a boyfriend. Sort of."

"Aren't you sure, then?"

"We don't go out much. We're busy."

"That's a tragedy."

She bristled. "Why?"

Liam leaned toward her. She smelled nice, this human. He liked her hair, all silky and curly, and he wanted to bury his nose in it.

"If I had someone like you, love, I'd be with her all the time. I wouldn't want her out of my sight. And I definitely wouldn't let her run around Shiftertown by herself. What is this man thinking about?"

Kim looked annoyed. "He doesn't know I'm here."

"He needs to take better care of you."

Indignation now. "He doesn't need to take care of me at all. I'm my own person."

"Maybe." Liam leaned closer, feeling his eyes change as he inhaled her scent. "But when you're in Shiftertown, *I* take care of you. No one will bother you here, I promise you that. They'll answer to me."

"I doubt I'll come to Shiftertown again."

"Even so."

Liam slid his arms around her and drew her close. She resisted. He traced patterns on her lower back and rested his cheek on her hair until she softened a little. He was right; her hair was silky and warm.

Kim started to relax against him, her body reacting to his. He needed to protect her. He'd made that decision the minute she'd walked into his office, to protect her from all other Shifters, most of all the leader of his own clan. "Everything will be all right now."

"Why do I want to believe you?" She sounded skeptical.

She had a nice voice, low and contralto. He imagined her whispering to him as she lay next to him in bed. Her hair would tangle on his pillow, and wouldn't she be pretty? He could understand keeping his human form for lovemaking if the human was Kim Fraser.

He straightened up and brushed a curl from her face. "Give me your cell phone."

"What for?"

"So I can admire the fine technology a human woman can afford to buy." He held out his hand. "I want to give you my phone number. What did you think?"

Kim pulled her cell phone out of a pocket of her briefcase and handed it to him. The phone was fancy, as he'd suspected, with all kinds of buttons and extras. Shifters were allowed to have only old models, recycled, most of the features disabled. Not that some Shifters didn't futz with them on the sly.

Liam started punching buttons. "I'm programming in my private number. For you only. If you need something, you call me. Any time of the day or night."

Kim watched as he tucked the cell phone back into her briefcase. "Anytime?"

"Anytime."

"What if I call every hour to check on your progress?"

"Then you do."

Her brows rose. "You trust me a lot."

"Because I'm asking you to trust me."

Kim chewed on her lip, making it red and cute. "I suppose I can see that." She held out her hand. "Thank you for your help, Mr. Morrissey. I'll be in touch."

Liam put his arm around her waist and turned her around. "I'm not leaving, love. I'm walking you back to your car."

"Why? It's only a few blocks away."

"I told you, when you're here, you're under my protection. Do you think that means I'd abandon you right here on the sidewalk?"

"I haven't the faintest idea what you mean."

"I mean I'm walking you to your car."

She made a noise of exasperation. "Whatever."

Liam wanted to laugh. She was adorable, his fox terrier. And determined.

And bloody inconvenient. The phone call had been from his father, telling Liam news he'd been waiting to hear. Ms. Lawyer needed to get out of Shiftertown. Liam and Sean suddenly had other things they needed to take care of.

Liam liked Kim's curves against his body as they walked, her narrow waist under his hand. She didn't try to break away from him, resigned, it seemed, to let him walk with his arm around her. As if they were a couple, in human terms.

Something warmed inside him, a space filling. Liam abruptly cut off the feeling. He could not afford to get involved with her. Protect her, yes; enjoy her, no. No matter how tempting she was.

Kim was breathing rapidly at their pace, her ridiculously high heels slowing her down. He wished she'd kick off her shoes and peel off her stockings and walk barefoot in the grass. He imagined her strolling along beside him, shoes in hand, a smile on her face.

Too soon they reached her car, a black two-door Mustang. The car chirped as she pushed the button to unlock it.

Liam pulled her into another hug. Kim resisted again, but he scooped her against him, letting his mouth rest on the curve of her neck. She was warm, her skin salty, her pulse beating under his lips.

"Good-bye then, Kim. You take care."

He meant it. There was danger out there, and Brian's troubles were only part of it.

Kim took the card from her pocket that she'd tried to hand him earlier. "You'll call my office as soon as you have anything for me, right? Anything at all?"

Liam turned the card around in his fingers, savoring the feel of the raised letters of her name. "Of course, love."

"Even if you don't think it's relevant?"

He didn't bother to answer. Liam opened the car door for her, and Kim gave him a flustered look before tossing her briefcase inside.

Liam smoothed her hair from her face. He could stand all day looking at her, breathing in her scent, touching her sleek hair.

He let her go. He wasn't allowed to have her, no matter that he was hot and hard for her. She was beautiful, but not for him.

Kim gave him a smile, one that heated his blood, and slid into her driver's seat. She cranked the engine, let it roar to life, then reached over to switch the AC to high.

She rolled down the window, sending a trickle of cool air over his skin. "Thanks, Liam," she said. "I don't mean to sound ungrateful. I'm just worried."

"We all are, love." He stood up, patted the roof of the car. "You go on, now."

The window slid silently upward. Kim gave him one last nervous smile, then pulled the car onto the street. The taillights flashed red before she turned a corner, and then she was gone.

Liam might never see her again. The emptiness of that hit him.

No, that wouldn't happen. She was under his protection now. He had her phone number and her address. He'd make sure she'd need to speak to him again, and he'd make sure she had to see him in person to do it.

When Liam reached home after picking up Sean from Sandra's, their father Dylan was there. Three generations of males lived in the Morrisseys' two-story bungalow—father, two sons, and Liam's nephew, Connor.

Connor was twenty, tall and lanky, still a cub by Shifter standards. By human standards, he was old enough to go to college, and Connor had been attending a community college this year. Shifters weren't allowed to apply to the prestigious UT Austin, but it had been voted to allow them some college-level education. No degrees. Wouldn't want Shifters taking over professional jobs or learning enough to be a threat.

Connor's classes were out for the summer, and he passed the time catching up on DVDs. Laws forbade Shifters access to TiVo or premium cable for some reason, so movie rental outlets near Shiftertown did big business. Connor was watching *The Howling* and laughing his ass off.

"You'll have to go with him, Liam," Dylan said as soon as Liam walked in, continuing the conversation he'd had with Liam on the phone.

Liam gave a grim nod as he got himself a Guinness from the refrigerator. Dylan had told him that Fergus's trackers located a feral Shifter east of town, one that had slaughtered a Shifter woman and her cubs a few nights ago.

May hell rot all feral Shifters, Liam thought. He and Sean had found the bodies, a devastating sight that made his heart ache. As Guardian, it was Sean's duty to dispatch the feral, but Liam was looking forward to exacting some justice of his own. Besides, no way he'd let his brother face the attacker alone. Not after what had happened to Kenny.

"I'll go too," Connor said. He'd come silently out of the living room and leaned against the breakfast bar in the kitchen. "If it's a simple takedown."

Dylan gave Connor a look of compassion. Dylan's dark hair had gone gray at the temples in the last few years, finally making him look older than his sons. But a Shifter's eyes, not his human shell, betrayed his age. Dylan's eyes had seen much.

"No, Connor."

"I'm not a cub anymore, and I need to learn to fight these bastards."

Connor's father, Kenny, had been ripped to shreds by a feral Shifter. Their family had avenged the death long ago, but Connor had been too young to participate. The need for personal vengeance burned in him. But not only did Connor look twenty, he *was* twenty in human years. His fighting ability would take another decade or so to hone.

Liam drew his lanky nephew into a hug. "Like you said, lad, it's a simple takedown. We'll get him and go out for pizza." Liam kept his voice light, though he was buzzing with adrenaline. He was more than ready to get on with it.

Connor rolled his eyes as Liam released him. "You and Sean are so condescending it makes me sick. You have human scent all over you, Liam. What have you been up to?"

Sean grinned as he pulled a beer out of the refrigerator. "You should have seen him. He meets this human lady, and ten minutes later he's massaging her feet. He wouldn't leave her alone."

Liam threw his bottle cap at him. Sean snatched the cap out of the air and threw it back.

"She needs protecting," Liam said, catching the cap in turn and tossing it to the counter. "She's busting her ass for Shifters, the little idiot."

"Brave for a human," Dylan said. He was the only one in the room who didn't look amused.

"She's brave, but she's innocent. I scent-marked her so other Shifters will leave her the hell alone. They'll know that if they bother her, they answer to me. That goes for Fergus's thugs too."

Dylan watched him closely, and Liam pretended not to hold his breath as he drank his beer. Whose side would Dylan take? The clan leader's? Or Liam's? It was never certain.

Dylan gave Liam a slow nod. "If Fergus asks, I'll tell him I sanctioned it."

Liam relaxed. He went to his father and clasped his shoulder in thanks, then returned to the refrigerator. "We might as well eat while we wait. How about old-fashioned burgers on the grill?"

"Grand idea." Sean sauntered into the living room and threw himself on the couch. He crossed his feet and leaned his head back on his folded hands. "Make mine medium rare and put a slice of cheese on it, why don't you?"

Connor sprawled on the floor and took the DVD off Pause. "Rare for me, Liam."

"Gobshites," Liam growled, but he pulled the meat out of the freezer and stuck it in the microwave to thaw.

As he started up the grill outside and formed the burgers, leaving out all the onions and salt and crap that humans littered their meat with, he thought about Kim. How she smelled, how she felt. How her blue eyes could open so wide that her lashes curled against her skin. Her dark hair had gleamed in the sunlight, revealing golden highlights.

He wondered what she was doing now. Back at her office, hunched over a desk? Talking to Brian at the jail? Reading thick law books to see what she could do for a Shifter?

She'd go home soon. Liam had easily found where she lived when her secretary had contacted him earlier this week. A simple computer search had sufficed, even on dial-up—no cable modems for Shifters. Why the human government thought not allowing Shifters cable or wireless or good cell phones would slow down their communications, he didn't know. Humans had weird ideas.

What would Kim do when she got home? Peel off that severe gray suit, most likely. Would she wear sexy underwear beneath it? Did all-work-and-no-play Kim Fraser buy herself shimmering lingerie?

Liam pictured her in a silk camisole that barely contained her lush breasts, maybe bikini panties baring most of her butt. Or not a camisole, but a tiny lace bra that pushed her breasts up and barely covered her nipples. Stockings, not panty hose. With a garter belt. She'd walk around her house in that, loosening up after work, pouring herself a glass of wine. Or maybe she was a down-home Texas girl who'd reach for a cold beer.

Liam imagined the beads of moisture on the beer bottle in the humid summer evening. Kim's lips would skim the bottle's mouth until she upended it and poured a cool stream of beer down her throat.

He imagined it so vividly that Sean's and Connor's burgers traveled way past rare to well done before Liam could rescue them.

Kim got out of her leisurely bath and went back to her bedroom with one towel around her torso and the other turbaned over her hair.

She'd gotten used to living by herself—unless Abel came over—no parents or siblings or anyone else. No dogs or cats, either, because she was gone most of the day, and she didn't want to subject a pet to so much neglect. Or maybe she just didn't want to mourn when it grew old, died, and left another hole in her life.

Tonight she felt the emptiness. She'd tried to fill it by e-mailing her friend Silas, a Pulitzer Prize–winning journalist doing research for a documentary on Shifters, and then taking a luxurious soak. She'd tried to lose herself in a delicious novel in the tub, but her thoughts kept drifting and she gave up.

She reached for an emery board and started sanding her nails. Maybe she felt the emptiness because in Shiftertown she'd noticed the fullness. The kids playing in the front yards, neighbors waving at Sean and Liam, the easy bond between the two brothers.

She thought about how she'd spilled her guts to Liam and let him massage her aching feet. The rubbing had felt *good*. She could still feel his touch, the warmth, the sensual firmness of his strong fingers.

Even better had been his lips on her neck. The man was *hot*. She had no idea whether Shifters did it like humans, but she knew that if she were a Shifter woman, she'd be working to get him into bed.

Strangest of all, Liam had listened to her. Kim had told him more in ten minutes than she'd told Abel in the year she'd been dating him.

Did that say something about Liam or something about Abel?

Kim set down the emery board and picked up her cell phone. She punched Abel's number and listened to his phone ring.

"Yes?" he answered. He sounded rushed.

"Hey, it's me."

"Kim?" He sounded baffled. "What is it? Was I supposed to meet you tonight?"

"No. I just thought we could talk."

"Oh." Pause as he rustled something on the other end of the phone. "Can I call you back? I'm in the middle of about ten things."

Kim waited for her anger to come. But she felt—nothing. "Sure."

"Tomorrow. Sleep tight, honey." *Click*.

"Yeah. Sweet dreams, babe." Kim keyed off the phone and dropped it on the table. Abel was a workaholic trying to make a name for himself at the firm. Of course he was in the middle of ten things. He always was.

Maybe it's time to cut that tie, a little voice in the back of her mind said. *Maybe it's beyond time.*

You know you didn't think that until you met Liam . . .

Kim picked up the phone again and scrolled to where Liam had typed in his name and number. It looked so normal, the four letters of his name, then an area code and seven-digit phone number like everyone else had.

You call me, any time of the day or night.

Had he really meant that? Or was it a mere platitude? *Call me, honey. Except when I'm busy, watching TV, out with my friends, or not interested in you right now.*

Just to be a pain in the ass, Kim pressed the button to call the number. One ring, and then Liam's warm voice filled her ear.

"Kim!" As though this was the best call he'd received all day. "You all right, love?"

"Yes, I'm fine," Kim said, her entire body warming. "I was . . ."

"Checking to see if I'd answer?" Liam's amusement came across loud and clear.

"Something like that. How's Sandra doing?"

"Better. Sean talked to her. You're not still working, are you?"

"I'm always working, Liam. Cases don't keep a nine-to-five schedule."

His chuckle sent a shiver down her spine. "You need to stop now and again, sweetheart. Take it from me. I know."

Kim realized. "Oh, you're at work now, aren't you? At the bar. I'm sorry, I shouldn't have interrupted."

"I told you, love. Anytime. You rest easy, now."

Take that, Abel. "Thanks, Liam. You too."

A pause. It stretched on.

"You still there?" she asked.

"Yes." He sounded suddenly subdued. "Good night, Kim. Call me again tomorrow, all right?"

She promised to, clicked off the phone, and held it to her lips. Her own boyfriend might or might not remember to call her back, but this Shifter had sounded happy to hear from her, even if he was up to his butt in bar receipts. She wasn't sure whether that made her feel good or lonelier than ever.

Chapter Four

Liam slid his phone into his belt as he mounted his Harley, waiting for Sean to join him. Kim's voice touched the raw sexual being inside him, the one that had wanted to unfasten her straining blouse buttons in his office. Even more warming was the thought that she'd made the choice to call him.

He'd stopped himself from asking, *What are you doing right now? What are you wearing? Or not wearing?*

Liam thought again of the directions to Kim's house he'd easily brought up on a computer search. Maybe after this takedown, he'd drive out there to check up on her. Maybe she'd let him in, and maybe he could persuade her up to her bedroom for another foot massage . . .

"Everything all right?" Sean asked as he straddled the bike behind Liam.

Liam shifted uncomfortably, willing his growing hard-on to calm down. "It's fine. Why wouldn't it be?"

"Because that thing in your pants looks painful."

Liam never found it easy to lie to his brother. "I was talking to Kim."

Sean started to laugh. He moved the sword strapped to his back to a comfortable position, then slid his arms around Liam's waist. "You have it bad, Liam. Give up the dream and go shag a pretty Shifter. Annie maybe."

Liam started the bike. "She works at the bar now. I never get involved with the help."

"I didn't say get involved. I said shag her. She's been happy to oblige you in the past."

"It's you she wants, Sean. I see her sweet gaze following your ass."

"Can we get a move on? I'd like to make this kill and be done with it."

Liam didn't reply. He knew Sean needed to calm his nerves, and stirring up his big brother was his favorite method.

Liam glided the bike, a Harley he'd bought for next to nothing and restored, into the street, then turned the corner and drove out of Shiftertown. He headed through crowded streets to the highway that would take them east out of the city. In his rearview mirrors, the skyline of downtown Austin glowed against the dark sky, the lit-up dome of the capitol a yellow beacon.

They turned down an inky-black road past Bastrop and rode across open country. Fergus's trackers had called right after Liam and Sean had finished their burgers, saying they'd followed the feral to some abandoned warehouses way east of town. The feral had made camp there, and the shit wasn't going anywhere, so could Sean and Liam please bestir themselves and come do their jobs?

If the trackers ran true to form, Liam knew they wouldn't show their asses if there was any kind of fight. They'd hightail it out of there as soon as Liam and Sean arrived. It was the trackers' job only to point the way, after all.

Liam parked well down the road from the warehouse, he and Sean doing the last stretch on foot. A chain-link fence surrounded the property of the once-prosperous business, but the flimsy barrier had been sliced open in plenty of places, with one whole section of it knocked flat. Crickets chirped in loud profusion outside the fence, but once Liam and Sean stepped over the fallen chain link, all animal noises ceased.

Liam smelled the stench right after that. Even a human would notice it, but to a Shifter the smell was like a body blow. Liam felt his lips curl back, his teeth elongate into fangs.

He tried to suppress his killing instinct, but it wasn't easy. Dylan seemed to think he and Sean would come out here and solve the problem in cool detachment. But Dylan hadn't seen the Shifter woman's body, hadn't found her children. Liam wanted to savage, no offers of mercy. So did Sean, probably even more than Liam did.

Without a word, the brothers separated, Sean unstrapping the sword from his back. Liam moved noiselessly through the shadows of the warehouse and stepped through a door that gaped open to the night.

The stench made him gag. Liam's cat's eyes adjusted to the dark, and he walked forward, scanning each sable shadow.

Before Liam had made it halfway across the warehouse floor, the feral stepped forward to meet him. He didn't look as wild as Liam had thought he would. He was dressed in jeans and a T-shirt, sweat-soaked in the humid Texas night. Except for being caked with dirt, not wearing a Collar, and his oppressive BO, he looked like any other Shifter from Shiftertown. Of course his neck was so black with filth, Liam wouldn't have been able to see a Collar if he had one.

"Don't you take baths, man?" Liam asked.

The Shifter snarled, his face elongating into something between human and wolf. A Lupine. Bloody wonderful.

"There's good soap nowadays," Liam went on. "Makes you sweet as a garden. You should try it. That is, if you're not busy killing wee ones like the bastard you are."

The Lupine grated, "Traitor. Collared pet."

"No, lad. Survivor. We don't go around murdering

anymore, didn't you hear? Especially not the cubs, and damn you don't know how much I want to kill you for that."

"I wanted the woman. Not her spawn by another Shifter."

"Those days are over, lick-brain." Liam took the Collar out of his pocket, feeling the strength of the steel, the bite of magic that wound through it. "I'm offering you this chance because my father makes me play by the rules, no matter what. Me, I'd rather kill you." He stepped forward. "One size fits all. Come on, take it like a man."

"I'm not a man. Neither are you. Are you too weak to fight me, Feline?"

"No," Liam said. "But you have two choices. Face me, or face the Guardian."

The other Shifter tensed. "The Guardian isn't here."

"Yes, he is." Sean stepped out of the shadows behind the Shifter. He drew the broadsword, its blade ringing in the still air.

The Shifter swung to Sean. He inhaled sharply, then whirled back to Liam and did the sniff-fest again.

"I only smelled . . ." The Shifter broke off, his light blue wolf eyes fixed on Liam.

Liam held out the Collar, still offering. "You take the Collar, I might resist killing you. Maybe you didn't understand what you were doing. I have about two brain cells that believe that. You refuse . . . Well, let's just say our Sean is even more pissed at you than I am."

Liam felt the air contract as the man shifted all the way. He didn't bother taking off his clothes; he let them fray as his wolf's body split the fabric. Sean waited, and Liam wondered if the Lupine understood how much Sean was holding back. The brothers' instructions were to kill the feral only as a last resort.

The wolf shook off the remains of the clothes, his eyes filled with rage. Liam didn't move. "Come on, lad. Shiftertown pretty much wants you dead without quarter. Dylan convinced me to give you a chance. Don't throw that away."

The wolf snarled. He rose on his hind legs, returning to human form. Now he was naked, not a pretty sight.

"I smell it on you." His nostrils flared in contempt. "A human. You scent-marked a human woman." How the Shifter could smell anything beyond his own stink, Liam didn't know, but his blood ran cold. "Abomination," the Shifter hissed.

"You know big words, do you?" Liam asked. "Let me give you some short ones: *Take the fucking Collar.*"

With a crackle of bones, the Shifter morphed back into a wolf. Liam braced himself for the attack, but the wolf abruptly whirled and sprinted in the other direction.

Sean was there, his sword biting into the Shifter's side. The wolf didn't slow. He howled, leapt out of the warehouse, and ran off into the night.

"*Shit.*" Sean brought the sword up again. "Idiot!"

He could have meant Liam, the Shifter, or himself. Liam balled his fists as fear poured through him. "Bloody hell, he's going to track her."

"What are you talking about?"

"Kim. He smelled her on me."

"He's been wounded by the Guardian's sword. He won't get far. We'll ride after him and finish it."

"Not wounded enough." The feral had seemed unusually strong—he must have been to kill a Shifter female guarding her cubs. Shifter females didn't go down easily, and one protecting her precious young would fight twice as hard. Liam could taste the feral's adrenaline spike in the air, a more vicious tang than it should have had. Something was wrong with him that sharply ramped up Liam's fear.

Liam started swiftly out of the warehouse, running by the time he hit the weed-infested parking lot.

"Liam." Sean sprinted after him. "If he makes it, he'll track the scent back to Shiftertown first, and Dad will make short work of him."

"Not if he's as good as I think he is. He'll track both my scent and hers. Kim took that double-scent home with her."

He started the bike, and as soon as Sean leapt on he roared away. Sean might be right, and the feral Shifter might go nowhere near Kim, but Liam couldn't take that chance.

Liam raced the bike back down the highway to the city, then north on the freeway. He dove off and angled west, through the main city, circling fine homes that clung to the hillside above the river. The night was hot and dank, but the air rushing past the bike felt chilled.

He thought of the red dot on the computer map that indicated Kim's house. To him, the red dot was a target, an announcement of her vulnerability. He needed to warn her, protect her, *hold her, taste her* . . .

If it wasn't too late.

Chapter Five

A muffled tinkle of broken glass trickled from the kitchen downstairs. At first Kim rolled over in bed, not paying attention. This was a safe neighborhood, never any break-ins.

When hinges of the kitchen door squeaked, she sat up straight.

Kim hadn't been asleep. She'd been staring at the dark ceiling for the last hour, absorbed in thoughts of Liam. How his warm, friendly voice tickled her ear, how the corners of his eyes crinkled when he smiled, how nice his butt looked in those tight jeans. Now her heart pounded, adrenaline pumping as she heard someone moving around her kitchen.

Should she trust her martial arts classes? In her baby-doll nightie?

Screw that. The magic numbers were 911.

Kim lifted her cell phone from the nightstand, thumb reaching for the numbers. She smelled a sudden sour odor, and then the phone flew across the room and shattered against the wall.

Before she could scream, strong hands lifted her by the neck. Kim found herself staring into white-blue eyes in a hard male face that had half changed to a wolfish form. Lips lifted from pointed canines, and the breath that washed over her smelled like rotten meat. Kim fought frantically as the half-shifted man's hands cut off her air, claws raking hot pain. He was going to kill her.

Through her dimming vision she realized that this Shifter wore no Collar.

Then suddenly she was free. Kim crashed back into the bed, gasping for breath, as the Shifter was ripped from her. She dragged her hair out of her face in time to see a wildcat slam the Shifter to her bedroom floor. Snarling filled the room, not angry doggy snarling, but the real thing, wild animals in red-hot fury.

Sean Morrissey stood inside Kim's bedroom doorway, holding a broadsword that gleamed with light of its own. Sean's eyes were midnight dark and full of rage. His gaze fixed on the fight in the middle of the floor, but he didn't rush to interfere. He watched, waiting.

The creatures upended Kim's dresser and nightstand and shoved her bed across the room like it was a cardboard box. Sean didn't *do* anything, just stood there with the sword ready. Kim heard herself shouting, but her words were lost in the animal screams as the two creatures fought.

The wildcat—ears back, canines extended—snapped its jaw across the wolf's throat. The wolf yelped once. Its paws scrabbled hard against the wildcat's body, drawing blood, before the wolf's head lolled to the side and it fell to the carpet, lifeless. The wildcat sat back, sides heaving, watching the corpse as though expecting it to get up again.

Kim fought the urge to laugh hysterically. *Excuse me but there's a deceased wolf and a wildcat in my bedroom!* She wasn't certain what kind of wildcat it was—tawny like a cougar, muscled like a leopard, with a hint of stripe like a tiger. It also had the huge jaws and massive paws of a male lion. But the cat didn't look weird, like a mishmash. It was lithe, beautiful, powerful.

Sean finally moved. The wildcat backed off as Sean

raised the sword, then drove its point into the dead wolf's chest. The wolf shimmered, became the half-shifted man who'd attacked Kim, then slowly disinte-grated to ash. At the same time, the wildcat rose on its hind feet and flowed back into the form of a very naked Liam Morrissey.

Mmm, he looks good, the back of Kim's mind said. Rip-pling muscles, smooth skin, wiry dark hair spreading across his chest. Tight abdomen, massive thighs, huge . . . *Oh, man.*

As soon as air poured back into Kim's lungs, screams hurtled out of her mouth. She tried to stop them, but hysterical reaction grabbed her and wrung her in its grip.

Liam's big body was next to her on the bed, his hand covering her mouth. "Hush, now, love. It's over."

Delayed shock. Understandable. I'll be all right.

Liam's hand was warm, somehow comforting, even though he was trying to keep her quiet. After a moment he gave her an inquiring look, and she nodded, indicat-ing she'd finished screaming. Liam lifted his hand away, and Kim dragged in a deep breath, inhaling his heady male scent.

"Liam, man, get yourself dressed," Sean said. "You'll scare the woman."

"No, it's all right." Kim closed her eyes, felt Liam's bare arms and legs encircling hers. Nope, didn't bother her at all. She opened her eyes again and looked at Liam. "What the *hell* just happened?"

"We killed him," Liam said. "We had no choice. The bastard would have killed you."

"Is that what happens to Shifters? They dissolve into dust, like vampires on TV?"

Sean didn't answer, standing stoically with the sword still pointed at the floor.

"No." Liam eased himself away from Kim, She wanted to reach for him again, have him enclose her back into that so very nice, naked embrace. "Only the ones Sean runs through with that sword. Sean is our Guardian."

Sean's eyes narrowed. "Liam."

"What's a Guardian?" More nonverbal cues flew between the brothers, not telepathy, but body language so subtle she couldn't catch it all, let alone understand it.

"A protector," Liam said. "Of Shiftertown, in this case."

"I didn't see a Collar on the Shifter." Kim shivered suddenly, violently. "I was going to die, wasn't I?"

"He would have killed you. He was feral. That means he was dangerous, to you, to me, to our families. He'd already killed a Shifter female and her children."

Kim gaped. "Wait, I heard about the Shifter woman dying. I thought she and her kids were killed in a car accident on a back highway in Hill Country. Weren't they?"

"No, lass." Liam looked so sad. Sean stood apart, incongruous in jeans and T-shirt with the medieval-looking sword. "She was murdered. Sean and me, we put her body in her car and pushed it into that ditch and set it alight."

"Why?" Kim got off the bed. She realized all she wore was a short, silky baby-doll, and she grabbed for the robe she'd tossed to a chair. "Why not report the crime and have the Shifter brought in?"

"Because it's our responsibility." Liam's gaze took in her body as she hastily shrugged on the robe, but his voice rang with anger. Sean gave a nod of agreement.

"No, it isn't," Kim said. "Shifters live in the human world now—that means human law prevails. You signed the agreement. The Shifter should have been arrested and tried like anyone else, not killed vigilante-style by you and Sean."

She ran out of breath. The two men weren't listening to her but looking at each other, still talking without talking. The weight of the Shifter's death pressed on the room.

Finally Sean shook his head and slid his sword into a leather sheath. "You're effing crazy, Liam, you know? You do what you have to, I'm reporting in to Dad."

"Do that. Take my bike."

"What, you think I'd be hitching a ride with a sword strapped to my back? I'll see you at home."

With a final scowl, Sean turned and left the room, carrying the sword by its sheathed blade. Kim heard him on the stairs, and then the back door slammed beneath them, shaking the house.

"Come on." Liam got up, still naked and unembarrassed about it. "Get dressed and go downstairs. I'll cook you some dinner—you look peaky."

"The Shifter—he's . . ." Kim swallowed. "All over my carpet." Gray dust coated the rug she'd bought at an antique store out in Fredericksburg. "Ew."

Liam enfolded her in his arms and kissed her neck, his warmth like a blanket on her cold skin. "I'll take care of this, love. Go on downstairs and wait for me."

Kim didn't want to. She wanted to stay here for a while and run her hands along Liam's broad, strong shoulders. His body was solid and reassuring, and so was his smile. She could stand here in his arms all damned night.

Liam kissed her neck again. "You'll be all right. Go on, now."

Kim was never sure how she made herself back away, grab her clothes, and scoot across the hall to her guest bedroom to change. As she made her way downstairs, she strained to hear what Liam did in her bedroom, but all was silent.

Liam found his clothes where he'd thrown them off in Kim's kitchen and slid them on. His adrenaline was still high, his heart pumping hard and fast. He wanted to run, hunt, grab Kim and have unbridled sex with her. Containing himself wasn't easy, but his body running so hot would continue to stave off the pain that was coming. And then he'd pay. Damn, would he pay.

Kim hunched on a sofa on the other side of the breakfast bar. She had no kitchen table and chairs; instead, a couple of stools stood at the counter, and she'd filled the rest of the room with a couch and two comfortable-looking chairs.

Her loose hair straggled over the blouse she'd put on, her blue eyes enormous as she watched Liam dress. He'd cleaned himself up in her bathroom after he'd vacuumed what was left of the feral Shifter from the rug. The bugger wouldn't come out all the way out, though.

"You'll have to send that carpet out for cleaning," he said.

Kim whitened. "Oh, God."

"I'll do it for you. It's my fault the shite came here at all."

"Why do you keep saying it's your fault? Not everything is your responsibility. You live in the human world now."

She was trying to hold on to what she knew, what she'd been told. Humans liked to comfort themselves like that.

"It's my responsibility because I let you come to Shiftertown. The feral smelled your scent on me and decided to hurt me by hurting you. That way, even if he died, he'd know I'd be grieving. It's the feral way—take ven-

geance on your enemy even while they're killing you."
Liam shook his head as he moved to the refrigerator. "I've
never seen a Shifter move that fast, or be able to track
that quickly. There was something wrong with him."

That bothered him more than he cared to admit. Ferals, ironically, were weaker than Shifters with Collars,
because Collared Shifters were well fed, well rested, and
had plenty of time to exercise. But this feral had been
fast and had brushed off Sean's first sword thrust as
though it were an insect bite.

Kim shivered. "Are there any more of them out
there?"

Liam didn't know, and that bothered him more than
he cared to let on, but he made his tone reassuring.
"Shouldn't be. We keep track of the ferals pretty well."
Or so Fergus claimed. The refrigerator's shelves were
bare except for a few containers of yogurt and a rubber-
banded bunch of greens. "You have no food, woman."

"It's in the freezer."

That compartment revealed stacks of boxed frozen
meals, all with "Lite" or "Low-calorie" written on them.
"This isn't food," Liam said. "It's a travesty."

"I have to watch my weight."

Liam remembered how Kim had looked in her wisp
of a nightie—lovely breasts, sweet waist, and thighs he
wanted to lick. "I don't mind watching it for you, love.
There's nothing wrong with your body."

She went a deep shade of red, and Liam slammed the
freezer door. "I can't cook you up my famous mile-high
pancakes with this crap. Come on. I'll take you out for
some real food."

"I can't go anywhere. My back door is broken."

Two small panes had been smashed, the lock ripped
out. "I'll take care of that."

Liam unhooked his cell phone and made some calls.

Voices on the other end promised to come and replace the glass and fix the lock in half an hour. *"Does the human woman have any beer?"*

"Bring your own," Liam growled and clicked off the phone.

Kim had a stunned look on her face. "What are you doing?"

"I keep telling you, sweetheart, it's my fault the bastard attacked you. I have friends who will take care of things, as a favor to me."

"Shifter friends."

"What other kind? Come on, we'll leave them to it."

Liam somehow convinced her to walk out of the house and open the garage, but he took the car keys from Kim's shaking hands and drove her back to Shiftertown himself.

Sean was right, Liam was effing crazy, but he had to do this. Kim needed protecting, but then, so did the Shifters. Liam would have to combine the two needs. Dylan would be livid, but Liam also had the feeling that Dylan would understand. Fergus, now . . . Well, Liam would deal with Fergus when he had to.

"This is where you work," Kim said, as Liam parked behind the bar in the tiny space reserved for him.

"Well spotted, love. They do a mean chicken-fried steak."

Kim's eyes flared with sudden hunger. Did she starve herself, the little sweetheart? She had a man, she'd said. Why didn't the idiot take care of her?

The bar was full when they walked in. Shifters predominated the crowd, with a handful of humans who'd either become friends with Shifters, had come in to gawk, or were Shifter groupies. Most patrons hovered at the long wraparound bar, but Liam guided Kim to an empty booth and sat her down.

Liam's heart was thumping, his adrenaline still high. He'd have to endure the agony sooner or later, but he hoped it held off long enough for him to enjoy his meal.

"Two chicken-fried steaks, Annie, and a mess of chips."

The tall, svelte Shifter woman who'd come to wait on them rolled her eyes. "We call them french fries over here, Liam. I tell you all the time. Not chips."

"I don't see anyone French in this bar," Liam said, continuing the usual banter between himself and Annie.

"The new cook is Cajun. Close enough."

"And we'll need something to drink," Liam said. "What will you have, Kim?"

"White wine?"

White wine. She was precious. "You don't want to drink the wine here. Bring me a pint of plain, Annie."

"Guinness," Annie said, noting it on her pad. "For you, miss?"

"A Tecate," Kim said. She glared at Liam. "With a lime, please."

"You got it." Annie whisked away, her tight barmaid shorts clinging to her trim behind. Every male in the bar turned to watch her pass, but once she'd gone their gazes swiveled back to Kim.

"Why is everyone staring at me?" Kim whispered. "I'm not the only human here."

But she was the only one scent-marked. Every Shifter, male and female, had caught what Liam had done. Nostrils widened, eyes flickered in acknowledgment. Kim belonged to Liam, and anyone who bothered her would answer to Liam. Message sent and received.

"I'm looking after you, and they know it."

"Why did you want to come here? We passed two IHOPs on the way."

"It's safer."

Kim glanced around. "For you or for me?"

"For both of us."

He quieted as Annie set down one sweating bottle of Guinness and one of Tecate, lime firmly wedged into the opening.

"Are you going to explain why you didn't call the police on that Shifter?" Kim shoved her lime entirely into the liquid and lifted the bottle to drink. Her tongue came out and touched the bottle's opening before her lips closed around it.

Goddess help me, it's hot in here.

Liam clenched his beer bottle, but the cold bite on his palm did nothing to calm him. "What do you think would happen if your human police found out he was on the loose?" he asked. "Shifters would be hunted, and the hunters not too worried about whether they brought down a Collared Shifter or a feral. Just so long as they got one."

"All right, I can see that. With one Shifter already on trial, people would freak if another one went crazy." Kim leaned forward, letting Liam see that this blouse didn't stay fastened any better than the last one had. "Do you think *he* killed the girl Brian is supposed to have murdered?"

"I wish it could be that easy. We weren't aware of him until a few nights ago, when he killed the Shifter woman. He wasn't around before that. Brian's girlfriend died months ago."

"How do you know he wasn't here?" She wrinkled her nose. "Of course, you'd have remembered smelling him."

Liam acknowledged that with a laugh.

"What did you mean by 'Collared Shifters'?" Kim

went on. "Sounds like collard greens. Before tonight, I thought all Shifters wore Collars. It's the law."

This was getting complicated. Liam sifted through what was safe to tell her. Hell, none of this was safe. "Not all Shifters took the Collar. Your human government knows that, but they keep it to themselves."

Kim's slim fingers toyed with her beer bottle, but she didn't drink again. She watched him with intelligent eyes. Beautiful eyes. *Damn, it's been way too long . . .*

"You make it sound like wearing the Collar is a choice."

"It is, love," Liam said. "It's a choice we were given twenty years ago, and we made it. Most of us. Some Shifters chose to remain wild."

"You mean free."

"Hunted. Dying. Pushed out. We might have survived maybe five more years if we hadn't taken the Collars."

"Are you saying you chose subjugation to save yourselves?"

Liam shrugged, pretending to agree. "Our lines were dying out. We weren't fertile, and children that managed to get born often didn't last their first year. Now look at us."

Kim moved her gaze from him to the filled room. At the bar Jordie Ross stood with his four sons, all tall and bulky, talking and laughing loudly. Their mother had survived their births—she was sitting in a booth on the other side of the room with a couple of friends.

Another Shifter woman held her hand on her swelling belly while her husband kept a protective arm around her. She was prudently drinking bottled water, leaning back against her husband.

"Liam." A tall figure cut his vision. "Nice human you've got there."

Liam looked up and scowled. "Ellison. Get lost, man. I'm trying to convince her that Shifters are civilized."

The tall man laughed. As usual, Ellison wore a black button-up shirt and jeans, cowboy boots, and big hat. He loved Texas, had adopted the state when his Shifter clan relocated from Colorado. Some of his clan missed the cool air of the Rockies, but Ellison Rowe embraced Texas Hill Country, even with its humidity, mosquitoes, bad traffic, and state congressmen.

"Don't believe him." Ellison thunked into the booth next to Liam and smiled at Kim. "Liam doesn't have a civilized bone in his body." Even Ellison's grin was wolfish.

"I'm sure she's comforted, hearing that from a Lupine."

"Lupine?" Kim wrinkled her brow. "I heard you say that before."

"Means I'm a wolf, baby," Ellison said. "Not a pussy-cat."

Kim's eyes took on a touch of fear. Liam reached across and touched her hand. "It's all right. He's a good wolf."

"Don't tell her that. I'm the Big, *Bad* Wolf."

"Like the feral Shifter," Kim said softly.

Ellison instantly lost his grin. "What?"

Liam shot Kim a warning look. "A rogue. I took care of it."

"He was a wolf? *Damn.* I'm sorry, Liam."

"I said I took care of it."

Ellison frowned, his big body folding in on itself, his sunny nature dimming.

"Two chicken-fried steaks, extra gravy," Annie said, depositing the food in front of them. "And a mess of fries. Anything else you need?"

"Bring me a beer, honey." Ellison glanced at Kim's and Liam's bottles. "A good old-fashioned American beer, nothing Irish, Mexican, or German."

"We got some strawberry blonde ale in the back," Annie said. "Made right here in Austin."

She swished away before Ellison could protest. "Aw, I *hate* microbrew. Yuppie beer."

"Then I won't invite you to the annual microbrew tasting party," Kim said, as Liam munched a crispy, hot chip. They were *chips*, damn it. What asshole came up with *french fries?* "Brewers from around the county set up booths and give free tastings all day long. You have to be invited, but I'm allowed to bring guests."

Ellison's face fell. "Well, maybe it's not so bad. Some of these brews are downright good."

Liam laughed at him, but his heart warmed. Kim was no wilting flower. She was scared, angry, uncertain, and unhappy, but she wasn't going to hunch in on herself and cry.

Good. She needed to be strong to take Shifters. She'd have to take the lot of them, now, because she wouldn't be going home tonight.

Chapter Six

Kim ate hungrily. Getting attacked and watching her attacker die did that to a girl.

This was all so weird. The cowboy sitting next to Liam, sipping his pale beer while watching Liam put away his chicken-fried steak, made jokes, but his eyes were wary, watchful—going from dark blue to light and back again as he and Liam talked.

Ellison seemed very upset that the feral had been a wolf Shifter. Why? Because Liam and Sean, who'd killed him, were big cats? Kim didn't understand what difference that made. A Shifter was a Shifter. Wasn't he?

Kim sensed that she'd stumbled upon something with layers and layers of complexity. She'd been so confident she could help Brian, striking a blow for Shifter rights at the same time, but now she wondered at her ego. The more she'd learned about Shifters today, the more she realized how very little she knew.

Ellison eventually moved off to talk to others, taking his microbrew with him. Kim wiped her mouth with the extra napkins Annie had brought. "Thank you. I guess I needed the food."

"A good meal with a good friend is one of the joys of life," Liam said, sounding like he meant it. "Even if it's in a Shifter bar."

Kim's chest felt suddenly hollow. She yearned for this kind of simplicity, but her life was chaotic and stressful and so damned busy. How long had it been since she and her girlfriends had met for a meal, to talk and catch up?

To laugh and wallow in memories of friendship? Too long. One of them had moved out of state since the last time the group had met, and the others were caught up in their own lives. Kim hadn't talked to most of her friends for more than a minute in months. Silas was the only exception and that was only because of his interest in Brian's case for his documentary. But even his e-mails were brief.

She put down her fork. "I really should get back home. Your friends have probably repaired my door by now, and I have to work tomorrow."

"You're working on a Sunday?"

"I'll work at home, but I have a lot to do. Cases to prepare, appeals to file. Brian's only one of my responsibilities."

Liam piled his silverware on his plate, pushed his plate and hers aside, and clasped Kim's hands. His movements were jerky, and his skin was hot. "You need to come home with me first."

"Why?" Not that, with his hands warm on hers and his sexy blue eyes gazing at her, she wanted to argue much.

"Sean will have told Dad what happened, but Dad will want to hear your side of the story."

"My side of the story? I don't have a side. I saw what you saw."

"This is a Shifter problem. Dad needs all the information he can get."

Kim let herself squeeze his hands in return. "All right, but not for long. I really have work to do."

"Dance first?"

"Sorry?"

The jukebox was going full blast, some country music tune Ellison had keyed in. "I need to work off some energy. Are you too much of a city girl that you can't do a Texas two-step?"

"You're Irish," she said as he pulled her up. "Don't you—you know, jig?"

Liam laughed, a sound so warm that everyone around them who heard it smiled. His eyes crinkled, and his laugh drove out the lingering horror of the wolf Shifter's attack.

Something should bother Kim about what had happened—something more than dead Shifter wolf and Sean with his sword and Liam being a snarling wildcat, that is. She needed time to sit, think, let her adrenaline shut down while her brain took over.

Liam didn't want to let her shut down. He pulled her out of the booth and to the middle of the floor. Other couples were already dancing—very close—but they were Shifters, so Kim couldn't tell the difference between couples who were lovers and those who were friends. Shifters liked to touch.

Liam pulled Kim into an embrace, his feet finding the rhythm of the dance. Kim knew the steps, but she hadn't danced in a long time, and she moved stiffly.

Liam ran his hand along the curve of her waist. "Relax, darling. I'll take care of you."

Kim's eyes were so blue, Liam thought. If he were into poetry, he'd say *blue like an Irish sea*. But he hadn't seen Ireland in such a long time that he couldn't be sure if the waters around it were still so pure blue they would break your heart.

Kim set his already pounding heart to racing. Her lips were red, full, luscious. Liam didn't kiss—when he bedded women he was too busy to do any kissing, and besides, he and the female were usually in animal form. But touching Kim's lips with his suddenly seemed like a good idea.

His libido was getting ahead of his brains. This woman wasn't, and could never be, for Liam. She was

here temporarily, dragged into Shifter troubles she
didn't understand. She didn't understand how deeply
she was in them, either. When she figured it out, she'd
sure as hell not be in the mood for any kissing.

His libido told his brains to shut the hell up. Her scent
was exciting, sweet. She looked up at him and smiled,
and her small hands moved to his waist.

Warm supple woman slid against his body, and Liam's blood flowed toward his groin. He imagined her
under him, hips lifting as he slid into her. Her blue eyes
would close, her round breasts would press his chest,
and her legs would rise to twine his waist.

Gods, he needed sex. After a fight he always ran in his
cat form to get it out of his system, before he paid the
price. He hadn't had the chance to run tonight, so his
body urged him to do an even better thing, take this
woman home and love her.

If he'd been doing what Sean suggested, having a
good night's shag with a Shifter woman every night,
Liam wouldn't be sweating now, fighting his urges and
his Collar. He'd never, ever had urges to be with a human woman.

Then again, he'd never met Kim.

Liam pulled her closer, hands moving to her hips. *I'm
the Shifter who doesn't need anyone, who puts the good of
Shiftertown before everything else.*

Right.

Kim laughed. "I forgot how much I liked to dance,"
she said over the music.

"Doesn't your man ever take you out on the town?"

"Abel? We go to fancy dinners, usually with a group
of lawyers he's trying to impress. No dancing."

"His name is Abel, is it?"

"Yeah, Abel Kane. Can you believe his parents named
him that?"

"He could change it. I hear humans do that." As though a name were a mutable thing. Humans were crazy.

"He says people remember it," Kim said. "I guess he's right."

"But he doesn't dance."

Kim laughed. Apparently thinking of this boyfriend dancing was hilarious. "No, he doesn't dance. I didn't know Shifters did, either."

"We do a lot of things." Liam twirled her once, pulled her against him again, and then the song drew to a close.

Couples dispersed. Jordie Ross kissed his wife on her upturned lips, stroking his fingers over her throat. The fond look she gave Jordie as she walked back to her girl-friends stabbed through Liam's heart. His own parents had looked at each other like that once. So had Kenny and Sinead. Mates for life, they'd thought.

Liam kept hold of Kim's hand. "Time to go."

Kim's wariness returned as he led her out of the bar. "Go where?" she asked.

"Home."

"You mean your home." And his father. Would Liam's dad be elderly and kind, with the same blue eyes as his son and a warm smile, or a rigid patriarch who terri-fied every person who crossed the threshold?

Liam nodded silently, his eyes giving nothing away. His sudden quietness made Kim nervous, but then she thought about her own house waiting for her, how large and lonely it was.

The place had never warmed up again since Mark's death, no matter how hard she and her parents had tried. There'd been a hole in every Christmas celebration, ev-ery Easter dinner, every Halloween night's trek through the neighborhood. The family had gone through the rituals each year, realizing that rituals were unfulfilling when someone you loved was missing from them, but they'd been unable to do anything else. Kim had tried to liven up the house with remodeling a few years ago, having a party to celebrate, but while the house looked more modern, it was still empty.

Kim thought about Shiftertown, how alive it was, how these people had been forced to reside here but had made it bearable with the closeness of family and friends.

"I'd like to see where you live," she decided. "Even if I have to be interrogated by your father."

"He won't interrogate you." Liam's smile returned. "Like Ellison said, we're pussycats."

Kim wasn't sure what to make of that, but she followed him through the crowd that had gathered outside the doors and in the parking lot. They were mostly Shifters, laughing and talking and waiting for a chance to ooze into the packed interior.

The night had cooled, the humidity lessening. Overhead, stars poked through the lights of the city against vast blackness that stretched to eternity.

"What a nice night," Kim said. "Do you live far? Can we walk?"

How weird that she wanted to. In this city of cars, walking was what you did along Lake Austin or in Zilker Park or on Sixth Street on Saturday night. You didn't walk to actually get somewhere.

"It's not far," Liam said, "but we'll drive. It will be safer to leave your car inside Shiftertown than out here."

He had a point—this was a bad part of town. Liam drove again, and Kim was content to look out the window. This late, no kids lingered on the lawns, but the houses glowed with light. People sat out on lit porches to talk or simply watch the night.

Liam pulled the car into an old-fashioned driveway—two strips of concrete with grass in the middle—about two blocks from where Brian's mother lived. Liam got out of the car and came around to open the door for her.

Kim looked up in surprise as Liam helped her out and shut the door, a courtesy she wasn't used to. In her world, a woman had to pretend she didn't want or need little courtesies from men. If she wanted a man's job, she had to act like a man. Be even stronger than a man, actually, and more ruthless. Kim knuckled down and played the game, and she was surprised at how much Liam's gentlemanly gestures pleased her.

Liam's house was a bungalow, like Sandra's, two stories with square brick pillars on the porch. One corner of the porch held a picnic bench and a table, the other, a porch swing.

"I've always wanted a porch swing," Kim said. "Stupid, but I was never allowed to have one. Homeowner's association didn't approve."

"You're welcome to lounge on our porch swing anytime you want."

"Anyone ever tell you you're a sweetie, Liam? Isn't it a little late for a visit, though? Will your father be up still?"

Liam's smile answered her. "We're night people."

"Like vampires? Hell, I've had too much beer."

"No. Not like vampires." Liam opened the front door and ushered her into his house. "Vampires are different."

Kim wasn't certain what to make of his answer. Was he teasing? But heck, Shifters existed. Why not vampires?

She'd definitely had too much beer.

The front door led straight into the living room, which was dominated by a big box of a television. The couch and chairs had been grouped around it, with folding TV trays for end tables. The tables were littered with soda cans, beer bottles, bowls holding crumbs of corn chips, and stacks of videotapes and DVDs. It looked as though they'd had a movie night. The floors were polished wood with mismatched rugs and runners on them, unlike Kim's cool tile floors with plush hand-woven carpets.

As Liam led Kim inside, Sean and another man came down the stairs to her left, and a young, lanky Morrissey bounded out of the kitchen that opened beyond the living room.

"Is that her?" the young man asked.

The oldest man moved past him and held out his hand to Kim. "I'm Dylan."

Liam's father. He didn't look any older than forty, but like Sandra, his eyes held the weight of years. Those eyes assessed her, much as Liam's had, but without the warm interest. His grip was strong, not overpowering, but it let Kim know he *could* overpower her anytime he wanted to.

Kim decided that if she'd met Dylan instead of Liam, she'd have hightailed it out of Shiftertown and never looked back. No wonder Liam was the one Brian said everyone approached. You had to be brave to look into Dylan's eyes and not quail.

Sean stepped off the stairs. "Connor, why didn't you clean up this crap? I told you Kim was coming."

"I'm doing it." The young man started gathering the jetsam into his big hands.

"My nephew, Connor," Liam said. "Our brother Kenny's son."

The brother who'd died. Kim watched the long-limbed Connor shoulder his way into the kitchen, trying to carry everything at once.

Liam gestured for Kim to sit down. A couch, which had seen years of bouncing children and men's booted feet, sagged when she sat on it. Connor reappeared and handed Kim a cold soft drink. Kim wasn't in the mood for one, but she thanked him, opened the can, and took a sip. No reason not to be polite.

Liam sat down next to her, close, as he had at Sandra's. Shifters really didn't understand personal space. Or if they did, they didn't care.

Sean stood ill at ease, his hands in his pockets. He wore a frown, as though he didn't like having Kim there, but not because he didn't like Kim. Dylan watched also, but with a quietness that the younger men of the family didn't have. He was closer to the predator than any of them.

And here I am, the gazelle.

To calm her nerves, Kim looked around at the décor, which was mostly bachelor clutter. "Hey, I have a suitcase just like that." She pointed at a black bag with metallic studs that stood next to the TV set. "Wait a minute, that *is* my bag." She glared at Liam, who didn't look the slightest bit guilt-stricken. "Gee, I wonder how it got here."

"Remember my friends who went to fix your back door? They brought it."

Kim set her can carefully on a TV tray. "Want to tell me why? Or do you have a fetish about stealing other people's luggage?"

It was Dylan who answered. "Because you're staying here, Kim. Liam knew you'd want your things."

"What do you mean, staying here? Spending the night? I haven't had *that* much to drink."

Liam slid his arm around her, strong, holding her there. "You need to stay."

"The Shifter wolf is dead. You and Sean killed him. I'm safe now." Finally the thing niggling at her broke through the fog in her brain. "Liam, *how* were you able to kill him? Your Collar should have stopped you from fighting, even against another Shifter. Right?"

Liam said nothing. She felt Sean standing above her, Connor's awkward uneasiness, and Dylan's strong silence.

"Liam?"

Liam's eyes were blue, hard, holding her gaze. "I'm sorry, love. That's why we can't let you go."

Chapter Seven

She took it well. Liam had to give her that.

No screaming, no outraged swearing, no gibbering in terror. Kim simply looked at him, her eyes unreadable.

"Why not?" she asked steadily. "If I can prove that Brian had nothing to do with the murder, it won't matter whether his Collar can malfunction. I have no reason to share the information far and wide."

"You should let someone else take over Brian's defense," Dylan said.

Now the anger came. "Oh, no, no, no. This case is going to make my career. Besides, I'm your best hope of springing him."

Dylan's eyes were hard. "Brian understands the need to protect the Shifters."

Kim struggled from Liam's embrace and sprang to her feet. "Are you saying you'd let him go down? Make him pretend *his* Collar malfunctioned to keep everyone from knowing the Collars don't work at all?"

"This isn't about the Collars," Liam said. "And anyway, the Collars do work."

"You're crazy. If Brian's found guilty, he gets the death sentence for Shifters. Do you know what that means?"

"He won't die at the hands of the human government," Dylan said. "If he's convicted, we'll take care that he doesn't face an executioner."

"What, you'll send Sean to turn him to dust?"

Sean looked away, unable to meet her eyes.

"No, not Sean." Liam stood up beside her. "It's not his job."

Kim gave him an uncomprehending look; then her eyes widened. "You mean it's *yours?* Oh, Jesus effing Christ, Liam."

"It's a Shifter problem," Dylan said in his quiet voice.

"And now *I'm* a Shifter problem? You can't take my word that I won't tell anyone? Liam, you saved my life tonight. I owe you."

"It's not up to us," Sean broke in. "We don't make the law."

"The oldest excuse in the book. Aren't you the leader around here, Dylan? Can't you make, you know, an executive decision?"

Dylan shook his head. "These are clan matters and Shifter secrets. Only Fergus can override the law."

"Who the hell is Fergus?"

"The leader of the South Texas clan," Liam answered. "Dad thinks you should have a hearing with him. I don't agree."

"Why not? Maybe this Fergus will see reason."

"Fergus? Reason?" Liam wanted to laugh. He thought about the big man with the long black braid, the thugs he surrounded himself with. Fergus hadn't been happy when Kim managed to get Brian a jury trial. He'd wanted Brian to plead guilty and be done, the human prodding into Shifter business over. Liam still didn't understand why Fergus was so ready to wash his hands of Brian, but Brian had been ready to obey.

Until Kim had persuaded Brian to fight. Of course she had. Kim was a fighter. Fergus had been livid when he learned Brian had a competent defense attorney.

"He's dangerous, Kim," Liam said, his voice sharp

with worry. "All Shifters are dangerous, Fergus especially so. You shouldn't have come to see me at all."

"I owe it to my client to try to help him get free."

"And now you know too damned much."

"Keep it quiet, Liam," Dylan growled. "I can contain this, but not if the neighbors hear you . . ."

Kim looked wildly out the window to the house next door. "What? What happens if the neighbors hear?"

"They might go to Fergus," Sean said. "We might not be able to stop them. We're your best protection."

"You can't keep me here." She had good lung power for such a small woman.

"We can and we will," Dylan said, eyes glittering. "We protect the clan."

Connor looked distressed. "Stop it, Grandda'. You're scaring her. She's going to think we're all crazy."

She'd not be far from wrong, Liam thought. Kim quivered with rage and fear, and Liam felt the overwhelming need to put his arms around her and soothe her. She needed to be held in the same way he and Sean had held Sandra, calming her nerves, easing her worry.

Holding Kim would calm Liam as well. His adrenaline was wearing off—he could tell by the dull buzzing in his head. Very soon now, he'd start to pay the price for killing the feral Shifter. Sean didn't look as bad, but then Sean hadn't fought; he'd only dispatched the feral's soul.

"Keeping you here is the safest thing," Liam said to Kim. "If Fergus thinks we have you under control, he won't send anyone to make sure you are."

Kim's anger would have knocked a weaker man sideways. She'd started to trust Liam, and now she felt betrayed. "Under control?"

"Kim, love, when I said I'd protect you, I meant it. That means from everyone, my own father or my clan leader if necessary. If you go home tonight, Fergus will send Shifters after you. I'd have to stay with you, bodyguard you day and night." Liam ran a finger along her chin. "Not that I'd find that a bad thing."

Kim stared at him without softening. He wished he could make her understand that she'd put herself in danger the minute she'd taken Brian's case. Dylan and Fergus had argued long and hard when Kim had sent word she wanted to talk to Liam, and now Kim was in greater peril than ever.

Someone banged on the front door, and Liam caught a scent of Lupine overlaid with a large dose of Oscar de la Renta.

Sean rolled his eyes. "Perfect. She's all we're needing."

"Your door's locked," a woman's voice called through the wood.

"Let her in, Sean," Dylan said, resigned.

"About time." A tall woman dressed head to toe in black walked in when Sean opened the door. She wore tight pants and a sleeveless silk shirt and had folded her blonde hair into an intricate French braid. Silver highheeled sandals studded with rhinestones completed her outfit. "Why'd you lock the door? You never lock it." She fixed white-blue eyes on Kim. "Who's this human woman, and why are you all yelling?"

The newcomer was lithe, with athletic grace, the kind of female Kim had despised when struggling with teen self-esteem. This Shifter lady could be a model for a fashion doll, except that she exuded personality with a capital P. Even her Collar gleamed.

Liam, Sean, and Connor viewed her with irritation. Dylan looked downright uncomfortable and avoided her gaze. *Interesting.*

The woman put a long-fingered hand on one hip. "I'm getting into bed when I hear my big cat neighbors trying to calm down a shouting woman. What am I supposed to think?" She pinned Kim with her predatory stare. "What are you doing to them, honey?"

Kim looked the woman up and down, pretending she wasn't unnerved. "*That's* what you wear to bed?"

"Depends on who's in it with me." The woman's gaze slid sideways to Dylan, who pretended not to notice. "Who is she?"

"None of your business, Glory," Connor tried.

Of all of them, Connor seemed to be the most oblivious to her overt sexuality. But then, if this Glory had something going on with Dylan, his grandfather, Connor would probably think her impossibly old. Even if she looked thirty at most. Damn, Shifters had good genes.

Glory sniffed the air, nostrils flaring. "Liam's scent-marked her. I never knew your tastes ran to humans, Liam."

Liam slid an arm around Kim's waist, and Kim wished it didn't feel so good there. "I'm protecting her from nosy Shifters."

"Sure you are." Glory's light blue gaze moved up and down Kim with too much perception. "But who protects you from *her?*"

Liam's grip tightened. "Good night, Glory."

Glory smiled a knowing smile, her lipstick coral pink. "All right, I won't pry." She gave Kim another assessing look. "Big cats are sensational, sweetie. I keep some extra-large condoms handy if you need them." She spun on the toes of her shiny shoes and sauntered out, black-clad hips swaying.

"I can see why you worry about your neighbors," Kim said as Sean closed the door again. "She's really something."

"Glory's a Lupine," Connor said. "She's always giving us grief. Why she wants to live in a big cat neighborhood, I don't know."

"She doesn't have a choice, does she?" Liam looked out the window, probably making sure that Glory went back to her own house and stayed there. "I'm taking Kim up to my room—alone. We need to have a chat."

"To your room?" Kim stared. "Why?" She wished she weren't so intrigued at the thought. She needed to be afraid of these men, to flee them, to not let them keep her here.

Then she thought of the feral Shifter in her bedroom and her big empty house with the dusty Shifter remains on her carpet. Contrasted with this bright, warm house, her own place suddenly had too many ghosts.

"You'll sleep up in my room," Liam was saying. "It's the cleanest. I even do hospital corners." He picked up Kim's bag, then put his arm around her waist again. He liked doing that, as though she naturally belonged in his embrace.

"Wait a minute. You expect me to stay overnight in a house with four single men?"

Sean grinned. "We're perfect gentlemen, Kim. Everyone knows that. Don't let us worry you."

"I'm not worried about my reputation, I'm worried about the state of the bathrooms."

Liam laughed softly, his warm breath tickling her ear. "They did a cleanup when I told them you were coming. And if they didn't, they'll be doing it now, *won't they?* This way, love."

Liam took her to a roomy upstairs hall with three bedrooms and bath and a stair that led to an attic. Kim had to admit everything looked nice. Polished wood, freshly painted walls, clean carpets. But the house was definitely missing feminine touches, which made it a little sad and incomplete.

Liam led her into a large bedroom with only one picture on the wall, a travel poster of a green vista in Ireland.

"Interesting neighbors you have," Kim said. "Do she and your dad have something going on? I noticed a lot of tension there."

Liam closed the door and dumped Kim's bag on the floor. "She and Dad have an on-again, off-again affair. When they get along, it's a beautiful thing."

"And when they don't?"

"We head for the hills. Right now they're in neutral."

"*That* was neutral? I see what you mean about heading for the hills. She's a wolf Shifter, Connor said, but your dad is a big cat like you?"

"Not exactly a match that would have happened before we took the Collar. But they care about each other. Deep down inside."

Must be *very* deep down inside. "I'll take your word for it."

Liam laughed his warm, throaty laugh. "I'm skeptical too, love, but it works for them. Come here." He sat on the bed, putting his back against the headboard, and patted the mattress beside him.

"On the bed. Of course." Kim put her hands on her hips. "If kidnapping and arguing don't work, try seduction."

"No seduction." How Liam could claim that while looking at her with those sinful baby blues, she didn't know.

Why did *no seduction* sound so disappointing? Maybe because Kim had felt a tingle of attraction for him since the moment she'd met him? As she'd talked to him throughout the day, she'd been lulled by his deep voice with its Irish lilt, softened by the warm blue of his eyes. Even him turning into a wildcat and killing a wolf on her bedroom floor hadn't quite brought her to her senses.

Kim gave up and sat down beside him, stretching her legs out next to his. His hard thigh warmed hers.

"What did Glory mean when she said you 'scent-marked' me? That sounds disturbing." Kim didn't smell anything different about herself, but then she wasn't a Shifter.

"Protection, love. Shifters know their families and friends faster by scent first, then sight. I made sure that when they smell you now they smell me and know to leave you alone."

"I don't remember you spraying me or anything." She wrinkled her nose.

"When I hugged you outside Sandra's house, I let my scent twine with yours."

"Oh." She'd remembered that hug all day, his body hard and strong against hers, his arms so comforting. She'd thought it part of the Shifter's strange need to touch. "But I went home and took a shower."

Liam gave her the smile that made his eyes sparkle. "It's more than smell—the scent-mark is a little bit magic as well. It fades with time if you never see the Shifter again, but for now, everyone in Shiftertown knows I'm taking care of you."

Kim was uncertain how to feel about that. She didn't like being "protected," but then again, having Liam charge in to save her from the feral had been a good thing. She'd also noted how the Shifters at the bar had sized her up. Without Liam's mark, would she have been fair game? Unnerving thought.

Liam had fallen silent, as though lost in thought. His big body took most of the bed, leaving Kim only a tiny portion. She wondered what it would be like to sleep in this small bed with him. A woman would have to cuddle up to him, maybe spoon against his back. Her arm would snake around his waist, and she'd want to tickle his belly button.

"Do Shifters have belly buttons?" she asked.

Liam's preoccupied look dissolved into a smile. "You're a treasure, lass. The gods sent you to us, I think."

"It just occurred to me."

Liam eased his T-shirt upward. His jeans rode low on his waist, baring his flat stomach and the indentation of his navel.

"I'm human in every way when I'm in this form," he said. "It's not only our appearance that changes. It's everything. Bones, muscles, organs. It's hellacious painful when we first do it."

"How old were you when you shifted the first time?" Kim couldn't drag her gaze from his abdomen. She wanted to taste his belly button and slide her tongue down from there to his low-riding waistband.

"I was about five as humans count years. I was still a cub. I remember thinking I was dying."

"It must have been weird to suddenly be a wildcat—whatever kind of cat you are."

"It's called a Fae-cat. But you've got it the other way 'round, love. I lived as a wildcat for five years before I shifted to human. Standing up on two feet and having eyes that couldn't see so well in the dark—it scared the bejesus out of me."

"You were *born* a cat?"

"My parents were both full-blood Feline Shifters, so yes. When there's a mix—wolf and cat Shifter, or wolf and bear, say—then you're born a human babe. You shift to whatever is the dominant gene when you're about five or six."

Interesting. None of her research had told her any of this, which made her realize just how little humans knew about Shifters. "What is a Fae-cat, exactly? I couldn't decide if you were mountain lion or leopard or what."

"It's hard to explain to a non-Shifter. We're a unique breed, left over from times before humans populated the earth. The Fae made us. They bred in the strengths of all members of the big cat family, at least the big cats of ancient times, the ancestors of wildcats that exist now. We're fast like cheetahs, can see in the dark like leopards, have the power of lions, the cunning of tigers. That's why we call ourselves Felines, not a specific breed. The Lupines are wolves, but not exactly like any wolves you'd find in the wild."

"In other words, the best of the entire species."

"You could say that."

"So, if you can crossbreed, like you said, then your dad and your next-door neighbor could produce children. In theory."

"In theory, though cross-species fertility is not as high as fertility within a species. Dad's only about two hundred, so he can still father cubs. Glory won't tell her age, but she's still in the fertile range."

"Dylan is two hundred years old?" Kim asked in amazement. "He doesn't look much into his forties. How old are you?"

"I was born in 1898, as humans count years. Sean came along in 1900."

Holy shit. "You look damn good for a centenarian. What about Connor? Don't tell me he's eighty-two."

"He's twenty. Born right after we took the Collar. His mum died of bringing him in, poor lass."

Kim's thought of Connor downstairs, with his good-natured smile and his worry about them frightening her. "Oh, Liam, I'm sorry."

Liam shrugged, a shrug that meant he'd resigned himself to it. "It happened often enough when we lived outside of humankind. It's one of the reasons the clan leaders decided to take the Collar. We were a dying people."

"She was married to the brother you lost, wasn't she? Kenny? That sucks. Poor Connor."

"Aye. A feral got Kenny ten years ago. We've looked after Connor, but it's not the same for him."

Kim leaned against Liam's strong arm, suddenly wanting to comfort him. "And I thought I had it bad growing up. But I was always cared for, never had to worry. Even when my parents passed away, they'd taken care of me to the end. I was already working, but they'd left me the house and plenty of money. I never wanted for anything."

The corner of his mouth quirked up. "Poor little rich girl."

"It let me do work I believed in. I don't have to take cases based on how much they pay."

"No, you're free to help hapless Shifters."

Kim sat up. "You all sound like you don't take this seriously, like you don't want me to get Brian free. Brian's mother is barely holding it together. You and Sean had to do the comforting sandwich with her, remember?"

"Aye." Liam went silent. His T-shirt had slid down again, covering his honed body. Damn.

"Believe me, when I'm defending someone, I make certain he gets a fair trial," Kim said. "It's a right we all have that can get lost if we're not careful. And besides, I think Brian's innocent. I seem to be the only one who does."

"Kim." Liam cut through her diatribe. "Brian *is* innocent. He couldn't have killed that girl. But to prove it, you might reveal secrets that could destroy all Shifters, everywhere."

"Secrets like the fact that the Collars don't work? Or that some Shifters don't even wear them?"

Liam gazed into the distance. "It's not quite that simple."

"Then explain to me what's going on." She softened her tone. "Believe me, I'll do what I can to get Brian exonerated, but bringing down your family isn't what I had in mind."

"I'm glad to hear that," Liam said mildly.

"So how *is* it possible that you killed that Shifter?" Kim asked. "The Collars really don't work?"

"Oh, they work, love." His eyes were clouded. "They work."

"May I look?"

Liam nodded. Kim knelt back on her heels to examine the thin black and silver chain around his throat. She lifted his hair at the back of his neck, wishing it wasn't all warm and silky and distracting.

The chain had no clasp and was fused to his skin, the links snug but not tight. A Celtic knot rested at the base of his throat. When Liam had been in his wildcat form in her bedroom, she'd seen the glint of the Collar against his fur.

"How did it not strangle you when you shifted?"

"When the Collar goes on, it becomes a part of the Shifter. Don't ask me to explain the technology or the magic, because I don't understand it myself. The Collar allows us to change to our animal forms—because if we were denied that we'd die. Our animal form is part of us, with us at all times. So the chain adapts to it."

Kim ran her fingers around the Collar, feeling the cool contrast of the silver with his hot skin, the bump of the Celtic knot. "What do you mean by 'the magic'? It's triggered by your adrenal system, isn't it? To shock you or tranquilize you when your chemical balance changes, right?"

Liam chuckled. "You saw me shift from cat to man, and the wolf die away to dust under Sean's sword, and you still don't believe in magic?"

"Not really. There's an explanation for even the most bizarre things."

"Remind me to take you to Ireland someday. I'll show you magic. An Irishman made these chains, an old man who was permeated with magic himself."

"A leprechaun?"

Liam laid his head back and laughed. Kim's hand was still on his neck, and catching his head in her palm felt intimate and warm.

"No, sweetheart, no little men in green with shamrocks. The man who made the first Collars was half Fae. Your government—and others in the world where Shifters are allowed to live—agreed that the old mage could supply the chains that keep us weak."

"You keep talking about *Fae*. What's Fae?"

"Sometimes called Fair Folk or fairies, but they're not cute little people with wings. The Fae are ancient and arrogant beings who once regarded the earth as theirs. Terrifying, they are. They made Shifters to be their pets, their hunting beasts, but we weren't having any of that."

Kim wasn't certain how much of this she bought, and she couldn't tell if he believed it himself or was having her on. "You said the man who made the chains *was* half Fae. Do you mean he's dead now?"

"He is. But he passed the knowledge to his son. The son stays hidden away in Ireland and sends the Collars as they're needed."

"How was it that you could fight and kill the feral

Shifter then? Or do the Collars work only if you try to attack humans?"

"No, like you said, the Collars are keyed to our adrenal systems. Doesn't matter who we're violent toward. But some of us have found ways to . . . delay . . . the system. It's painful, but it can be done."

Liam met her gaze calmly, but something raged behind his eyes. He'd changed since he'd come into this room, but she couldn't put her finger on how. "You've learned how to override yours, you mean," she said.

Liam shrugged again, but his shoulders remained hunched. There it was—the key. Instead of Liam the strong and protective, he'd withdrawn into himself. He'd talked with her and smiled at her, but his thoughts were far away.

"I have," he said. "I only override it when necessary."

"Like tonight." Kim touched his chest, feeling his heart beating too rapidly beneath her fingers. "And that hurt you?"

"It did, love. That's why I'm sitting quietly on this bed and leaving your beautiful self alone. My entire body is brutal raw with pain."

Chapter Eight

Liam hadn't lied; he hurt like hell.

Kim's eyes went wide with shock. "But we were dancing half an hour ago."

"I can hold it off for a long time, especially if the excitement of the kill is high." He let his gaze drift over her delicious little body. "And dancing with you—let's just say I wasn't letting anything stop me from enjoying that."

She looked worried. "And you're in pain now?"

"Excruciating." Agony bloomed behind Liam's eyes and in every nerve ending, every muscle. His spine felt as if someone had twisted it with a giant pair of pliers. The punishment didn't even spare his smallest toes.

"Liam, I'm sorry. I didn't know."

"A man doesn't like to admit when he's hurting. It shames us."

"Can't you do anything for it? Would ibuprofen help? I have some in my purse."

He wanted to laugh. Ibuprofen wouldn't make a dent. "Nothing to be done but wait it out. Having you sit here with me is nice."

Kim watched him in concern for a few more moments, then snuggled down against him. Liam smiled as he gathered her close, reflecting on the ironies of life. On the one hand, the pain was driving him crazy. On the other, Kim would likely never have draped herself over him if he hadn't admitted his suffering.

"What about Sean?" she asked. "Is he in pain too?"

"Probably a little, but he didn't make the kill. He only cleaned up after."

Kim smoothed his T-shirt over his abdomen. "Why would you do this to yourself? I mean all Shifters. Live with the possibility of this hurting?"

"We had to." Liam stopped, talking becoming too much of an effort. The pain would recede, probably by tomorrow morning, but he'd have horror to go through first. It wasn't so bad this time, maybe because he'd been fighting to protect Kim. He'd acted on instinct when he realized she was in danger, not even worrying about the price he'd pay.

"You make me want to kiss you," Kim said.

His heart beat faster. "What a sweetheart you are. But I don't kiss."

She lifted her head. "What are you talking about? You've kissed me plenty today."

On her hair, her neck. Liam moved as his cock started to harden with memory, even through his pain. "I don't kiss like humans do, on the lips. I don't see the point."

"You mean Shifters don't kiss at all?" Kim's eyes narrowed. "Wait a minute, I saw a Shifter kiss his wife in the bar. That was his wife, wasn't it?"

"You mean Jordie? Yes, she was his mate. I didn't say all Shifters don't kiss. I said *I* don't. When I'm with a Shifter woman we have other things on our minds."

"You mean you hump her without intimacies? Figures. Tragic that someone who looks as good as you isn't interested in the woman's pleasure."

The pain receded the slightest bit. "What shite are you talking? There's plenty of pleasure when I'm with a woman. On both sides."

"Huh. You don't even take the time to kiss her."

"Since you're not a Shifter woman, you wouldn't understand. It's fast and furious, no time for much else."

Kim shook her head, her curls tickling through his shirt. "You have no idea what you're missing, Liam."

"I've never been with a human." Liam liked her face close to his, her scent filling his whole body. "You're right, I don't know."

"All right, then. Hold still."

Kim knelt beside him. Her jeans tightened against her thighs, and her blouse gaped open, giving him a glimpse of soft breast swelling above lace.

Her scent was driving him crazy. Liam had used protective marking before, but he'd never smelled such a heady mixture as he did now—his scent and Kim's blended in almost equal parts. As though they belonged together.

Kim's hesitant fingertips brushed his cheek, her caress so different from her forthright manner and sassy speech. "Am I hurting you?"

She was worried about him, the sweetheart. "The pain's backing off."

"That's good."

She came close, closer. The warmth of her skin, the scent of it, made Liam's hard-on throb, his lust start to break through the excruciating pain. Kim's lashes swept down as she touched her mouth to his upper lip.

Something shook in Liam's core, and the hurting began to lose the battle. Liam moved his lips in response, clumsily catching her mouth with his.

The satin-smooth slide of Kim's lips took his breath away. He *had* kissed in human form before, but they'd been quick, affectionate pecks with friends or female members of the family. He'd never experienced the full sensations of a slow, hot kiss, lips moving and exploring.

He cupped Kim's neck, encouraging her to continue, and nearly jumped off the bed when she thrust her tongue into his mouth.

Kim jerked away. "What? Did I hurt you?"

"No." Liam laced his fingers behind her neck, under her warm hair. "You surprised me, is all. Is that your way of kissing? I like it."

"My way? I think it's everybody's way. Don't tell me Shifters don't French kiss."

"I'm Irish."

Her smile was gorgeous. "Well, well, something I know that the all-powerful Shifter-man doesn't."

"Let's try it again. I'm a quick learner."

Kim cupped his face. "I shouldn't be doing this."

"You should. It's helping me." *Stay with me.*

"I can't get involved with you, and besides, you're trying to keep me prisoner in your house. Not that you'll succeed, by the way."

"It's for your own safety, love. I'm responsible for what happens to you."

"I do feel safer here." It cost her to admit that, Liam could see. "If I were alone in my house right now, I'd be scared. Being attacked by that feral—it was so fast. I always thought I could defend myself, and I suddenly realized I couldn't."

Liam kneaded her neck. "Here you don't have to worry." He tugged her closer. "Let's try the French way again."

Kim wanted to resist—Liam saw hesitation in her eyes. She wanted to say no, to pull away, to walk out. He also sensed her wanting. She craved to be touched, and she thought he was harmless, sitting here in so much pain it made his teeth ache. Never mind that she was mostly right.

Kim closed her eyes before their lips met again. Was

this required for a kiss? Liam kept his eyes open, liking to watch the way her lashes curled against her skin, how one lock of her hair slid over her cheek.

She put her tongue inside his mouth again. Liam caught it, licking, lapping, playing. He tilted his head so he could better fit their mouths together.

Damn, this was good. Humans had something going with this kissing, even if they gave it a French name, like the fries he insisted on calling chips. Liam's erection was getting massive now. He wasn't sure whether he'd be embarrassed if the tip peeped above the waistband, or whether he'd be pleased to show her how much he wanted her.

Playing catch-me with Kim's tongue, Liam slid his hands to her thighs, wishing she still wore the skirt from this morning. If so, he could inch his way under the hem, latch his fingers over the tops of her stockings, unhook the garters, peel the stockings down . . .

Kim eased back, her eyes half closed. "Liam, you're going to kiss my lips raw."

Liam smiled. "You say that like it's a bad thing."

"I thought you were hurt."

"I'm feeling so much better." Liam dug his fingers into the denim covering her thighs, his strength returning. He could roll her over onto the bed, press her down into the mattress, have her teach him some more about human kissing.

He touched her lips again. "You're a sweet, beautiful thing, do you know that?"

"For a human?"

"For an anything, love."

He kissed her one more time, then made himself push away and sit up. This was getting dangerous. His strength was growing and with it, rampaging lust.

Kim looked at him in confusion, her lips swollen and

red, her eyes dark, pupils wide. "What's the matter? I thought you wanted more lessons."

"Afraid not, sweetheart. I have to get out of here before you regret it."

She smiled a little. "I don't regret a little kissing."

It would be so much more if he didn't leave. Goddess, she was delectable. "You'll be safe here tonight, I promise you. No one, not even Fergus himself, will get through Dad, me, and Sean. Even Connor's a good fighter, young as he is. They like you, and we've taken you in. You'll be protected like you were one of the pride."

She looked surprised, then thoughtful, as though she hadn't considered it that way. "I admit I'm afraid to go back home right now. But I can stay only until morning. All right?"

Liam didn't answer as he stood. He knew damn well she could see his erection—how could she miss a thing of that size pushing at her? If she asked him to, he'd unbutton and unzip to let her see him, or touch him, or take him in her mouth.

Bloody hell, he had to get out of here.

Kim wet her lips. Liam put his hands on his hips, his pulse thumping so hard his fingers hurt. Her mouth was lush and red, lips plump, making him want to bite them.

"I should sleep now," she said, sounding as though she had to make herself acknowledge it. "I have a lot to do tomorrow."

Sleep. In his bed, her head on his pillow, her body damp and warm. Maybe wearing that little wisp of a silk thing she'd been in when he'd rescued her tonight.

"See you at breakfast then," he made himself say.

"What do Shifters eat for breakfast?"

"Wheaties. Or I can fix you my pancakes, like I promised."

Didn't she look mouthwatering, sitting cross-legged

on the bed, her blouse half unbuttoned, her nipples hard enough to press through her bra and the white fabric? He could push her back onto the pillows, close his mouth on one taut point through the shirt.

Kim picked up a pillow and hugged it to her chest, cutting off the beautiful view. "Good night, Liam."

"I won't be sleeping much, that's for certain. Not thinking about you down here in my bed."

"Down here? Where will you be?"

He pointed at the ceiling. "Connor's got the whole attic floor. Plenty of room for me to bunk down with him. Want me to knock on the floor, let you know when I'm there?"

Kim got off the bed, still hugging the pillow. "What I want is to sleep and forget about this awful night. Then get up and go home. I don't mind staying here tonight because I'm scared, but tomorrow, when I'm done being afraid, I'm going home."

She wouldn't be going home. Liam wouldn't argue with her right now, though. No point in it.

He smiled at her, forced himself to turn his back on her compact body and pretty eyes and leave the room.

He had to stand in the hallway a long time after he closed the door, waiting for his fierce hard-on to go down. He needed to talk to Dylan, but he couldn't face his father with an erection that could stop a train.

Seeing the light go off under the door behind him and hearing the squeak of his bedsprings as Kim climbed into his bed didn't help deflate him at all.

An hour later, Glory opened her back door to admit a moody Dylan Morrissey.

Glory had never met a Shifter who turned her on faster than Dylan could. So what if he was a Feline? Glory's friends didn't approve, but they could eat their hearts out. Dylan was tall, broad-shouldered, and temperamental, with the best ass she'd ever seen on any male, Shifter or human.

Glory let Dylan pace, happy he'd responded to the veiled invitation she'd thrown out when she'd talked to the human girl. Dylan didn't always respond to hints; he did what he pleased. *Damned alpha male.*

"You're giving me motion sickness," she said after a time. "What have you decided to do about the little human? Let Fergus kill her?"

"I don't know what I'm going to do about her." Dylan finally stopped and rested his broad fists on her kitchen counter. "Liam just spent an hour talking me out of taking her to Fergus, which means I disobey Fergus's direct orders. *Fuck.*"

If only.

Glory knew damn well Liam hadn't talked Dylan out of anything. If Dylan thought the girl should go to Fergus, nothing Liam could do would stop Dylan from taking her there.

"Why do you think Liam's right?" she asked.

Dylan's hard blue eyes sparked with anger, though he flicked his gaze away before his dominant rage could fix on her.

"What makes you think I agree with him?"

"Because if you didn't, you'd have her ass in your truck and be hauling her down to San Antonio instead of standing in my kitchen with me."

Dylan slammed his fists into the counter. "I know that. But Liam . . ." He straightened up and shook his head. Glory glanced quickly at the counter, but Dylan hadn't dented it. This time.

"But Liam what?" she asked.

"He cares about her." Dylan ran his hands through his hair, mussing it in a sexy way. "I've never seen him like this. I thought he wanted to protect her because Liam always protects the weak. But it's more than that. Let's say I'm surprised he's letting her sleep alone tonight."

"You think he'll claim her?" Glory started brewing coffee to cover her nervousness, not to mention her rampaging horniness. "She's human."

Dylan leaned his backside against the counter and folded his arms. "You know how high the ratio of males to females is in Shiftertown. It's doubtful Liam will ever mate with another Shifter."

Glory poured fragrant ground coffee into her coffeemaker and closed the lid. "You'd let him take a human as mate?"

"Never in the old days, but those days are gone." He looked exhausted, Dylan who'd lived so long and seen so much. "She seems robust, and she's not afraid of us."

Glory snorted. "If she's not afraid of you, it's because she doesn't know any better. Though I agree, she's got spunk." She admired the way the human girl had said what she'd really thought, though Glory would never admit it. In Glory's experience, most humans she encountered either avoided eye contact with her, pretended contempt, or simply ran away.

"Another reason I don't think Liam will claim a Shifter woman is because he thinks too much about the good of the clan," Dylan was saying. "He pushes potential mates on other Shifters rather than claiming them himself. I asked him why, once. He said that Shifters lower in the hierarchy have more time to breed and raise a family, and that's what Shifters need most. Cubs, not testosterone contests."

"How self-sacrificing of him."

"I also think he's never come across a female who stirs him. For sex, yes. As a mate, no. But this one . . ."

"This one he's not likely to charitably pass down to the next mate-seeking Shifter. She's human; she needs his protection. And Liam is a protector at heart." Glory smiled. "Like his dad."

Dylan finally looked straight at her. He'd been sliding his gaze from hers, trying not to pin her with his angry uncertainty, trying not to demand submission. What a sweetie. He must know that if he wanted Glory to go down on her knees, she'd happily oblige.

"It's my job," Dylan answered irritably.

"No, it's you. You're one big protecting hunk of male. The only reason Fergus leads your clan and not you is because he's a ruthless bastard. You don't challenge him, because you fear he'll retaliate on the innocent, Connor in particular."

Dylan's expression went harder still, and it was all Glory could do to stay upright in her high-heeled shoes. His eyes were tinged with red, a sign that he was ready to lose it.

"You only met Fergus the once," Dylan said, tight-lipped.

"Once was enough. I never want to see him again. People respect you, Dylan. They fear Fergus. There's a difference."

She started to turn away, but a steel-strong hand clamped her arm. "What are you trying to do, Glory? Sow insurrection in my clan?"

Glory looked at him in surprise. "Insurrection? Are you kidding? What for?"

Dylan's grip softened, but Glory saw he had to make himself ease off. "Then why are you so interested in me challenging Fergus?"

"Because you're a better man than he is. I've always thought that, and I'm not the only one."

Dylan closed his eyes. He clenched his jaw, a muscle

twitching. "The clan's survival is more important than me confronting Fergus."

"I know." Glory dared to step closer to him, now that his awful gaze was shielded. "If we start challenging and fighting one another like we did before the Collar, we'll be dead within a few short years."

"I'm glad you understand."

"See, sometimes I listen when you talk."

Dylan opened his eyes then, the red gone, the beautiful blue so deep it made her heart ache.

"Glory," he said softly.

"Yes?"

"Shut it."

Dylan wove his fingers through her hair, loosening it until it spilled over his hands, and he covered her mouth with his.

Glory rose into the kiss, excitement pumping through her. No one could screw like Dylan could. And Dylan surpassed even himself when he was pissed off and warring with his dominant instincts.

She decided not to fight too hard when Dylan lifted her and deposited her on the counter. She wrapped her legs around his hips, unbuttoned his pants, and leaned back to enjoy herself.

Chapter Nine

Liam was wrenched out of sleep the next morning by Kim banging on the attic door and shouting his name. His instincts had him on his feet and wrenching open the door before his brain even knew he was awake.

He found Kim in the hall, her eyes blazing, in a big black T-shirt with a Guinness logo on it. Kim had obviously slept in the rumpled T-shirt, which she must have found in Liam's dresser drawer. Liam knew she'd be warm and very naked beneath it, and then he realized he was naked himself, prepared to shift.

One part of him was shifting already. "Gods, Kim, why are you out here yelling like a banshee?"

Kim held up a small bit of satin fabric, her eyes wide with fury. "Who packed this? It was a *man*, wasn't it?"

"Probably. Why?"

She shook the red satin patch. "This is a *thong*. Have you ever worn a thong? Do you know how it feels to have a string up your ass all day?"

Liam sensed the rest of his family listening: Connor sitting up in bed behind him, Sean in the hall below, Dylan behind him in the same clothes he'd worn last night, which meant he'd slept next door.

"What's wrong with a thong?" Liam asked her. "I bet it's sexy on you." He pictured it, and immediately clamped down on his imagination. *Gods*.

"Oh, right," Kim said. "I'm standing in a courtroom, trying to think on my feet while the prosecution is laughing its butt off at me, but that's all right—*at least my underwear is sexy.*"

Liam leaned on his arm, trying hard not to laugh. He heard Dylan retreat, quietly, into his bedroom. Sean, too, departed, chuckling. Connor folded his arms around his knees, watching this female display in puzzlement.

"Why do you have them, then?" Liam asked.

"Friends buy them for me, all right?" Kim snapped.

"And you hang on to them?"

"I don't want to hurt their feelings. They think they're doing me a favor."

Liam let his grin break through. "They think it's a favor to let you . . . how did you put it . . . wear a string up your ass all day?"

Kim rolled her eyes. "Never *mind*. I'm taking a shower and going home. You got rid of the feral Shifter, so it's not like he's coming back. I'll be perfectly safe."

Liam felt Connor's tension behind him, his troubled worry. Liam relaxed his stance to try to convey to Connor that everything was under control. *Right.* "Kim, love, I'll make you breakfast, and you write out a list of what you need. I'll send someone 'round to retrieve it all for you. Someone female this time. How will that be with you?"

Kim planted her fists on her hips. She shouldn't have done that; the movement thrust out her breasts and let the T-shirt outline her nipples. "Are you still insisting that you won't let me leave?"

"Not yet. It's not safe."

"It's perfectly safe. The feral Shifter is dead, and you had the lock on my door fixed. Make your damn pancakes if you want to, and then I'm leaving. I won't tell *anyone* what happened last night or repeat what you told me about the Collars. I know how to keep a secret, all right? And you can just get over it."

She stomped back down the stairs and slammed her own door so hard the sturdy walls rattled. Liam sensed her beneath the boards at his feet—her rage; her frustration; her warm, pliant body filling out his shirt. Her closed door would be no barrier to him if he chose to charge in and confront her.

Connor was watching Liam with concern. "What are you going to do?"

He meant, was Liam going to subdue her, and would he hurt Kim doing it? Connor was young, still uncomfortable with his own instincts, not yet certain where he fit in the clan and pride hierarchies. Things were more difficult for him than they had been for Liam or Sean, because Connor had grown up a captive Shifter, and boundaries were fuzzier now than they'd been in the wild. Connor didn't yet understand when you showed dominance and when you tolerated, and *what* you tolerated. Plus, he'd been raised by mateless males and had never seen an example of an intimate relationship.

Not that anything Liam had with Kim was going to be straightforward. Educational, maybe. Straightforward, no.

Liam tamped down his own instincts, dousing the pheromones that were putting Connor on edge. "What am I going to do?" He shrugged and headed for the attic bathroom. "What she asked me to. I'm going to make her pancakes."

Kim descended to the kitchen, showered but still irritated. Liam's friends had packed not only the underwear she never wore, but also her shortest skirts and lowest-cut tops, a garter belt, and a bunch of stockings. Nothing remotely comfortable, not even shorts and sandals for surviving Austin in the summer.

She paused at the kitchen doorway, surprise cutting through her annoyance. Liam in a tight T-shirt and jeans, spatula in hand, glared at a griddle full of pancakes. Behind him in the narrow kitchen, Sean scrubbed dishes in the sink.

Every woman's dream—two gorgeous men in the kitchen, cooking and cleaning.

Dylan sat at the table, tipping his chair back on two legs while he watched a sports report on a television that had to be twenty years old. Connor sat next to him, flipping through a car magazine. The air was somewhat tense, as though words had been cut off when they'd heard her coming.

Something else wasn't right about this domestic picture, apart from tall, muscular men working in the kitchen to fix her breakfast. Kim realized that Connor didn't have his nose in the Internet or a video game or a cell phone. Nor did he have an iPod glued to his ears.

Were those more technologies forbidden to Shifters? Or could the Morrisseys simply not afford them? She knew that Liam had a job, which he seemed to take casually. What about Sean and Dylan? Did they work? They seemed in no hurry to rush to an office. Abel was always out of bed as soon as the alarm went off, through the shower and into his suit and tie in fifteen minutes. *"Come on, honey, we're going to be late."* No time for pancakes, coffee, or a chat, never mind a morning cuddle.

Liam took a plate from the stack next to him and flipped pancakes onto it. "These are done. You're supposed to have the table ready, Connor." Liam smiled at Kim, but something in him seemed subdued, the sparkle that had been in his eyes earlier that morning gone. What was going on?

Connor hauled his tall form out of the chair and shuffled to the kitchen. When his body filled out, he'd be as muscular as his two uncles and Dylan. He looked unfinished right now, like a young horse, all arms and legs. But he was handsome enough, probably already drove girls crazy.

"I'll help," Kim offered. She took the bottles of syrup Connor had snatched out of the cupboard and carried them to the table.

Dylan rose. "Sit down, Kim. You're a guest."

Kim opened her mouth to say, *No, guests are allowed to leave*, but she shut it again. There was plenty of time to argue, and besides, the pancakes smelled terrific.

In any case, she had no intention of arguing with them. She'd simply get into her car and leave.

The pancakes tasted as good as they smelled, tangy, sweet, and laced with cinnamon. Damn Liam for being so gorgeous and skilled at cooking too.

"Did you sleep well, Kim?" Connor asked her around a mouthful.

Kim had fallen into a heavy sleep and dreamed about two things—being attacked by feral Shifters and kissing Liam. Both experiences had been intense.

"Sort of."

"Liam didn't," Connor said. "He thrashed all night. The springs on my extra bed squeak something awful. Drove me mad."

"I wasn't used to the bed," Liam said, sitting down next to Kim with his pancakes.

For a man who'd slept restlessly, especially after claiming to be in excruciating pain, Liam looked damn good. His face was freshly shaved, his hair still damp from his shower. She smelled soap and shaving cream on him, which sent her imagination into the shower with him, his body dripping wet and soapy.

Dylan, on the other hand, looked extremely pissed about something. He glowered as he ate, hunkering over his plate. Sean went through his pancakes quickly, without speaking, and returned to the kitchen for more dish scrubbing.

"Do you always make Sean do the dishes?" Kim asked. "Seems unfair."

"We take it in turns," Liam answered. "It's Sean's day to do the washing up."

"Mine tomorrow," Connor said glumly. "I swear I'm taking a mate as soon as I'm of age, so I don't have to do it anymore."

Kim ate her last mouthful of pancakes and wished for more. Screw eating light; these were *good*. "That's going to be your offer, Connor? 'Marry me so you can clean up after me, my two uncles, and my grandfather'? I'm sure every woman would jump at that."

At the sink, Sean laughed. Liam smiled, but distractedly. Connor frowned as if she'd given him something new to think about, but even his enthusiasm was dampened.

The four Morrisseys were certainly wound up this morning. The worst tension was between Liam and Dylan—and Kim gave herself three guesses what they'd been fighting about.

Kim set down her fork. "Let's keep this simple. I'm going to go upstairs, get my stuff, and leave. I'll call you and let you know what's going on with Brian's case—keep you in the loop. I promise. And I won't reveal anything I learned about feral Shifters, Collars, or your werewolf neighbor in glittery shoes."

Dylan looked up from his meal, his eyes dark but tinged with red. Despite his handsomeness, he was damn scary, and Kim again realized why humans sought out Liam instead of his father.

Liam shot Dylan an angry glance, but when Liam spoke to Kim his voice was gentle. "You need to stay a little longer, love. A few more days at least."

"No." Kim wiped her mouth and put down her napkin. "I have a job and a life. Tomorrow is Monday and I have to be at my office, where I work to earn my living. Remember Brian and his case? You do want me to get him free, right?"

"You'll go to your office," Liam said. "I'll go with you."

"Oh, right. A Shifter walking the halls at Lowell, Grant, and Steinhurst. I don't think so."

"It's that or you don't go at all."

Kim shoved back her chair and stood up. "Listen, Liam, I didn't ask to be dragged into your problems. I didn't ask for that—*thing*—to attack me. I'm real sorry I found out about the Collars, but all I want to do is get Brian released and back home to his mother. You don't seem to remember that I'm on your side."

Liam had gotten to his feet with her. Connor watched, worried, and Sean turned from the sink, scrub brush dripping.

"It's not up to me, Kim," Liam said.

"You're damn right it's not up to you. It's up to *me*." What was the matter with them? "Y'all are *Shifters*. You could be arrested for kidnapping me or holding me hostage—hell, for even talking to me sharply. They'll do to you what they're doing to Brian. A sham of a trial and an execution."

Dylan finally spoke. "We weren't planning on telling anyone. Or letting you tell anyone."

Kim's heart beat faster. Yep, Dylan was the scariest one in this room, all right. Her powers of argument died under his red-tinged stare. The feral Shifter who'd attacked her now seemed like a puppy dog compared to Dylan.

Liam's voice went hard. "Dad, you promised this was mine to handle."

"Aye, but you're not handling it," Dylan answered. "You know what you have to do."

"Let me do it then. In my own time."

"No, you need to do it *now*. It's the only way."

Kim backed up a step. "Do what now?"

Liam wouldn't look at her, while Dylan glared and Sean turned away. Connor had his mouth open, clearly not knowing what they were talking about, either.

"Do what now?" Kim repeated.

If she ran for the door, would she make it? How fast could Dylan, Liam, and Sean move? Liam didn't look ready to spring, and neither did Dylan, who sat loosely, but these men weren't human.

What was the matter with her? Yesterday, she'd been nervous about coming to Shiftertown and talking to a Shifter who wasn't behind bars. Then Liam had looked at her with those Irish blue eyes, and she'd melted. She'd even slept in their house without putting up much fuss. She'd done everything on their terms, and Kim never did anything on anyone's terms but her own.

Now she was reminded of how dangerous Shifters were. She'd blithely walked into their lives, and she knew they wouldn't let her blithely walk out again.

Kim balled her fists. "Liam, please reverse the scent-marking. I don't do the dominant-submissive thing."

"Kim."

Oh, damn, even him saying her name made her want to flow to his lap and put her arms around him.

"What?" she growled.

"The scent-marking is for protection, not subjugation. Besides, you're less submissive than the highest alpha female I've ever met."

"Oh, sure. You're telling me that Glory is submissive?"

Dylan rumbled, "She's not an alpha. She's fairly far down in her pack."

The surprise of that stopped Kim's speech for a moment. But only a moment. "That explains why she puts up with you. But not me. I'm out of here. I'm sorry, Liam, but you're going to have to trust me."

Liam stepped around her to cut off her retreat. No, she wouldn't have made it to the door. His hands went to her shoulders, and she found herself pinned against the nearest wall.

"And you're going to have to trust me," he said.

This wasn't fair. He smelled too good. His blue eyes held the hint of red that Dylan's did, but she sensed that Liam was holding himself way, way back.

For one giddy moment she wondered what it would be like if he let loose. Would he press her to the wall, cover her with the weight of his body? Watching him lean around the bedroom door frame this morning, stark naked, had made her breasts ache and her thighs grow damp.

I have lost my mind.

The moment hovered, Liam towering over her, Kim's knees wanting to bend. She could slide down Liam's body and press her face to the front of his jeans. Wouldn't that be nice?

"Ow!" Connor shouted. He folded over, arms around his stomach.

"You all right, Connor?" Kim asked worriedly.

"No. Crap." He moaned in sudden pain.

"What's wrong? Are you sick? Geez, Liam, what did you put in the pancakes?"

A plate shattered on the kitchen floor. "Shite," Sean whispered, and at the same time his eyes flooded with pain.

Liam shoved Kim from him. "Kim, get away from us. Now."

All four Morrisseys started growling, eyes changing. Connor moaned pathetically.

Kim didn't know enough about Shifters to know what the hell was the matter with them. Were they shifting? Or sick? Sean slid to the kitchen floor at the same time Liam fell to his knees. Dylan got out of his chair and tried to go to Connor, but he collapsed before he made it to his grandson.

Liam raised his head, lips peeling back from fangs. "Go!" he shouted at her. "Run!"

Kim didn't waste time arguing. She fled through the kitchen, wrenched open the back door, and ran outside into hot, humid Austin air.

She could leap into her car, roar the hell out of Shiftertown, go home, and change all the locks. Move. Quit her job, never see Shifters again. They could keep her clothes; she didn't like most of what they'd packed anyway.

When she reached the bottom of the porch steps, Connor started screaming. The anguish of it made Kim stop, turn back. Connor was the youngest, the weakest of them, and whatever was happening hurt him most of all.

Kim ran back up the steps and into the house. Connor's keening split the air. Dylan and Liam were both crawling toward him, and she realized that they were trying to touch him, these people who comforted each other with bodily contact.

"Liam, what can I do?"

Liam cranked his head around and looked up at Kim. His eyes were bright red. "No, Kim. Get out."

"I can't leave you like this. How do I help you?"

Liam couldn't or wouldn't answer. He managed to reach Connor, who screamed even louder when Liam touched him.

Damn it. Kim didn't know enough about Shifters—she who'd thought she'd researched everything about them. This could be anything from their Collars going wrong to some kind of weird virus.

"Hang on. I'll be right back."

She had no idea if Liam heard or understood. Kim ran out through the kitchen again and headed down the dirt path to the house next door. She banged on the back door, cupping her hands to peer through the window.

"Glory?"

She heard nothing, and for a few seconds she feared that Glory, too, writhed on the floor, moaning. Maybe everyone in Shiftertown did. *Shit.*

Glory wrenched open the door, as tall and stunning as she'd been the night before. She wore a hot-pink halter top that clasped her throat and hid her Collar, skintight black leather pants, and pink spike-heeled pumps. *Not an alpha, my ass.*

Glory was breathing hard, as if she'd been working out, but there wasn't a drop of perspiration on her face, not a hair out of place. "What?"

"There's something wrong with them. Something Shifter-wrong. You have to help them."

Glory jerked her gaze to the Morrissey house. "With Dylan?"

"With all of them. I don't know what's happening."

Without a word Glory stepped past her and hurried down the porch stairs. Kim had to jog to keep up with the woman's long stride, and this with Glory wearing mile-high shoes.

Glory shoved open the back door of the Morrissey house as though she belonged there. She stopped short, and Kim nearly ran into her. Liam had his arms around Connor now, but Connor still keened with his heart-breaking wail.

"What's wrong with them?" Kim shouted.

"I don't know. I've never seen this before."

Fat lot of help that was. Glory strode to Dylan, who had his eyes closed, his now elongated teeth cutting his lips. Glory grabbed his shoulder. "Dylan!"

She had to shake him and yell at him before Dylan finally looked up, his eyes now yellow swimming with red. He rasped a word Kim couldn't understand, but Glory nodded. She turned back to Kim with a grim look.

"They're being Summoned," she said.

"Summoned? What the hell does that mean?"

"It means their clan leader is calling them. He's put a compulsory spell on them—they'll be like this until they reach him and he lifts it."

A spell? "I thought you said you'd never seen this before."

"I haven't. Summonings happen only about once every two hundred years, because clan leaders who use them indiscriminately don't stay clan leaders long. Shifters don't like being coerced. Fergus must want you bad."

"What, he couldn't use the phone like everyone else?"

"He did use the phone. Yesterday. He commanded Dylan to turn you over to him, and Dylan refused. So Fergus did this."

From Glory's expression, she fully blamed Kim. Glory's shirt might hide her Collar, and Dylan might claim she wasn't high in her pack, but she was still a Shifter, still strong, still deadly.

"You have to get them to San Antonio," Glory said.

"San Antonio?"

"That's where Fergus is. You have to get them to Fergus—they can't drive like this."

"To this Fergus who's demanding that I be 'turned over' to him, whatever the hell that means? Why can't you take them?"

Glory snorted. "Respond to a Summoning from another clan leader? I'm Lupine. I walk into a gathering of Felines, they'll take my head off before I can speak."

"What about *my* head?"

"You'll have to risk it. Fergus will expect you to come with them anyway. Come on, help me get them into your car."

"They won't fit in my car."

"Make them fit." Glory grabbed Dylan under the armpits and hauled him to his feet. The big man could barely stand, but he leaned heavily on Glory and let her drag him across the kitchen. "There's no other choice."

Glory kicked open the kitchen door. It banged against the wall and began to drift shut, small flakes of plaster floating from the ceiling.

Liam snaked one clawed hand around Kim's ankle. "No," he rasped. "Run."

The pain in his eyes broke her heart. Liam was right; she *should* run. She should leave the Shifters to their fate and emigrate to Australia. Kim was coldly terrified at the thought of facing this Fergus, the man who could render four powerful Shifters helpless from seventy-five miles away. But Liam's anguish kept her with him.

"Kim," Glory shouted. "Come *on*."

Kim leaned over Liam. "We have to go, Liam. It's the only way, Glory says."

Liam tried to speak, but his words came out as unintelligible grunts.

Glory charged back inside and grabbed Sean. Kim finally persuaded Liam off the floor, and Liam hauled Connor to his feet. Somehow, the three of them got out the door and to Kim's two-door Mustang.

Sean had already folded himself into the tiny backseat, while Dylan leaned heavily on the car. Dylan seemed the least debilitated, but he was older, probably stronger. Glory took charge of Connor, and Dylan helped her slide Connor into the back next to Sean. Dylan himself cramped in beside his grandson, leaving the front seat for Liam to collapse into.

"What the hell?" A male Texan voice reached Kim. The big Lupine she'd met the night before, Ellison, came running at them from across the street. "Glory, what's going on?"

"Summoning," Glory said tersely.

"Holy shit."

"Kim's taking them to Fergus."

"Aw, man." Ellison's light blue eyes filled with distress. "And I can't go with you, damn it. Liam's got my cell number. You call me and keep me posted, all right?"

"Sure." Kim numbly got into the car.

"Wait." Ellison dashed into the Morrissey house, then out again, carrying Sean's big sword in its leather sheath. "Take this, in case."

There was no room for it in the packed car. Kim opened the trunk and Ellison dropped it inside.

As Kim slammed her door and started the car, Ellison stepped close to Glory and put both arms around her. She leaned into him, not in a sexual way, Kim real-

ized, but for comfort, like Sandra had with Sean and
Liam yesterday.

Kim pulled out of the driveway, her fingers cold
and shaking despite the July heat, and headed out of
Shiftertown.

Chapter Ten

They'd better be grateful for this. Kim sped down the I-35 as fast as she dared, cursing under her breath at the crawling traffic. It was Sunday—shouldn't all these people be in church or something? But no, they were meandering along the freeway between Austin and San Antonio, clogging the ramps, driving slowly in the left lanes, cutting her off . . .

She drove as swiftly as she was able, though she didn't dare risk being pulled over for speeding. She imagined herself trying to explain to the nice police officer why she had four half-crazed Shifters stuffed into her car and a big sword in the trunk.

Connor's moans had turned to whimpers. Kim had no idea how this Fergus had caused their state from so far away, but she wanted to scream at him. Liam was the strongest man she'd ever met, and to see him hunched up in the seat next to her, rocking in pain, made her furious.

"It's not much farther." She had no idea if Liam could hear her, and he didn't respond.

The freeway had never seemed so long. Signboards with German-sounding names slid by: New Braunfels, Gruene, the ever-popular Schlitterbahn water park, which Kim had loved as a kid.

When they reached the northern outskirts of San Antonio, Liam at last took his hands from his face. "This exit."

Kim dove for the off-ramp, which took her to a freeway that looped around the city. "Then where?"

Liam flicked his fingers at the road, which she took to mean, "Keep going." Dylan sat up behind her. In the rearview mirror, Kim saw him draw Connor to him, cradling the boy against his chest. Sean had his eyes closed, but Kim couldn't tell whether he slept.

When they'd reached the southwestern edge of town, Liam gestured for Kim to take another exit. He directed her down a road that became a highway, running west out of town again.

"There's a Shiftertown out here?" Kim asked, as they left the city limits behind.

Liam didn't answer. Sean was sitting up now, leaning against the window. Their breathing had calmed, no longer tortured rasping, but they still looked gray and drawn.

About twenty-five miles later, Dylan leaned forward between the seats, long arm pointing out a side road that wasn't signposted. "There."

They'd left Hill Country behind and had reached the deserts of south Texas. The land was flat and dry, grasses clumped and yellow instead of soft green. On the left side of the road, behind barbed wire, a few cows grazed.

No barbed wire lined the right side of the road, the land open and flowing to the white-blue horizon. The humidity had dropped considerably, Kim's sweat was quickly evaporating in the dry air.

"It's coming up," Liam said. He sounded almost normal, and his fangs had receded.

Two wooden fence posts with no fence and no gate marked a dirt road that reached a pale finger across the land. Kim turned down it, silently cursing the ruts that banged her car's underbody. Maybe she could charge this Fergus for the damage.

A cluster of houses lay about three miles down this joke of a road, and a hand-painted sign read: WELCOME TO SHIFTERTOWN! POPULATION: FIFTY-TWO SHIFTERS, TWENTY HORSES, FIVE DOGS, AND FIFTEEN CATS.

The houses were long, low adobes with tiny windows, probably ranch houses left over from earlier in the twentieth century. Like the houses in Austin, these had been fixed up and painted, but instead of having yards, they were grouped around a somewhat sad playground where no kids played. Pickups were parked haphazardly in the dirt around the houses.

A steel pole corral that surrounded open stalls with corrugated steel roofs sat at one end of the street. A dozen desultory horses moved between pens and corral, paying no attention to the car hurtling toward them in a cloud of dust.

One of the town's five dogs lounged at the front door of the house in front of which Liam told Kim to park. The house was no bigger than the others and had a green-painted door flanked by two windows to either side of it. The dog got up, stretched, and wandered toward them, tail wagging.

"Are you sure this is right?" Kim asked, as she got out and yanked the seat forward to release the others.

"Very sure," Liam said.

The four men had returned to almost normal, except for the tension. Connor leaned against the car once he'd gotten out of it, his face still tight.

"Why did he Summon Connor?" Kim asked Liam in a low voice. "If he wants me, why didn't he just get you and your dad to bring me down? Or can't he pinpoint who he wants?"

"No, the spell can be very specific. Fergus decided who he'd cast it on."

Kim looked at Connor, who had walked away to retch into a stand of tall grasses. "What kind of asshole is this guy? Connor doesn't have anything to do with me."

The Liam who looked at her was no longer the affable, sexy man she'd met yesterday. The Liam next to her sparked with contained fury and would have scared the shit out of her if she'd walked into the bar's office and seen him like this behind the desk. She realized that Liam had showed her the "nice" Shifter, the one humans could talk to. The one she could sit with on a bed and kiss.

No, wait, she could kiss him even now. She'd taste his fury and let him know she shared it, while he ran his hands over her body.

How would sex with Liam be when he was like this? Raw and wild. Against the wall or on the hood of the car—all-out, good-time sex. *That's what I'm talking about.*

Liam opened the door of the house and walked in. The inside didn't impress Kim. People obviously lived here, but they just as obviously didn't much care about cleaning up the place.

Liam strode through the cluttered living room and kitchen littered with dirty dishes, and opened a door. Cool air poured up stone stairs beyond. Cellar? Storm shelter? A place like that could house snakes, scorpions, black widows . . .

"In there?" she asked. She thought she could face a hostile Shifter, but spiders? Not so much.

Liam passed her without a word. Thank God for the Shifter custom of the male entering a place first. If there were spiders down there, Liam could stomp on them before she went down.

Dylan nodded at Sean, who'd retrieved his sword from her trunk, indicating he should enter after Liam. Then Dylan, then Connor.

Kim hesitated at the top of the steps, still thinking about spiders—and Fergus. She could run, make it to her car, and hightail it back to Austin. No one was behind her; she could get a good head start.

Connor looked back at her, the light from the kitchen glinting on the fear in his eyes. He was terrified and, from the greenish cast to his face, still nauseated from the Summoning. Would the bully Fergus try to hurt Connor if Kim ran for it? Probably.

"Bastard," she growled, and started after Connor. She couldn't do that to the kid.

Connor flashed Kim a nervous grin and kept going. Kim picked her way along, feeling out of her depth and refusing to touch the stone walls.

The Morrissey men waited for them in a tiled corridor that was completely incongruous with the house above. The walls were polished wood and, to Kim's astonishment, filled with paintings and beautiful photographs. Real paintings by real artists that museums paid major money for, photographs by people like Ansel Adams. Spanish-style, carved wooden doors with small square windows lined the corridor between the priceless artwork.

What the hell kind of place was this?

Liam led the way to the end of the hall and opened a door to a cavernous room. Dylan went in first this time, then Liam, then Sean, then Connor. Kim, in most need of protection, entered last.

The room was huge, meant to hold several hundred people. The walls were paneled with warm wood, the purple-red hue speaking of exotic Oriental forests. The ceiling was arched like a cathedral, the arches intricately carved and marching toward an enormous fireplace at the end. Money and artistry had gone into shaping the chamber, which was far larger than any of the houses above it.

The room was also filled with Shifters.

There must have been a hundred of them, each as physically honed as Liam, Dylan, and Sean. The sign outside said that only fifty-two Shifters lived in this Shiftertown, so these must have driven in for the occasion. Every single one was male.

The crowd parted as Dylan led the way forward, past the looming arches, through the sea of Shifters, to the center of the room. Four men waited for them there: a big guy with a long black braid and a leather motorcycle vest, surrounded by three equally thuglike men.

"Let me guess," Kim whispered to Liam. "That's Fergus."

Liam nodded grimly. Fergus turned hard blue eyes to Kim and gave her the Shifter once-over.

"This is her?" he asked. His accent was more Southern than Texan, and his tone said he'd expected her to be more formidable.

Liam set his mouth, and Dylan became their spokesman. "This is Kim Fraser, the defense attorney for Brian Smith."

All eyes on Kim. Nostrils flared as the Shifters took in Kim's scent and the fact that Liam had marked her. Every single Shifter in here wore a Collar, but it dawned on Kim that the Collars might not make a damn bit of difference if she tried to run or fight. These were dangerous men, watching for now because they chose to.

"Crap," she said under her breath. "And me without my pepper spray."

"We like pepper spray," Liam answered.

"Figures."

Fergus pinned her with a blue stare, then looked at Sean and held out his hand.

Sean unstrapped the sword on his back and took it to him. Fergus didn't say thank you; he just grabbed the sword from Sean and passed it to one of his underlings. As he turned, strands of braided leather swung across his hip from a handle hooked to his belt.

"Is that a cat-o'-nine-tails?" Kim asked Liam.

"Most like."

"Why, in case he loses his own?"

Liam's sudden smile burst over his face. Connor laughed openly.

"Shut it," Dylan hissed.

Fergus's attention riveted to Kim. "Come here, woman."

Kim remained where she was, not about to trot obediently to him. Liam stood beside her, his body solid and warm, making her feel suddenly safe.

"I *said*, come here."

Kim lifted her chin. "Do the words 'screw you' mean anything to you?"

Fergus's eyes glittered as the Shifters muttered to each other. Fergus's three henchmen folded their arms and glared. One had a shaved head and a neck covered in tattoos, one had a sandy blond ponytail, and the third had short black hair. He looked ex-military, although Shifters weren't allowed to join the military.

"Bring her to me," Fergus said curtly to Liam.

Liam didn't move. The room was silent, the tension ramping high. Fergus's eyes changed from blue to white-gray.

Kim didn't know what all Fergus could do—another Summoning to make Liam drag her across the room to him? Kim felt like a sapling in a tall forest; Shifter males were mostly over six feet tall, and she was five feet high in flats. And where were all the women Shifters? Baking cookies?

"You know you can't kill me," Kim said in her brisk courtroom voice. "There's already one Shifter in jail because of a human's death, and even though *I'm* convinced he didn't do it, plenty of people think he did. If I disappear or turn up dead, you'll have your county sheriff and possibly the feds all over you."

Fergus just stared at her, then turned to Liam. "Does she ever shut up?"

"Not that I've noticed."

"Not a point in her favor."

"I don't know," Liam said with a faint smile. "I kind of like it."

Fergus's lip curled. *"Bring her to me."*

"Sorry, Fergus," Liam said. "I'll be leaving that choice up to her."

The room held its collective breath. Kim didn't have to be an expert in nonverbal cues to see that Fergus's whole stance now said, *Obey me or suffer.* Liam's stance said, *No way in hell*, but Kim noticed he wouldn't meet Fergus's eyes.

"I'm not going to hurt the woman," Fergus said, tight-lipped.

"No?" Kim broke in. "Why am I not reassured?"

"He's telling the truth." Liam's voice warmed her ear, his voice so tight she realized how much he must be holding himself back.

"Could have fooled me."

Liam turned Kim to face him. He touched her cheek, his eyes wary but with a sparkle of excitement deep within them. "He doesn't want to hurt you, love," he said softly. "That was never his intention. When Fergus called Dad last night, he ordered us to bring you down here so he could claim you as his mate."

Kim's blue eyes went wide, shining with anger, fear, and astonishment. "You've *got* to be kidding me."

Liam smoothed a lock of her hair, trying to soothe her with his Shifter touch. "Don't worry, love. I'm not going to let him."

It struck him suddenly that he'd been waiting for something like this. Maybe all his life. He'd told himself he'd passed up potential mates to give other Shifter males a chance at happiness, but he realized now that he'd simply not found a woman he wanted to be with. Easy to be altruistic when he wasn't making much of a sacrifice.

But when this sassy human female had walked into his office yesterday, with her blouse buttons straining, her short gray skirt smooth over her sweet rump, when she'd started laying out a heated, well-reasoned argument why he should help her before Liam could even speak, his well-ordered world had overturned. She'd managed to touch something that Liam had always kept protected. Maybe she'd touched it because he hadn't kept his guard up, hadn't expected a human to reach what no Shifter had ever reached.

Last night, when Dylan had broken the news that Fergus expected Liam to bring Kim to him so Fergus could claim her as mate, Liam had flat-out refused. Dylan had argued, not understanding. What was the fate of one human against the good of all Shifters? Fergus could control Kim, and that would be the end of the matter.

Liam had nearly punched his father in the face, something he'd never in his life dreamed of doing. Kim would go to Fergus over his dead body, he'd said. Dylan had regarded Liam first in amazement, then comprehension, even sympathy. He'd stopped arguing, told Liam he agreed to disobey Fergus, then walked out of the house.

Mate. Mine. Protect.

Liam wanted to hold Kim and not let her go. He wanted to kiss her, screw her, make her pancakes the next morning. The instincts that hadn't manifested in a hundred years of living suddenly rose and raged.

"Why would he want me to be his *mate?*" Kim was asking. "Whatever that means. He's never met me before today."

Goddess, how could a male *not* want her? But she had a point.

"He wants to control you," Liam said. "Because you're right. It would cause him major problems if he killed you. But if you're his mate, you're subject to him and clan law. And no longer a threat to Shifters."

"And if I refuse?"

Fergus wasn't going to let her refuse. Liam wasn't certain how Fergus planned to subdue Kim—drugs, spells, terror—but the man wanted Kim under his thumb.

Fergus also likely wanted to see how far Liam would go to protect her. Once Fergus knew what Liam felt for Kim, the better he could manipulate Liam and the rest of his family. Either way, Kim would be watched, controlled.

"You won't have to," Liam told Kim.

Fergus gave them a narrow stare. "Does this mean you make the Challenge for her?"

Liam sensed Dylan and Sean move in behind him, their instinct to protect manifesting, no matter how bloody stupid they thought Liam was being. Liam wished Connor would get the hell out of here. Connor was a kid, a cub, and he wasn't ready yet for this kind of confrontation. Liam didn't think Fergus would take that into consideration when he started meting out punishment.

Liam slid his hand into Kim's, looked Fergus straight in the eye, and reached for a Texas phrase that would make Ellison proud.

"Damn straight."

Chapter Eleven

Fergus's gaze locked with Liam's, and Liam felt a surge of triumph.

"Dylan," Fergus snapped.

Dylan answered in a calm voice. "My son is not yet mated. It's his right."

Don't defend me, Dad. Walk away. This isn't your fight.

Dylan remained in place. Liam hadn't really thought he'd be wise and disappear. Dylan would never desert his offspring, even if it meant his death.

"Ex*cuse* me," Kim burst out. Heads swiveled to her, a hundred pairs of Shifter eyes pinning her, but she didn't flinch. "I don't like all this talk about *mating*, thank you very much—especially when it involves me."

Liam wanted to laugh out loud. She was a treasure. Shifter instincts were starting to blot out his human reason, making him yearn for Fergus's blood under his claws and then Kim in his arms.

Sex with Kim would be glorious, even if he had to stay in human form for it. He'd gotten a taste of her last night, her sweet mouth, her kisses, her touch on his body. He wanted to lie on top of her, practicing more human kissing as he slid inside her and made her his.

Fergus's own pheromones rolled off him, thick and strong, polluting the air. Smelling them, Liam realized Fergus didn't plan to make Kim mate in name only. He wanted Kim, wanted a furious fuck. Liam would die before he let that happen.

"Silence her," Fergus growled at Liam.

Sean stepped to Kim's other side, Even without the sword, he stood like a warrior, ready to fight. "Liam has made the Challenge," Sean said. "Nothing we can do but see how it plays out."

"Screw that." Kim tried to twist out of Liam's hold, but Liam wasn't about to let her go. "Connor," she said over her shoulder. "Can you find something for me to stand on? A chair or something?"

Her question jolted Connor out of his frozen terror. Good for Kim.

The Shifters parted to let Connor leave the room. Liam hoped it would take him hours to locate a chair, or that he'd think better of returning at all, but Connor came back almost at once with a stepstool.

"Good enough." Kim told him to put it on the floor in front of her, and Liam released her long enough to let her climb on it. He kept his arms around her as she straightened up, both to steady her and to keep her in his protective hold.

"That's better," Kim said. The stool let her stand half a head taller than Liam, and now she could look across the crowd of Shifters.

"There doesn't need to be any violence over this," she said. "What y'all don't understand is that I can be the best *friend* you've got. You have a Shifter in jail, and the world howling for his blood. If I can prove he didn't kill his human girlfriend, think what terrific PR that would be for all of you. Shifters are viewed with suspicion and hostility. If I show the world that Brian was wronged, make him a sympathetic figure, even a hero, imagine what an amazing step forward that would be. They might let you integrate more, let your kids go to schools that aren't held in abandoned warehouses."

Silence. Not one expression changed.

"Hey, maybe they'd even let us have cable," a Shifter

in the back drawled. The room rumbled with male laughter.

"I'm serious. I'm good at my job. I can do this if you help me."

Fergus's mouth drew to a thin line. "Liam, shut her up."

Liam wasn't about to. Kim had Fergus baffled, and he liked that.

"You act like you don't want Brian released." Kim went on. "He didn't kill Michelle. Why should he be executed for it? Why would you let him be?"

Fergus drew the cat-o'-nine-tails from his belt. "Liam."

"He's going to whip me?" Kim asked Liam in amazement.

Liam lifted Kim off the stool. "Time to stop talking, love. Fergus, if we're doing this Challenge, let's get on with it, man."

"Not until I teach the bitch some manners."

Connor stormed forward despite Sean's attempts to restrain him. The young man's face was red, his large hands in fists. "Leave her alone! She's not doing anything to you. She's just talking. How can that hurt you, you bastard?"

"Connor, shut it," Dylan said fiercely.

Fergus's gaze chilled the air as it rested on Connor. "Come here, boy."

"He's a cub," Dylan tried. "He doesn't understand."

Connor wiped his eyes. "I understand, Grandda'." He glared at Fergus, though he dropped his gaze almost immediately. "I meant it too."

Fergus was livid. Cords stood out on his neck, and his eyes burned with the intensity of a feral's.

Liam knew full well how Fergus had envisioned this

cozy scenario: Liam and family would scurry down to San Antonio, hand Kim over in abject apology, then hurry away again, letting Fergus do whatever the hell he wanted.

Instead all four Morrisseys had defied him—twice. The first time by refusing to respond to his verbal summons, yesterday. Now, in Fergus's own lair, Kim had lectured him, Liam had made the Challenge, and Connor had broken the rule of a cub not confronting an alpha before he was of age.

Cubs could get away with a lot on account of their youth—Goddess knew Liam had been a pain in the ass during puberty—but flouting Fergus in front of the whole clan could not go unpunished. Connor was too young to fight for dominance, so he'd have to be swatted, as a lion might bat aside a cub who'd gotten too rambunctious.

"Come here," Fergus repeated.

The magic in the command propelled Connor toward him. Sean started after him, but Liam shook his head. "No, Sean, let me."

Sean opened his mouth to argue, then nodded, his eyes bleak. He turned away, unhappy, but knowing why he had to stand down.

"Let you what?" Kim asked Liam.

Her eyes were wide in her white face. She was afraid and angry, and so damn beautiful she made his heart ache.

Liam cupped her face in his hands. "Kim, my love, stay here with Sean and Dylan. Don't even think about coming after me, and please, *stay quiet.*"

Kim's lips parted as though she wanted to protest. Then she closed her mouth and nodded. *Good girl.* Liam turned from her and swiftly followed Connor.

Liam was the same height as Fergus. He and the big man looked at each other eye to eye, Liam without flinching.

"If you do this," Fergus said in vicious fury, "then when I answer your mate Challenge, I'll wipe the floor with you."

Gods, what an arrogant bastard. "Just get on with it."

Connor's eyes held tears, but his head was up, though he couldn't meet Fergus's gaze or even Liam's. "No, Liam. Leave it."

"It's my right, nephew," Liam said quietly.

Two of the thugs, the one with the shaved head and the black-haired one, divested Connor of his shirt. Connor couldn't meet their eyes either.

Liam stripped off his own shirt and dropped it on the floor. The thugs ignored him. They turned Connor around and bent him forward at the waist, exposing his young, unblemished back.

Fergus raised his cat-o'-nine-tails. With a grunt, he brought it down. Before it could strike Connor, Liam leaned over his nephew and took the blow directly across his own back.

"What the hell?" Kim shrieked. "What is he doing?"

Horror filled her as Fergus, eyes fixed, mouth curled in vicious enjoyment, struck again. The sound of the leather swished through the silence, followed by the slap against Liam's skin.

Dylan moved toward them, grim-faced, tugging off his shirt to reveal a back as broad and muscular as Liam's. When he reached Connor and Liam, he leaned over Connor as well, father and son enclosing the boy in a protective Shifter embrace. Fergus continued to ply the whip as though he didn't notice, lips pulling back from teeth that had become fangs.

Kim started forward, but Sean stepped in front of her, blocking her way. "Stay here. Let it finish."

Sean's eyes held anguish, but she saw he wasn't about to try to stop Fergus. She also sensed that if Sean hadn't felt the need to keep Kim bottled up here, he'd have joined the human shield around Connor.

"This is insane," she said, heart in her throat. Barbaric, uncivilized.

But they're Shifters, a voice whispered in her head. *Isn't that why they're forced to wear the Collars, to keep their barbarism under control?*

The Collar wasn't doing jack to keep Fergus from beating Liam and Dylan to bloody pulp. The leather straps opened Liam's flesh, and blood dribbled to the floor. Liam was taking the brunt of it, only some of the blows hitting Dylan, as though Fergus's aim was to debilitate Liam only. Nothing reached Connor, enclosed in a Shifter wall.

The other Shifters watched without comment, no murmuring, no growling, neither egging Fergus on nor trying to stop him. The beating went on and on, as though Fergus was taking out years of welled-up aggression on the Morrisseys.

"Why don't you do something?" Kim asked Sean, tears in her eyes.

"It's the Shifter way." Sean's mouth was set in a grim line.

"It's a fucked-up way."

Kim waited until Sean again turned to watch, then darted around him and ran through the pack. Short height could be an advantage—the tall Shifters weren't used to dealing with one small, athletic female slithering through their grasps.

She reached Fergus. "Stop this!"

Fergus gave Liam two more vicious blows, then

trained his awful gaze on Kim. He was far more frightening than Dylan, his eyes red with rage, a tinge of madness in them. She was looking at a man who would do absolutely anything, no matter how ruthless, to get what he wanted. No holds barred.

Liam jerked his head up. "Sean, take her out of here."

Sean was already behind Kim. Kim spun away and put herself right under Fergus's nose. Fergus snarled. His face had half changed, his lips peeling back from his red, angry mouth. She thought of the Lupine who'd tried to kill her, and realized that Fergus wasn't too far removed from that un-Collared Shifter's vicious rage.

"I'm not Shifter," Kim said. "I'm not afraid of you."

Big fat lie. The man was terrifying, and Kim had no doubt he could kill her fast. But Kim couldn't stand by and watch him beat on Liam, whose back was now coated with blood.

Fergus went for her, whip raised. Liam lunged at him with a fighting snarl. The sound filled the room, loud and inhuman.

Fergus's eyes glittered, not in fear, but in glee. A second later, Dylan was next to Liam, his skin glistening with sweat and blood.

"No, Liam. It's not your right."

"Let him," Fergus said.

"*No.*" Dylan's voice was hard.

As Kim watched, tiny sparks raced around Liam's Collar and into his flesh. Liam flinched as his muscles registered the shock, but he never took his eyes from Fergus.

So the Collars did work. Liam was in a deadly rage, his adrenal system signaling he was ready to fight and kill. The Collar was trying to stop him, to once again torture him from the inside out.

"Liam," she whispered. "Please don't."

Her words seemed to penetrate the haze of fury in Liam's brain. Liam broke the gaze lock with Fergus, turned his head, and looked down at Kim.

"I claim her as mate," he growled.

To Kim's surprise, Fergus's angry look receded until he almost smirked. He spread his arms, the ends of the cat-o'-nine-tails fluttering. "I hereby release my claim. I wouldn't want the bitch in my house, anyway, with my cubs. I wish you joy of her."

The Shifters let out their collective breaths, stances relaxing. *What the hell?* "Liam . . ."

Liam seized Kim's arm, his hand slick with blood. "I claim her before the clan, as is my right."

Fergus's eyes glinted. "The clan recognizes your claim."

"He changed his mind quick," Kim said. "Fastest one-night stand I ever had."

Liam laughed, the sound rumbling. Fergus looked triumphant, as if he'd won, his eyes glittering in a way Kim didn't like.

He wasn't giving in. He was planning something.

Fergus gave the rest of the room a flat stare. "Everybody out."

The Shifters started to leave, their voices growing louder as they wound down. Kim wondered how many truly supported Fergus and how many had been compelled here like Liam and his family. Glory had said Shifters didn't like clan leaders who used the Summons so maybe Fergus had simply bullied them into showing up.

Fergus stepped past the Morrisseys, followed by his thugs, the only ones who hadn't relaxed. His bodyguards, Kim realized. Fergus was the clan leader, the ultimate alpha, or whatever. But if he had such power over the clan, why did he worry so much that he'd lose it?

Dylan pulled his shirt back on, wincing when the fabric touched his raw back. Liam took his T-shirt from Sean and balled it in his hands, his back a bloody mess.

Liam had rushed to protect Connor from dire hurt, and Dylan had rushed to protect both his son and grandson. Kim understood love like that, the same that had reared up and kicked her when she hadn't been able to save her brother all those years ago.

She took Liam's T-shirt from his hands, giving him a watery smile as she shook it out and folded it.

The only one not pleased was Connor. When the last of the Shifters had left the room, Connor launched himself at Liam.

"Why did you do that? I could have taken it. I didn't ask you to stand in for me."

Tears of rage and frustration streamed from Connor's eyes as he beat on Liam's chest.

Liam grabbed his fists, his voice incredibly gentle. "Connor, lad, stop that now."

Connor jerked away from him. He started to strike at Dylan, then probably realizing that was a bad idea, rounded on Sean. Sean responded by wrapping his arms around Connor and pulling him close.

Liam moved behind Connor and stroked the young man's hair. "The punishment wasn't for you, Con. Fergus was pissed at me for not groveling enough. He couldn't come up with a legitimate reason to have me beaten, so he picked on you. It wasn't your transgression, lad, it was mine."

Kim saw Connor relax, the young man leaning into Sean. "Why'd you let him? Grandda', why didn't *you* fight him?"

"Not the time and place," Dylan said. "Come on, we have to go."

He turned and left the room without waiting for them, his boots clicking on the tiles of the hall. Connor finally unwound his arms from Sean and went after Dylan, wiping his eyes, and the other three followed.

"You are going to explain what the hell just happened, aren't you?" Kim asked, as she started up the stairs ahead of Liam. After the elegant surroundings in the basement, the stairs were dingy and musty. She thought about spiders again.

Liam ruffled her hair. "Kim, who likes everything nice and neat. What a woman."

He caressed her neck under her hair. He might have just gotten skin whipped off his back, but his touch still raised goose bumps on Kim's flesh. It was the touch of a man desiring a woman, nothing less.

Damn if she didn't want to turn around right there and jump his bones. Never mind that his father, brother, and nephew were only a few steps ahead of them. Kim wanted to kiss Liam as she had last night, maybe have him lift her so she could wrap her legs around his waist.

Liam kissed the corner of her mouth. "Come on, love. Let's go out to the sunshine."

Kim kissed him back, which did not dampen her fires; then she made herself turn and follow Sean up. They clattered through the silent house, then out the front door.

The Shifters were waiting for them, all of them, arranged in a semicircle between them and Kim's car. Kim's heart started to pound.

"Aren't they going to let us leave?"

"Not yet," Dylan said.

Doors around the group of houses were opening, and female Shifters emerged. With kids. Happy to be released from whatever confinement had been imposed on them, the kids raced to the playground, making the sad patch of grass suddenly come alive. The entire dog population joined them, tails waving.

Fergus had clipped his cat-o'-nine back to his belt, and now stood with arms folded, talking to some of the male Shifters. Kim almost fell over with shock when a woman moved through the crowd and slid her arm around Fergus's waist. She wasn't some wimpy thing, either—she was tall, strong, muscular, with a hard but beautiful face. Like Glory, though not as flamboyantly dressed.

"Who is that?" Kim asked Liam.

"His mate," Liam said. "Andrea."

"Wait, wait, wait." Kim waved her hands. "He was going on about taking *me* as his mate. Why, if he already has one?"

"Clan leaders can mate with more than one woman, and Fergus has two already. Selfish, because there aren't many females to go around, but it's true that mixed offspring have a better chance of surviving."

"Oh, for God's sake." Kim rounded on Liam. "Can *you* have more than one mate? Do you have three wives tucked away in Shiftertowns around the state?"

Liam burst out laughing, and Sean followed suit. Their laughter held a note of tension, as if they were happy they had something to laugh about. Liam put his arm around Kim. "I couldn't handle more than you, love. And I hope you can handle me."

His smile gave the double entendre impact. Kim flushed. "We need to talk."

"Not yet." Liam walked Kim out to the semicircle of Shifters. He didn't retrieve his shirt; his back had to be killing him under the burning sun.

Fergus faced them as they approached, Andrea letting go of him but remaining only inches from his side.

"Why would she want him?" Kim whispered. "Especially when he has another?"

"Because he is the most powerful man in the clan. Only Dad comes close to him for dominance. And I should have mentioned that Shifters have terrific hearing."

"Thanks."

"Liam." Fergus's voice rolled across those of the other Shifters and the kids playing. "Stand here."

Liam stopped in front of Fergus and turned Kim to face him. He brushed a finger over Kim's cheek, then held up her left hand in his right, twining their fingers.

Without waiting for everyone to quiet down, Fergus said, "Under the light of the sun, I recognize this mating."

He spoke in a monotone, the words rapid, as though he wanted to get this over with. He was ready to move on to the next thing, and Kim wondered what that next thing was.

Liam smiled at Kim. The other Shifters started clapping and cheering, and Connor threw his arms around Kim and gave her a breath-stealing hug.

"Thank you, Kim."

Before Kim could ask, "For what?" Connor was leaping away, whooping and yelling with the others. Fergus twined his arm around Andrea's waist and walked away with her.

Kim never knew where it came from, but all of a sudden beer foam showered the air. Sean shook a bottle and sprayed it over them, laughing hysterically. He'd gotten his sword back, she saw, the hilt protruding over his shoulder.

"Just what I wanted, beer in my hair," Kim said.

Liam rubbed his thumb across her chin. "We'll have time to wash it out later." He leaned down and pressed dry, warm lips to her mouth. "Is this kiss up to your standards? I'm still learning."

He smiled, but his skin was hot under her fingertips, his chest still sweating. "Are you all right?" Kim asked. "I saw the Collar shock you."

"I'll live." Another light kiss, Liam's hand stealing to her waist. "I'm thinking of another ache right now."

The stiff thing pressing her abdomen left no doubt about what he meant. "You're back's a mess," she said.

"So we'll be washing that along with your hair."

Liam kissed her again. Around them, the Shifters partied, a complete change from the cold resentment in the basement. They could have been at a block party, friends and neighbors coming together to celebrate. Dylan struck up conversation with some of the Shifter men, and Sean had been lured away by a couple of females. Sean and the ladies were flirting pretty fiercely, although Shifters liked to touch a lot, so maybe they were discussing movies or something while hands ran along arms and shoulders and backs.

Questions swam in Kim's brain—she'd thought she'd researched everything about Shifters, but she realized she'd only learned what they'd let humans learn. There was too much she didn't know, too many nuances she needed to understand. She hadn't argued about this "mating" with Liam because she saw that it let Liam walk away from Fergus, and Fergus stop trying to beat up on Connor and Dylan. And she definitely hadn't wanted to do any kind of mating with Fergus.

She'd smile and laugh with them, go along with their pretense that everything was all right, but once they got back to Austin, she and Liam were going to have a long talk.

A shadow fell over her, and Kim looked up to see Fergus looming next to them. "You accept the mating?" he asked Liam.

He asked *Liam*, not Kim. Asshole.

Liam's expression remained cool. "I do."

"You know what it means, then?" Fergus kept his voice soft, turning away from the other Shifters. "You are responsible for everything she does. She steps a toe out of line, it's you who pays. Your father won't interfere; he knows the rules."

Kim's anger flared. "You—"

She found Liam's fingers over her lips. "Not now," he said. "I know what it means, Fergus. You forgo the claim forever, then?"

"I do, but I have a condition."

"Why does that not surprise me?" Kim muttered behind Liam's fingers.

"Brian goes down," Fergus said. "You, woman, will let him, and Liam, you'll make sure she does it. He pleads guilty and takes the punishment. Those are my terms."

Without waiting for their answer, he turned from them and walked away.

Chapter Twelve

Liam knew that Kim didn't understand. He held her hand as she drove, and sensed the confusion pouring off her. He'd explain everything to her soon, but right now he just wanted to have her pull the car over so he could drag her off and sex her.

He burned with it. When a Shifter claimed a mate, the urge to procreate released. He'd always known that in theory but never realized it would be this much of a flood. It was all he could do to stop at holding Kim's hand. He wanted to slide his fingers under the waistband of her jeans, lean over and press kisses to her neck, unbutton her blouse and dip his hand inside.

The little sweetheart hadn't let him get into the car until she'd dragged a towel and a first-aid kit out of her trunk, demanded a bottle of clean water from one of the Shifters, and doctored Liam's back. She'd rinsed and dried the wounds, then applied antiseptic, which had stung a little.

Liam had tried to tell her he'd heal quickly, but she only clenched her teeth and doctored him anyway. He also couldn't tell her, with Sean and Connor hovering, that her touch fired his longing to open his pants and have a go with her right there.

The others must have sensed his craving, because the teasing had begun.

"So does a mate's touch really heal, Liam?" Sean had asked.

"I don't think he's going to last until we get home." Connor snickered beside him.

"You'll live, son," Dylan had said, clapping Liam on the shoulder. "It's worth it."

Kim hadn't known what the hell they were talking about, but from her blush, she'd suspected.

He squeezed Kim's thigh now, and she responded with a smile, albeit a nervous one. Not disgust, not, "Keep your hands off me, Shifter." Kim liked him. Would she like him after she fully understood what was happening?

"Damnation," Connor said from the backseat.

Liam looked over his shoulder. Connor's nose was buried in a magazine Kim had grabbed for him at the convenience store where they'd stopped for gas. Though Kim had offered to pay for gas, magazine, and cold sodas, Dylan had silently fished out some cash and pressed it into her hand.

It was a sports magazine, because the only thing Connor liked better than cars was sports, football in particular. Not American football with pigskin and pads, but *real* football, what Americans called soccer. Connor had never been to a true football game, in a stadium overflowing with raving crowds that made American fans look like a pack of knitting grannies. Connor watched it on telly when he could and avidly followed the Republic of Ireland national football team in the sports news.

"Ireland is playing today," Connor mourned. "Tonight for them, but today over here."

"Never on a major network," Sean said. "That would be a bloody miracle."

"Sportz 3." Connor lifted the magazine sideways, studying the grid of sports offerings for the week. "Satellite channel. Game starts in an hour." He sounded glum.

"Never mind, Con," Dylan said. He leaned against the window and closed his eyes. "It's a human game, anyway."

Dylan had never understood Connor's obsession with sports. But then Dylan had grown up two centuries ago, far from human society, while Connor had spent his entire young life immersed in it. Connor was what Shifters were trying to create by taking the Collar, a generation comfortable with human culture. Maybe in a few generations, the Collars could become a thing of the past, forgotten, Shifters fully integrated into human society.

Dylan wanted that. But it didn't mean he understood Connor's addiction.

"Ellison has a friend in Shiftertown North," Sean said. "He can sometimes get satellite channels. Maybe we can get you up there to see it."

"In an hour?" Connor shook his head. "And I've seen that jury-rigged TV. You have to turn off all the lights, tilt your head sideways, and squint. If he's lucky and can get a signal at all."

"There's bound to be a recording somewhere," Sean said. "Me and Liam will look around for it."

Connor threw down the magazine. "Stop babying me, Sean. I'll not see it, and you know it. It's not like the local DVD stores have a huge section on Irish football."

"Or you can watch it at my house," Kim said.

All four Shifters stopped and stared at her. "I have every satellite channel known to man," Kim went on. "Plus a new flat-screen. No beer, though. Sorry."

Connor shoved himself between the seats, eyes alight. "Are you serious? You'd let me watch your telly at your house?"

"Sure, why not?"

Dylan answered. "Because your neighbors might object to you with a houseful of Shifters. Police might be called."

"It's not against the law for a human to invite over

Shifters. Unusual, maybe. And anyway, we'll go in through the garage and no one will see us."

"'Twould be an imposition we can't ask," Dylan said, his tone holding finality.

Connor made a frustrated noise. Liam sympathized with his frustration but for a different reason. He'd pictured taking Kim to Shiftertown and locking them both in his bedroom for three days. But he understood that Kim was offering this hospitality to try to make up for Fergus dragging Connor into this mess—a mess she thought she'd caused.

Kim didn't know that the mess with Fergus was ongoing, that the incident today was a drop in the vast ocean of their struggle with the clan leader. Fergus had gotten what he'd wanted—control of Kim and how she managed Brian's case. Or so Fergus believed. Kim hadn't said anything after Fergus had given her his "terms." She'd scowled but kept her lips pressed together, which Liam didn't think boded well. Fergus seriously underestimated Kim if he thought she'd simply fall into line.

However, in theory, now Fergus could threaten Liam and the rest of the Morrisseys if Kim didn't cooperate. Plus Fergus's capitulation had made him look generous to the rest of the clan—he'd been unwilling to stand between a Shifter and his true mate. Wasn't that noble of him?

"But trying to hold me prisoner in Shiftertown *isn't* an imposition?" Kim demanded. "I'm driving the car, and we're going to my house so Connor can watch Irish football."

Connor hooted with joy and kissed Kim's cheek. "I love you, Kim. I'm so glad Liam claimed you."

Kim looked startled but said nothing. Connor thumped happily back in his seat, and Dylan made a "Whatever" gesture.

Of course, Liam thought as the Austin exits started to glide by, Kim's house also had a bedroom.

An hour later, Kim had four Shifters in her living room avidly watching guys in shorts running across a soccer field in rainy Ireland.

I could grow to like this game, Kim thought. No helmets or padding, just tight-fitting shirts, enticing glimpses of chest hair, and socks and shorts that emphasized muscular legs.

Not that the Shifters gave a damn what the men looked like. Not five minutes into the game, they were shouting and cheering, cursing or high-fiving. At least Sean and Connor were. Dylan watched with interest if not enthusiasm, and Liam restlessly left the room and followed Kim to the kitchen.

"You made them very happy." Liam leaned on the counter while Kim looked at her mostly empty refrigerator. She wasn't equipped to entertain men, that was certain. No beer, no chips, or whatever men chowed down on when they watched sports. She was pretty sure Abel watched sports, but she'd never caught him doing it.

"They won't be happy when they get hungry."

"They won't care." Liam slid his arms around her from behind. "Now, about that shower?"

"*Liam.* Your dad's in the living room."

"And likely to stay while the game's going. Your bathroom's upstairs, if I remember." He kissed her neck under her hair.

"It's true I'd like to take a look at your back again."

"Just my back?" Liam nuzzled her cheek. "Damn, woman, have mercy on a poor Shifter."

He licked her neck, his tongue hot and wet. Kim

closed her eyes, a shiver traveling from her breastbone to the cleft between her legs.

He wanted sex, and she knew it. Wanted it, craved it, and wasn't ashamed of it. Kim couldn't lie to herself. She wanted Liam back, with her whole body.

The crowd on TV roared, and Sean, Connor, and even Dylan were on their feet, shouting. Through the open door to the living room, Kim saw Sean and Connor slam together in a joyful hug.

Liam nipped Kim's ear. "Let's go upstairs."

"You can't be real. There's sports on TV, and you want to go off with a woman instead."

He slanted her a hot smile. "What you call soccer isn't my thing. Now if it had been *Gaelic* football . . ." He laughed. Kim had no idea what the difference was, but she liked the sound of his laughter.

Liam took Kim's hand and led her to the staircase. As they ascended, the others continued to relive the glory moment of the goal.

Kim's main bathroom was huge—when she'd gone through her redecorating frenzy, she'd combined a hall bathroom with the master bath for one giant bathroom fest. She had a two-person tub in the middle, a large stone-tiled shower on one end, and a gigantic vanity on the other.

"You put a refrigerator and a TV in here, and you'd never have to leave," Liam said.

"Funny. Get your shirt off."

Liam skimmed his T-shirt over his head faster than she could blink. His chest rose with his quick breath, strong bone and muscle under tight, smooth skin. Dark hair curled across his chest to his abdomen. His Collar gleamed, the black and silver links moving with his skin. It might be a symbol of his captivity, but Liam standing with bare torso, jeans riding low on his hips, and the chain around his neck was sexier than any male model could ever hope to be.

Kim wanted to touch every one of his muscles, trace them from shoulders to spine, pausing at his backside to spend a little time there.

The stripes Fergus had laid on Liam's back had already closed, though the bruises remained. In a couple of days, Kim guessed, no one would be able to tell he'd been beaten.

She gently touched the closing wounds. "How is this possible?"

"I told you, we heal fast." Liam gave her a smile. "That's not what's hurting me, love."

"What is?"

His pants came off a little slower than his shirt but only because he had to unzip them. His underwear followed in a flash, and then Kim found six feet, six inches of aroused male Shifter in her arms.

"*You* hurt me," Liam whispered. His skin was hot and satin smooth under her touch, glistening with sweat. "I need you, Kim. It's killing me."

"What's the matter with you?" she asked, worried.

"Mating instinct. It makes me want to fuck or die."

"You smooth-talker, you."

"I can't help it. I claimed you as mate, and my body wants to complete the process."

No kidding. Kim curved into his embrace, not unhappy to flow against his body. He might call it "mating instinct," but Kim called it desire, one so strong there wasn't a cure but to give in to it.

Liam kissed her forehead and dropped kisses in her hair. Kim let her hands rove his shoulders and then his back, down to his fine, firm buttocks.

"You feel good," she murmured.

"You feel good touching me. Your hands are so cool."

She went on stroking his buttocks, the muscles as strong as she thought they'd be. "You have a nice ass."

"So do you." Large hands clasped it.

"I shouldn't be doing this."

"Most natural thing in the world, mating. The Earth goddess and Earth father joining to make the seasons continue. We're a part of that."

She couldn't help laughing. "You know, I think that's the best pick-up line I've ever heard."

Liam licked the side of her neck. "Is it working?"

"Conflict of interest. I could compromise the case."

Liam kissed her, fingers loosening her blouse. He didn't answer, and she remembered Fergus's parting words, that Kim was to drop Brian's defense and leave the poor guy to take the fall.

The fall for what?

Kim had expected Liam to tell Fergus to stuff his terms, but Liam hadn't protested. Did Liam join Fergus in wanting to throw Brian to the wolves?

"Liam, we need to talk about this."

Talk was obviously not on Liam's agenda. He kept up the scalding kisses, hands stroking. Her body became pliant, the space between her legs moist and needy.

His hardness pressed her abdomen, the feel of it making her nipples tight. She slid her hand down before she could stop herself and closed it around his penis.

Damn. He was frigging enormous. The shaft pressed her palm, moving a little with his pulse. His skin was hot, and she'd never felt a man's need so obviously before.

Not a man. A Shifter.

What women speculated about Shifter men was obviously true. They *were* bigger. And stiffer and hotter. Kim rubbed her thumb over his tip, feeling it slick and needy.

"Why are you doing this to me?" she asked.

Liam didn't appear to hear her. His eyes flicked to slits, cat's eyes, and he growled low in his throat.

"Don't you dare turn into something while I'm holding you." Kim squeezed his shaft, and Liam let out a soft groan. "That would be just too weird."

"Humans." Liam nipped her ear. "Teach me more about kissing." His tongue moved to her mouth, slid briefly between her lips.

Liam might not know how to kiss with finesse, but he did it with fervor. He licked her mouth from corner to corner, hands roving her back. Downstairs, Sean and Connor gave another whoop of victory, and Kim wanted to echo it up here. Liam's teeth scraped her mouth, his kiss clumsy, but his hands were skilled.

He loosened her blouse and brushed the tops of her breasts with callused fingers. Her lacy bra parted.

"Let me see you."

Kim let go of Liam long enough to pull her blouse open, to let her bra fall to the floor. Liam's gaze roved her, his cheeks flushed, eyes dark.

Abel had never looked at Kim like this, as though she were some Greek goddess. Liam cupped her breast almost reverently and slid his thumb across the areola. The nipple rose and tightened, and Liam leaned down and tugged it lightly with his teeth.

"You are so beautiful," he whispered into her skin.

Abel had never said that, either. "For a human?"

"For an anything."

"I don't disgust you, then?"

Liam laughed softly. "Stand still and take a compliment, love. Your body is made for loving." He moved his hand down her abdomen and unbuttoned her jeans. "I like that your hips are so curved." The zipper went down, the jeans slid past her butt, cool air touched her thighs.

"Fat-assed, you mean."

"I'm not meaning that, and you know it." Liam's hands eased her jeans to her ankles. "So you wore the thong, then."

His big hand found her bare butt cheek, betraying the truth of the statement. He softly kneaded, and Kim shivered. Here she was, in nothing but a thong in the middle of her bathroom, pressed against the hottest man she'd ever seen in her life.

Liam kissed his way down her neck and licked up between her breasts, and Kim's thoughts ceased being coherent. Liam bit her lip, then her cheek, strong hand moving to her nape and holding her there.

The thought tapped on her brain that even with the Collar, Liam was three times as strong as any man she'd ever been with. He could toss Abel across a room without working up a sweat. He could rip away her clothes in a heartbeat.

As though he read her thoughts, Liam hooked his fingers around the elastic of the thong and twisted it until it broke. His fingers found the moisture between her thighs, and she gasped, arching into his hand.

Liam eased back from the long kiss, both of them breathing faster. He softened his grip on her neck, caressing a little as though in apology.

"I don't want to hurt you." His eyes were still the cat's, narrow, slitted, light blue.

"I'm pretty tough."

"You're such a little bit of a thing." Liam's voice went

soft with wonder. "You're so small, so fragile." The caresses on her neck changed to a light touch. "Goddess, what if I hurt you?"

Kim smiled a hot smile. "I've never heard a guy call me 'a little bit of a thing.' Usually it's, 'Are you sure you want to eat that, Kim? You know you're watching your weight.'"

"Screw them."

Kim touched her forehead to Liam's, looking into his scary eyes without flinching. "I'd rather screw you."

Another growl came from his throat. "I don't know if I can hold back. I've never done this before."

"A virgin Shifter? What do you know?"

"I meant not with a human woman." Liam furrowed her hair with strong fingers. "Especially one so soft."

Kim wriggled against his body. "We have to do this," she said. "I predict that we'll implode if we don't."

Another cheer erupted from downstairs, followed by prolonged shouting. Kim had to wonder which room was more charged, her living room or this one.

Liam's growl changed to an animalistic snarl, and he pulled Kim down with him to the bathroom floor. She found herself on top of him, straddling him, her fluffy white rug cushioning her knees.

Liam held her hips. "Do this, Kim. I don't trust myself."

Kim hardly trusted *her*self. She leaned forward and kissed his lips, at the same time shifting her hips so that his tip rested against her opening. "You're a hell of a man, Liam Morrissey. I only met you yesterday, and today you're sexing me on my bathroom rug."

Liam didn't answer, his face tight. Kim leaned forward a little more, then slid back onto him.

Oh, dear God in heaven. She closed her eyes, her head going back as a groan left her mouth. Liam was big, but she was so wet that she slid smoothly onto him, her body happy to accommodate him. But the feeling . . . She groaned again, she who never made noise when she had sex. She prided herself on being discreet, even delicate. She realized now she'd never wanted to make noise, never had reason to.

Liam's hard face softened, his eyes changing back to the deep blue she'd already come to love. He made a raw noise as his warm hands moved to her breasts, rough fingertips catching on her nipples.

"I never knew humans could be so beautiful," he said.

Kim smiled, her heart warming as it beat faster. *He* was the beautiful one. And skilled. She'd teased him about being a "virgin," but Liam obviously knew exactly what he was doing.

Kim felt the loops of her white rug on her knees, the fiery heat where they joined, Liam's soothing hands. He smelled of sweat and sex and himself. His chest shone with perspiration, the black curls damp across hard pectorals. His jaw was dark with unshaved whiskers, which glistened as he rocked his head back, eyes closing in ecstasy.

Kim leaned down and kissed him, tasting male musk and the cold soft drink he'd drunk in the car. He slid his hands to her waist, letting his hips rise and rise again, pressing himself ever deeper inside her. Kim's head lolled back, and she let sound come out unchecked, drowned out by the television and shouting downstairs.

Liam half sat up, helping her ride him. Their lips met, parted. His eyes remained dark blue, although once or twice they flickered to the cat's until he forced them dark again. He was holding back with effort, Kim sensed through her haze of pleasure. She wondered what Liam *not* holding back would be like. Delightful thought.

Sweat trickled down her skin. Liam gripped her waist and rose into her with strong thrusts, sending rivers of pleasure through her body.

"Liam."

Liam growled. His eyes moved to white, then snapped back to human blue. He pulled her down to kiss him. Their mouths locked together, and he rolled with her, putting her on her back on the sweat-soaked rug.

Could anything be better than this? Lying naked on the bathroom floor with a gorgeous, hard-bodied Shifter on top of her?

Kim lifted her hips to meet his thrusts. They were both panting, both groaning, Liam's face flushed, eyes half closed. The muscles in his arms and shoulders played as he made love to her, and the mirror across the room showed his fine buttocks tightening.

Kim's orgasm, when it came, was nothing like she'd ever experienced. The world went away except for the incredible feeling that pierced her where they joined. Nothing mattered, nothing existed, only the two of them, their sweating bodies sealed together and the madness ripping through them.

Kim's throat ached, but Liam was quiet as he thrust the final few times.

"Feel my seed, Kim," he whispered. "Take it, love."

Liquid scalded into her, the semen of a Shifter. Liam's mouth covered hers as his hips worked.

It occurred to Kim that it had gone pretty quiet downstairs when Liam finally collapsed on top of her, panting as though he'd never find his breath again.

Chapter Thirteen

So this was happiness.

Big-smile-on-his-face, heart-swelling happiness.

Liam rolled over on the rug again, gathering Kim on top of him. Kim kissed him, her lips soft and warm. Liam had never known such happiness was possible. This was his lady, his mate, the female he'd protect with his life.

Way down at the bottom of his mind lay fear—he'd seen what had happened to his father and then his brother when they'd lost their mates. Dylan had gone off on his own for a year. Kenny had folded up into himself, not speaking to or looking at anyone for weeks.

Liam understood their pain now. He'd hurt like hell if he lost Kim. And he'd only known her since yesterday. Right now their happiness was fresh, fragile. Imagine the hurt after years of being together, of learning each other, body and mind. To lose that . . .

Liam held her close. She was lush and curvaceous, her sweet breasts pressing his chest. Any man who'd told her she wasn't perfect as she was deserved to be shredded.

Kim looked down at him with a smile. "That was . . . Wow."

"*Wow?* This is the articulate lawyer talking?"

"Wow about sums it up."

He stroked Kim's hair and kissed her lips. "I'm catching on to this kissing."

"I think you need more practice."

"You keep on teaching me, love."

Kim licked his mouth. When she did it again, he caught her tongue with his. He pulled her down for the kiss, lacing his fingers through her hair. He could enjoy these lessons, even when their mouths were raw from lovemaking. He'd make sure he kissed her—real kisses— for the rest of his life.

Something burbled on the other side of the room.

"Oh, hell." Kim jerked up.

Liam let her go with reluctance. His reward was watching her crawl to her pants, her backside enticing him as she went. Kim yanked her cell phone out of her pocket and sat up, and now he got to watch her firm, creamy breasts tipped with dark nipples. Liam propped himself on his elbow and enjoyed himself.

"Yeah?" she said into the phone.

A man answered, loud enough for Liam to hear him across the room. "Hi, honey. How are you?"

Kim squeezed her eyes shut. "Abel."

"Did you want something?" he asked.

Her eyes popped open again. "What are you talking about? You called me."

The voice changed to one of tired patience. "Last night, when you called, you sounded like you wanted something. What was it?"

"It's not important now."

"Well, I'm going to be tied up all day, all this week, actually, but maybe next Friday I can come over."

Maybe? With this woman waiting for him? The man was a thrice-damned idiot.

"Abel." Kim gazed into the distance, folding her legs under her. "I won't be free Friday. In fact . . . Abel, we need to break up."

"Fine." The line hummed quietly while her words processed. "What did you say?"

"I said I'm breaking up with you."

"Why?" Abel sounded baffled. Not hurt, not angry, just puzzled.

Kim made an impatient noise. "If you have to ask why, then that's why."

"Kim, honey, you're not making sense."

"Don't *Kim, honey* me. I met someone. I didn't mean to, but it happened. You and I weren't going anywhere, so I figured, what the hell?"

"Oh." Again, puzzlement instead of anger. "Is it someone in the firm?"

"No. Like I said, someone I just met."

"Right. Well. I guess I'll see you around."

"Yeah, I guess so."

Abel clicked off. Kim sat staring, every muscle tense, and then she flung the phone across the room. It landed on the tiles and spun until it hit the big bathtub.

"Two years of my life I wasted on him, and all he can say is 'See you around'?"

Liam rolled over and braced himself on both elbows. "He sounds a bit of a fool."

"More than a bit." Kim pressed her hand to her forehead. "Do you know *why* I went out with him? I just now realized it. Because he would go out with me. No other reason. No compatibility. Convenience, for both of us. I'm pathetic."

Liam held out his hand. "You weren't pathetic, love. Lonely. There's a difference." He wriggled his fingers. "Come here."

Kim walked to him, no more crawling, until she stood over him. This was the best view of all. Liam roamed his gaze up her tight, petite legs to the slick tuft of hair between them, over her cute navel, her round breasts and bare neck, ending at her beautiful face.

"You're mated now," he said, as Kim knelt on the floor next to him. "You've no more need to be lonely. You have me."

"You and your ego."

"You make me laugh, love. You have me and my father and Sean and Connor. Ellison and Glory. All the Shifters."

"Even Fergus?"

Liam grimaced. "Him too. He's bent out of shape about Brian, and I don't know why, but usually he's a fair leader. Mostly."

"Fair? He tried to *whip* Connor for talking back to him!"

"I know, and it might be hard to understand, but Connor did wrong. He's a cub. He doesn't have a place yet, and attacking the clan leader needs punishment. Connor knew that. Any other time, he might have been let off with a warning, but in the middle of a moot, when our family was already in disgrace—Fergus couldn't let it go."

"So he whipped you and your father instead."

"Any member of a pride has the right to take a punishment for any other, but it has to be voluntary. Dad and I could take the lash; Connor never has. And I wasn't wrong about Fergus wanting to punish me instead. Connor gave him the excuse."

"This is one of those Shifter things I don't understand, isn't it?"

Liam let himself grin. "You'll get used to it. You'll get used to all things Shifter."

"No, I won't." Kim pulled her knees to her chin, shaping her body into delectable curves and shadows. "We can't date right now, Liam. Not until after the case is over and Brian is free. Then, I won't lie, I wouldn't mind getting to know you—much better. What we did today will have to be a one-off."

Liam laced his fingers through hers. "We're not *dating*, love. We're bonded for life."

Kim gently disengaged her fingers and scooted a few inches away. Liam let her go; this was new to her, and he had to ease her in a bit at a time. "That's what it means for Shifters to be mated."

"That's not the human way," she said. "I'd only be bound to you if I married you. Signed a piece of paper saying so."

"Shifters aren't allowed to get marriage licenses. Not under the current laws."

"I know. I'm sorry."

"Fergus pronounced us mated, in the Shifter way, under the light of the sun. In a few days, my dad will pronounce it so under the light of the full moon. Then it's you and me together forever. Because you're human, I'll seek a Fae to bond us as well, increasing your lifespan to match mine." He grinned at her. "Think of how many cases you can defend that way."

"The Fae can increase lifespan?" Kim's eyes widened. "Why isn't everyone out to find a Fae and stay youthful?"

"Because the Fae are bloody elusive to humans, and it only works if the human is bonded to a Shifter. That happens rarely, for obvious reasons, and only the Shifter can seek out the Fae. The Fae have certain obligations to Shifters, as much as they hate it, and this is one favor they grant us if we ask for it. Your natural lifespan will lengthen to match mine. When I grow old and die, so will you."

"Great, what if you get hit by a bus?"

"I said *natural* lifespan. It would be like a human relationship but longer."

Kim half smiled, shaking her head as though she thought he was talking nonsense. "That's not how it works."

She still didn't understand. She would in time, though; Kim wasn't stupid. And then—she'd kill him.

"It is working, love. Anyway, you've taken my seed. What will you say to the wee one that comes if you haven't bound yourself to me? It'll be embarrassed."

"Wee one? Oh, you mean if I have a baby. Don't worry about that. I take contraceptives."

"Contraceptives?"

"You know, birth control. I don't know if Shifters have that."

"I know what it is, Kim." Humans bred like rabbits, and they were always looking for ways to keep babies from coming. So few Shifter babies were conceived and so few survived that Shifters wouldn't dream of preventing them. Shifter women knew how dangerous it was to give birth, and yet they sought it with everything they had.

"I was taking it because I was going out with Abel," Kim said in reasonable tones. "It would look bad if he and I had a child together. No, let's be honest—it would be a hell of a complication if we'd had a child together."

"And if you had one with me?"

"You're a Shifter."

Liam lay back on his elbows, eyes narrowing. "This makes a difference?"

"Please don't be offended. If I had a half-Shifter baby, that would be the end of my career. I researched this when I took up Brian's case, because he was dating a human. There haven't been many hybrids since you took the Collar, but the woman in question gets shunned by human society every time. In fact, my theory about Michelle's death is that her ex-boyfriend killed her because she'd betrayed him with Brian, a Shifter. I imagine that made him crazy." Kim sighed. "Proving it is a bitch, though."

Liam heaved himself to his feet and stalked to the medicine cabinet over her pristine pedestal sink. He opened it and started pulling out bottles.

"What are you doing?" Kim asked.

"Looking for your birth control pills. I want to flush them."

"I don't take pills. I get injections from my doctor."

"Then stop."

"Excuse me?" Kim stood and planted her hands on her naked hips. "How is this your business?"

"Everything you do is my business."

"Liam, if you want someone to breed little Shifters with you, you have plenty of Shifter women drooling over you. I saw the waitress at the bar—what's her name?—Annie. She'd have gone to bed with you in a heartbeat."

"And she has."

"Oh." Did Liam dare hope that was jealousy in her eyes? "Did you throw away *her* contraceptives?"

"She's Lupine. I told you that the chances of conception in those cases are low, remember?"

"How lucky for you."

"You say *lucky* like you'd never want a child."

"I do want one." Kim threw him an exasperated look. "I like kids. But not right now."

"And not with a Shifter."

"If I decided to pick a Shifter, it would be you." Kim smiled her beautiful smile. "Maybe later, when I have a solid career, and if you're still available . . ."

Liam moved across the floor and had her in his arms before she could turn away. "Understand me, Kim. We are *mated*. That means I go to no other female unless I lose you to death, and even then it will feel like betrayal. I protect you, I take care of you, I bind myself to you, and you alone."

Her face lost color. "That's your custom?"

"It's not custom. It's Shifter law. It's magic that runs deep inside us. This mating brings you into my pride. Even Fergus can't touch you without going through me. That was the point of me claiming you."

Kim squirmed away, and Liam let her go.

"It was necessary," he explained. "If I hadn't made the Challenge, Fergus would have taken you as mate whether you liked it or not."

"How could he?" Kim asked. "I'm not bound by Shifter law."

"He could because we're animals. We look like humans and you put Collars on us, but we're born animals and only learn to become human later. The leader of the clan can claim whatever unmated female he wants, and we have to step back and let him unless we want to Challenge. It's his right. But Fergus is hellaciously strong, and most in the clan don't want to fight him, so he takes the mates he wants."

"But I'm not Shifter . . ."

"Do you think Fergus gives a damn about that? He wants to control you, needs to control what you tell the humans about us."

"Wait a minute." A look of horror moved over Kim's face. "Are you telling me that if I hadn't agreed to do this mating thing with you, Fergus might have taken me off and raped me?"

"Very likely."

"But he'd go down for that. A human court would crucify him."

"Would they? Or would they say it was your own fault for hanging out with Shifters? You just said that having a child with me would ruin your career, that you think Michelle died for associating with a Shifter. Shifter-whore is the term."

Her face went white, and she sat down hard on the edge of the tub. "Shit."

Liam came to her, crouched in front of her. "Don't be afraid, love. I'll never let Fergus hurt you. Ever. The mate claim overrides clan hierarchy. He can beat up on me, but never you. Even if he kills me, you'll still be protected by my family, my pride."

"But why would Fergus still want to kill you?" Kim asked in confusion. "He seemed to back off all of a sudden, like he didn't care about the mate thing anymore."

"Because he knew he'd won. He got me to promise to control you, for the good of all Shifters. If he'd pursued it further, for nothing but self-satisfaction, the clan wouldn't have approved, and even though he's leader, he can't afford to lose the clan's respect. Besides, Dad was there. Fergus has never been one hundred percent certain he's dominant to Dad, and he didn't want to put that to the test, especially not in front of the whole clan."

"So why doesn't your dad fight him, then? It's obvious none of you like him."

"To tell you the truth, love, I'm not sure," Liam said, troubled. "Dad won't talk about it. Maybe he knows he *isn't* dominant to Fergus, and if Dad were killed, he couldn't protect the rest of us from him. But I don't know. He's never said and gets pissed off when anyone brings it up."

Kim frowned, rubbing her arms. "But when Fergus came at me with the whip and you almost attacked him, Dylan stopped you, said it wasn't your 'right.' What did he mean? I thought you were *supposed* to fight."

Liam remembered the surge of adrenaline rising white hot, searing him like a brand on flesh, when he'd seen Fergus focus on Kim. Only Dylan's harsh voice had stopped him from making a fatal move, or this day would have ended differently.

"Because at that moment, I wanted to kill him. The Fae-cat in me wanted to go after Fergus in a clan dominance fight, to take him down for good. The mate Challenge isn't to the death—at least, not anymore—but fighting for clan leadership usually is, unless the clan leader surrenders before the fight. Dad stopped me from making it a clan dominance issue, thank the Goddess."

"Why? It seems like you could have saved him a step." She let out her breath. "Not that I want to see you in a fight to the death. I'm happy he stopped you too."

"Shifter politics." Liam tried to sound offhand, but something subtle had changed during the moot today, and he wasn't yet certain what. "Only Dad, as pride leader, has the right to fight for clan dominance. If I want to take out Fergus, I first have to take out Dad, and I won't be doing that anytime soon."

Kim gave him a faint smile. "Because you know he could kick your ass?"

Liam laughed. "No, because he's my dad, and I love him." Another laugh. "And yeah, he could probably kick my ass."

Kim hugged her chest. "I thought I researched Shifter law down to the last degree. I don't remember any of this."

"Because it's not written law. It's passed down through the generations, and it's based on instinct and what you call custom." Liam laid his hands on her shoulders. "It's complicated even for us. I'm going to protect you, Kim. Believe that."

She looked up at him with anguished eyes. "Liam, I can't be your mate. I only came to Shiftertown to get help building my defense for Brian. I'm fine with you keeping Fergus off my back, but I can't move into your house to become a Shifter baby-making machine. You're crazy if you believe I'll agree to that."

He traced circles on her shoulders. "I'd never believe you'd do anything you don't really want to, Kim Fraser."

Kim broke his hold, got to her feet, and reached for her clothes. "You got that right." She pulled on her jeans in short jerks. "Now if you'll take your family and go home, I *really* have a lot of work to do. I'm seriously behind."

"All right."

She stopped and stared at him. "You agree? Just like that?"

"Just like that, love."

"Stop calling me 'love.'"

Liam chuckled. "Now that, I can't do."

He watched Kim's breasts softly bounce as she scrabbled for the rest of her clothes. He wouldn't push her now—she was human, this was sudden, and it would take her time to get used to him. But Kim was *his*. His mate, his lover.

All mine.

She finished dressing and hurried out of the bathroom. Liam followed, not bothering with his clothes. He paused on the landing to watch her hips sway as she ran lightly down the stairs.

As angry and confused and hurt as she was—and as likely to make his life hell—Kim glowed with beauty. Her body was covered with Liam's scent, filled with their lovemaking. Beautiful, beautiful Kim.

Liam went down the stairs after Kim. Below him, she stopped abruptly, noting that the TV was dark, the living room quiet. Sean and Connor looked at her with innocent faces.

Connor grinned. "Everything all right up there? I thought the ceiling might come crashing in."

Kim flushed. "Where's Dylan?"

"Gone," Sean said. "Took the bus back to Shifter-town. Dad does his own thing."

"I see," she said, clearly flustered. "I can call a taxi for the rest of you."

Sean shook his head. "No need. Dad said he'd be back to fetch us."

Connor lost his smile. "Aren't you coming home with us, Kim?"

Poor cub. He liked Kim, was ecstatic about the mating, and probably assumed Kim would instantly become one of them. Connor had much to learn about females.

"Now that Liam says Fergus is no longer a threat, I'm going to stay in my own home," Kim said. "I didn't mind helping out today, and thank you for the pancakes, but I'm kind of tired and have a lot of work to do."

Liam shifted. His Fae-cat didn't wait for him to ready himself, and for the first time in his life, the shift didn't hurt. He leapt off the bottom step, the stairs creaking under his weight, and he tackled Kim. His big, sheathed paws sent her to the ground, and he landed on top of her, balancing so he wouldn't crush her.

In this form he could truly smell her, and she was better than the best field of blossoms. She combined her scent and his in perfect proportion, the sign of a perfect mate.

Kim tried to squirm out from under him. "Liam, what are you doing? Someone get this big cat off me."

Liam didn't mind her wriggling while his brother and nephew laughed at them. He swiped her face from chin to forehead with his large tongue, shifting back to human form as she turned her head and cried, "Eeewwww."

Incredibly, Liam did leave with his family, and Kim found herself alone in the house. She'd expected Liam to stay on his overprotective kick and insist she come back with them to Shiftertown for the night. Or maybe move his whole family to her house so they could watch satellite TV, she wasn't sure.

But Liam had gone back upstairs, put on his clothes, and herded Connor and Sean out through the garage just as Dylan pulled a big pickup into her driveway. As the others piled in, Liam slid his arms around Kim and kissed her.

"You rest now," he said, smoothing her hair. "We'll talk later."

Kim's lips tingled and she wanted more, but she made herself step back. "I'm going to work in the morning. I'm not dropping the case, whatever Fergus might think."

"I know." Liam lifted her hand and kissed her palm. "You wouldn't be yourself if you dropped it. But as you like to say, we need to talk."

Kim suddenly, inconsistently, didn't want him to leave. "Tomorrow?"

"Tomorrow."

Liam brushed another warm kiss to her lips and walked out. Kim resisted the urge to rush after him, to tell him to come back, to beg him to stay.

What was the matter with her? Liam and his family had imprisoned her in Shiftertown, and then she'd driven them a hundred or so miles to the middle of nowhere so she could endure the abuse of Fergus the Irish biker thug.

Then why did her heart ache as the pickup backed away, all four Morrissey men squished into the cab? Liam must have brainwashed her with his fine blue eyes and incredible smile, not to mention intense, mind-blowing sex.

As Kim closed the door, the emptiness of the house

pressed on her. The TV was dark and quiet, no male voices raised in jubilation. She stood in the middle of the living room and felt the silence.

Kim went through the rest of the afternoon on automatic. She showered, trying not to gaze at the rug where she'd ridden Liam so ecstatically. The tactile memory of his body on hers, of every finger press, every kiss, every slide of skin on skin was imprinted on her. Kim had never had sex like that in her life.

In a half daze she drove down the hill to her local grocery store. She found herself putting things in her cart that wouldn't have occurred to her a few days ago—steaks, ground beef, potato chips, and Guinness stout. *Why?* she wondered as she paid without meeting the cashier's eyes. *It's not like I'm going to invite them over again.* But just in case . . .

Kim took the food home and crammed everything into the refrigerator. She fixed herself a salad that she picked at, and then she opened her briefcase and laptop and flipped listlessly through files.

She needed to get her head around all this—Brian, the Collars, Fergus, this mating thing. She reread a note from her friend Silas asking Kim whether she could get him an interview with the Shifter leaders. Silas was a good, evenhanded journalist who didn't shrink from bald truth but didn't make something out of nothing either. Two days ago, she'd have eagerly set up an interview for him. Given what she knew now, she wasn't so sure it was a good idea, or if Liam would even agree to talk to him.

On the other hand, everything that had happened today helped Kim look at Brian's case from a new angle. Had Brian intended to make Michelle his mate? If so, wouldn't he have been as protective of her as Liam was of Kim? If Brian had decided to "claim" Michelle, that might mean he'd never dream of hurting her. Wouldn't he have done everything in his power to keep her safe?

Michelle's ex-boyfriend, on the other hand, might go ballistic. Brian, a Shifter, would be hard to kill, but not Michelle. And if Brian could get blamed for Michelle's death, so much the better.

Then again, why hadn't Brian been there to protect his girlfriend from her killer? Where had he been and what had he been doing to keep him from Michelle at the critical moment?

Kim sighed and rubbed her temples. She was getting nowhere.

After an hour or so of trying to think and failing, Kim went to bed. Mistake. She should have been exhausted after rolling on the bathroom floor with Liam, but instead she was wide awake, her pulse speeding as their lovemaking played over and over in her mind.

She'd never, ever felt like this before. Kim should be sated after that incredible sex, but she wanted more of Liam. And more.

"What is the matter with me?"

She sat up and snapped on the light. Three seconds later, her phone rang.

Kim picked it up, her heart pounding as Liam's rich Irish tones rolled over her. "Kim. You all right?"

Kim wanted to sigh with happiness. "I'm fine. Why wouldn't I be?"

"I wanted to make sure."

"I am fine." She lay back down on the pillows, feeling warm and content. "Really. Really, really fine."

"Good." He sounded as though it was the best news he'd heard all day.

Kim hesitated. "How's Connor doing?"

"Still not happy with me, but he'll be all right. Letting him watch Irish football has made you his superhero."

"I'm glad he's okay."

"I'm glad you're glad."

Kim wondered if Liam was in bed talking to her, if he was stretched, naked, on top of the bed she'd slept in last night. Her heart beat faster.

"I'm going to my office tomorrow." She said it firmly.

"I know you are. I wouldn't expect you to do anything else." Liam's voice softened. "Good night, love. You call me anytime you need me, all right?"

He meant it—his sincerity came through loud and clear. All she had to do was say, *Liam, I need you*, and he'd be there. So different from Abel and his *I'm busy, honey, I'll call you later*.

"Good night, Liam." Kim made herself click the phone off and set it on the nightstand, but it was a long time before she snapped off the light.

Outside Kim's big house, Liam tucked away his phone and kissed his fingers to her bedroom window. He faded into the shadows against the wall and settled in to guard her for the rest of the night.

Chapter Fourteen

The next morning Kim raced her car into her parking space at Lowell, Grant, and Steinhurst, half an hour late.

Late. On a Monday. Missing the Monday morning meeting. Kim scrambled out of her car, snatched up her briefcase, rushed for the front door, and stopped in dismay.

Liam leaned against the Harley he'd parked at the curb in front of the firm's walkway, smiling his wicked smile.

"Morning, love," he said.

"What are you doing here?" Kim demanded.

"Looking after you. Like I should."

July sunshine gleamed on Liam's dark hair and flat black sunglasses. With his black T-shirt and jeans, Collar around his neck, his jaw working as he chewed a piece of gum, he looked nothing less than a dangerous Shifter male. Which he was.

She made an exasperated noise. "Liam, I cannot bring a *Shifter* to work with me."

Liam lifted his sunglasses, blue eyes dancing. "I don't see any signs: 'No Shifters Allowed.' 'Shifters Must Keep Off the Grass.' 'Absolutely No Territory Marking Anywhere.'"

"Very funny. Go home."

"No." He lowered the sunglasses and took her elbow. "If you work here, I stay with you. I'm your guard dog. You won't even know I'm here."

"Because no one will notice a six-foot-six Shifter in my office."

"I'm staying, Kim. Or you're coming home with me. Your choice."

She jerked from his grasp. "You're a pushy pain in my ass."

"I'm not taking a chance that Fergus will leave you alone. He can't touch you anymore, but that doesn't mean he won't order other Shifters to make trouble for you. Some of Fergus's lackeys are . . . Let's just say they're fanatically devoted to him."

"You all are crazy, you know that?"

Liam shrugged. "Hey, you're the Shifter lover, which means you're crazier than we are. Come on."

Liam opened the heavy glass door and, Shifter-fashion, entered the building first. Once he determined that the polished granite and marble foyer was harmless, he nodded for Kim to come inside.

Kim knew of nothing that could make him leave, short of having him arrested, and even then the police would have to break out the tranquilizer guns. She also knew that, deep down inside, she didn't want him to leave. Kim didn't trust Fergus either, and Liam's presence made her feel safe. Embarrassed, awkward, and confused, but safe.

As they moved through the plush halls, lawyers looked up through open doors or stepped into the hall in astonishment. Liam nodded at the head of the firm who'd stopped short in his doorway. "Top o' the morning to you."

Kim scuttled into her office suite where the secretary, Jeanne, who worked for Kim and two other lawyers, typed on a computer keyboard. Jeanne looked up, gawked, and lost her place. "Who the hell . . . ?"

Liam smiled. "Top o' the mornin' to you."

"It's all right," Kim said in a hard voice. "He's helping me on the Shifter case."

Jeanne looked as though she'd melt through her chair. "Can I get you coffee?" she offered Liam in an eager tone.

"Coffee would be grand," he said.

Kim grabbed Liam's arm, shoved him into her cluttered office, and slammed the door behind them. She pointed at the leather couch wedged between two bookcases.

"If you're staying—*sit.*"

Liam grinned, removed his sunglasses, stretched out full length on the couch, and folded his arms behind his head. He looked good enough to eat.

Kim slapped her briefcase to her desk and popped it open. "What is this 'top o' the morning' crap?"

"It's how people expect the Irish to talk. That and 'faith and begorra!' I'll throw those in later."

"You are so full of shit."

Liam chuckled and closed his eyes. He looked prepared to lounge there the rest of the day, reminding her every second of their thorough sexing in her bathroom. She'd dreamed about it all night, the main reason she'd been late. When he'd rolled her over and driven into her, his warm weight on top of her, she'd never felt more connected or intimate with a man in her life. She'd felt . . . complete.

Forget the goopy, romantic stuff. The sex had been damn fantastic.

Kim had to stop thinking about it. She had to be professional and do her job. She had other cases to prepare for, a load of witness statements and evidence reports to go through. Brian's defense to figure out, the private investigator's weekend reports to read.

Once she won Brian's case, she'd be finished with

Shifters. Fergus's wishes would be a moot point, Liam wouldn't need to guard her anymore, and he'd go back to Shiftertown and leave her alone. For good.

Why did the world suddenly go colorless at that thought?

Kim dumped files back into her briefcase. "I need to talk to Brian. I assume you want to come with me? We'll take my car—I'm not riding to the county jail on the back of your motorcycle."

Liam didn't move. "You're not going to see Brian."

"I need to. I want to ask him about Michelle again, whether he planned to mate with her, whether he already did. If Brian thought of her as his mate, he'd never have hurt her, right? He'd come over all protective, defend her rather than attack her."

"You might be right about that, but you're still not going to see him."

Kim clicked the briefcase shut. "Why not? He's in jail. He's not going anywhere."

Liam finally came off the couch. "You're not going because Fergus told you to drop the case."

He was a tall, solid wall, blocking her way to the door. "We've discussed this. I say screw Fergus."

"I wouldn't. I hear it's not good."

Kim didn't laugh. "So you agree with him?"

"I didn't say that." Liam rested his hands on her shoulders. She'd never get by him, and she knew it. At the same time, she knew he wouldn't hurt her. He'd prevent her from leaving, but not by hurting.

"Then what are you saying?" she asked.

"That Fergus won't trust me to keep you off the case. I was the one who talked him into letting you come to Shiftertown in the first place. So he'll have sent his own men to watch you, to stop you. I'm here to keep them from tangling with you. If you go to the jail, there will be tangling."

Kim made a noise of exasperation. "Explain how I'm supposed to defend a man I'm not allowed to talk to. I need to ask him questions, important questions."

"Ask him some other way."

Kim tried to dart around him. Liam put one arm out and hauled her back against him.

"Liam."

He closed both arms around her and pulled her close. "Do this my way, love. Don't mess with Fergus more than you have to. He'll make you regret it."

Kim wanted to succumb to the wonderful, protected feeling of having his arms around her. Even her parents hadn't been this protective of her. After Mark had died, they'd wavered between being overly paranoid about her safety to backing way off when they realized they were smothering her.

They'd gone on like that until they'd died. She'd found herself alternately on a choke chain or floundering during her parents' "you don't even have to check in with us" moods.

Liam's protection was like a soft blanket, not a leash, but the tether was there nonetheless.

"I can't work like this," Kim said.

"We'll find a way." Liam kissed the crown of her head.

The warm touch of his lips electrified the memories of their lovemaking, reminding her that her throat was still scratchy from all the screaming. She couldn't help putting her hand on his waistband and sliding her fingers downward, her pulse speeding when she found that he was hard and hot behind his zipper.

Liam laughed. "Vixen." He tilted her head back and kissed her.

Liam was still learning how to kiss. Which meant he experimented and explored, his tongue sliding all over hers while he gripped her buttocks with one firm hand. He tasted like the gum he'd been chewing, minty fresh.

If anyone came in, they'd see his sun-browned hand planted against her gray business skirt, Kim letting a Shifter put his tongue down her throat. And they wouldn't know the half of it.

"Stop," she whispered. "Don't do this to me."

A gentle kiss to her forehead. "I'd never hurt you, Kim."

"It's not pain I'm worried about." Kim rested her head against his chest. His skin was hot through the shirt, his heart pounding at breakneck speed. "It's me."

"You're not making sense."

"I know what I mean. You are seriously damaging my mental health."

Liam broke away, but he was smiling. "You mean I make you spare."

"If that means crazy, then yes. That too."

There was a soft knock on the door, and Jeanne poked her head in. She carried in a tray of coffee, in real mugs, not Styrofoam cups. Kim turned from Liam, hoping she looked nonchalant.

Jeanne set the coffee on the polished side table. "Abel is looking for you."

"Abel?" For one crazy moment, Kim couldn't remember who he was. Ah, yes, buttoned-up, executive ex-boyfriend. The man who looked incredibly boring next to Liam. "What does he want?"

"To ask you about the judge you had on that indecent exposure case. He's got a similar case before the same judge."

"Oh." Business. Tips on what swayed a judge or pissed

him off. Kim had won the case, because the man they'd arrested had had erectile dysfunction, verified by a doctor, when the witness had sworn the defendant had been quite, um, pointed. "Set up a meeting with Abel," Kim finished. "I'm busy until tomorrow."

"He's here now."

Before Kim could answer, Abel Kane pushed around the door and strode into the office. Kim had always thought him good-looking—tall, blond, well-dressed—but he was a lightweight compared to Liam. And there was no comparison at all in the sex department.

"Can't this wait?" Kim asked him.

Abel was looking at Liam in curiosity. "Kind of in a rush."

Liar. He couldn't be paid to care about indecent-exposure cases; he'd used the excuse to come in here and eyeball Liam.

"Why?" Kim asked in an annoyed voice. "Client can't keep his pants on?"

Abel ignored her attempt at humor. "So the Collars really do fit all Shifters. What neck size would you say he has?"

"He can hear you, Abel."

Liam gave Abel his slow smile. "Top o' the morning to you."

"Will you stop that?" Kim snapped.

"Is he Irish?" Abel said in surprise. "I didn't know Shifters could be Irish."

"The Shifters in my family go back generations in Ireland," Liam said. "We had a castle on a hill and everything."

Abel continued to assess Liam like a scientist examining an interesting specimen. "Type up a report on him," Abel said to Kim. "It would be useful if we ever have to defend another Shifter."

"Abel, will you please stop talking about him like he's not in the room?"

"What's eating you, Kim? Is it the new guy you met or your time of the month?"

What an idiot. Abel hadn't connected Kim "meeting someone" with the extremely virile Shifter standing in her office. Abel couldn't imagine for one second that she'd dump him for a *Shifter*.

Liam's grin died. He'd been taking Abel for what he really was, a self-centered moron, but Liam's eyes narrowed at Abel's last statement. The predatory thing Liam did so well came out, proving that up until now, he'd been a wolf watching the sheep frolic.

"The lady said she's busy." Liam's voice held a hint of growl.

Without moving, Liam gained the attention of everyone in the room, plus Jeanne listening outside the door. A sheen of perspiration glistened on Abel's forehead.

"Right. I'll call you later, Kim. About that judge."

Abel couldn't turn around to walk out. Liam wouldn't let him. And yet, Liam did nothing but stand there, not moving, not touching the man. He hadn't even let his pupils go slitted.

Abel had to back to the door, one step at a time, before he finally turned and fled. He ran into Jeanne, who was plastered solidly against the crack in the door. They tangled a moment; then Abel fled and Jeanne slammed the door, leaving Kim and Liam alone again.

Chapter Fifteen

Kim took Liam out for lunch. Liam enjoyed riding in her small car, watching her gray businesslike skirt riding up her thighs. As he'd guessed, she wore stockings with lacy tops, held in place by garters. Thinking about skimming off the skirt and looking at her in only the garter belt and stockings didn't do his rising erection any favors.

What deflated his arousal was being turned away by the first restaurant they reached. The hostess took one look at Liam's Collar and got the manager.

Kim stormed away, furious, but Liam didn't know why she was surprised. Shifters hadn't been welcomed in most places for twenty years.

The next two restaurants wouldn't let them in, either. They ended up at a greasy spoon close to the north Austin Shiftertown, where the owners had figured out that Shifters paid for the food and didn't cause trouble, unlike the gang kids that roamed the nearby neighborhoods.

"How can you stand it?" Kim fumed as she dumped sugar into her coffee. "I never realized how blatant it was."

Liam blew on his coffee to cool it before he sipped. "Bans against Shifters? If you never witnessed it firsthand, I'm guessing you frequent places Shifters don't even bother trying to go to. But it doesn't much matter to me where I go. I don't really want to eat at a place where they don't serve Shifters."

"Stop being so blasé. They treat you like animals."

"We *are* animals."

"Be serious."

"Kim, sweetheart, I've lived a hundred years under various and sometimes nasty conditions. This life isn't so bad. There are certain people I keep out of my bar too. I'd ban Lupines altogether, except Ellison and Glory would try to wipe the floor with my butt."

"Be serious," she repeated.

"What for?" Liam looked straight into her blue eyes, trying to calm her rage. He liked her anger, though, because it meant she cared. "The way people treat Shifters can be amusing."

"Discrimination is never funny."

"You're a righteous woman, Kim. I like that."

"How can you just *sit* there?"

"I usually sit when I'm drinking coffee. Or I lean against something. If I lie on my back, it goes down the wrong way." Kim started to rage, and Liam reached over and took her hand. "I'm sorry, love. I'm glad you care so much. It's sweet. But I'm not bothered."

"How can you not be bothered to have people walk all over you? Abel acted like you were behind a viewing wall in a zoo."

"Because they don't walk all over me." He glanced around, but they were relatively alone in their corner of the restaurant. "We don't ever let them. Do you understand?"

"Not really."

Liam lifted his coffee again. "Neither does Fergus. That's why he chose the Shiftertown out in the desert. He can't stand for anyone to bruise his ego."

Kim sat in silence, running her finger around the rim of her cup. She spoke carefully, as though she had to choose each word. "What you mean is, you don't get upset when they won't let you into restaurants or forbid you having cable, because those things aren't important to you."

"Now, you're catching on."

"And Abel doesn't bother you because you don't value his opinion."

"Not really. On the other hand, he says anything nasty like that to you again, I'll crush him."

Kim had a sudden vision of a lion lying on a veldt in complete relaxation, swatting an obnoxious fly with his tail. The fly had Abel's head. The same lion would have cubs climbing all over him, which he'd turn and greet with a lick.

"It's like we live in a different world from you," Kim said. "And we don't even know it."

"Something like that."

The look she gave him was stunned. "I've been feeling sorry for you."

"Don't worry about that, love." He grinned. "If last night was a pity fuck, I'm all for them."

She turned bright red. "It wasn't. And don't talk about sex while I'm trying to get my head straight."

"I was thinking about doing more than talking about it."

"Stop." She pressed her palms flat on the table. "When you do that, I can't think."

"I'm glad. Thinking, it's an overrated activity."

"Liam, where does Fergus get all his money?"

Liam managed to look blank. "Does Fergus have money?"

"You know he does. There's that underground complex for one, and all that artwork for another. It didn't spring there overnight."

"Shifters live a long time, and some are good with money."

"But Shifters aren't supposed to have much money."

"No." Liam took a calming sip of coffee. Trust Kim to pry at their most basic secrets, leaving Liam to have to think of ways of explaining. He didn't want to lie, not to the woman he'd chosen as mate, but at the same time she wanted to rip the lid off everything they desperately needed to keep protected.

"How do you think we live, sweetheart?" he asked her, keeping his voice down. "We're only allowed low-wage jobs, and yet we're expected to feed our families, pay the rent. You don't think I live on what I make as a part-time bar manager, do you?"

"I did notice you had a casual attitude about going to work. As in, you never go."

"But I have the job. So the human committees can mark down on their sheets that I have employment and be happy that they've done well by me."

"So you do have money?"

"Now then, Kim, a man would think you didn't want him for his looks and his fine personality."

Kim flushed again. "You obviously don't want me prying, but you expect me to be your mate—for life—without explaining what's really going on with you."

Liam laid his hand lightly over hers. "I was teasing. Let's just say my family is provided for. As will be my mate and my offspring."

"Offspring. Now we're back in dangerous territory."

"I thought all women would want to know that their mate can take care of the cubs. But all right." Liam withdrew his hands. "Let's talk about Brian."

Kim looked surprised at the change of subject. "All right, let's talk about why Fergus doesn't want me to save him. Why he wants Brian to plead guilty."

"I wish I knew, love. Brian's no threat to Fergus, nowhere near challenging for leadership. Fergus has helped Brian and his family in the past. They aren't close, but not enemies."

"Maybe Brian pissed him off somehow."

"If he did, I never heard about it. I would have heard." It bothered him that he knew little of what had gone on between Brian and Fergus. Liam had always thought he had his finger firmly on the pulse of Shiftertown. He knew everyone, and they knew him. If a Shifter were in trouble, someone would tell him or Sean. That was the way it worked. In Brian's case, it hadn't.

Kim said, "When I first came to see you, you told me you didn't know much about Brian."

"I was trying to put you off. A human poking around in Shiftertown is dangerous."

"But you took me to see his mother."

"I liked you." That liking was growing into something far deeper, perilously deeper. The joy that flashed through him every time he saw Kim's beautiful eyes and sassy smile grew stronger each day. The thought should dismay him, yet it didn't.

Mating could start off as nothing more than a drive to reproduce, and some Shifters never moved beyond that. But others, like his father and mother, his brother Kenny and mate Sinead, had developed a relationship that went beyond mating, even beyond love. It was a bond humans couldn't understand, and Liam felt it forging between himself and Kim.

It was a heady feeling, and one he feared would turn into worse pain than any he'd ever experienced. The Collar's torture would be nothing compared to Kim breaking his heart.

Kim frowned at her coffee. "I can't believe that now that I have good questions to ask Brian, you won't let me near him. You're not making my job easy." She looked up, an idea lighting her eyes. "But wait a sec, I can't believe Fergus wouldn't let Brian's *mother* talk to him."

"Possibly. Clan rules are one thing; maternal ties are another. Sacred, you could say."

"The same way Fergus can't mess with me if I'm your mate."

Liam nodded. "He can't unless I let him."

"*Let him?* What's all this 'let' shit? Shifters don't understand the term 'feminism,' do they?"

"I wouldn't say that, love. Shifter females are no pushovers. But realize that Shifters have lived in small groups for thousands of years, the males protecting the females and the cubs. It's instinctive for us. This is the first time we've dwelled in close communities—we still had the clans, but we rarely saw others in our clan. It's taking us a little bit of time to adjust."

She watched him in curiosity, one finger still rubbing the rim of her cup. Liam thought about her sweeping the same finger over his cock and instantly got hard again.

"Where did you live before?" she asked. "I mean in Ireland, before you came to Shiftertown? You told Abel you had a castle."

"A castle. That we did."

"With battlements and everything?"

"It was mostly a ruin by the time we moved in, but we fixed it up and made it livable."

"What did the Irish think of you? This was before Shifters came out, right?"

"Oh, they had all kinds of explanations for us. The ones inclined to believe in ghost stories thought we were the Fae, and that wasn't far off. Lucky for them, Shifters are ten times kinder than the Fae. Others thought we were former IRA come to hide out. The more skeptical just said we were crazy. But everyone knew we kept the village protected, so no one tried to drive us out."

Kim was watching him now, a bit like her office colleagues had, but Liam didn't mind so much being subjected to her blue-eyed scrutiny. "Why did you come to Austin if you had a fine castle in Ireland, and everyone loved you?"

Liam shrugged. "Once the traitorous bastard Shifter in England sold his story and demonstrated that he could shape-shift, Ireland got a little dangerous for us. People who needed money started taking bounties on Shifters, dead or alive. Kenny's mate, Sinead, was pregnant, and we couldn't risk her getting hunted. We heard that in this country, Shifters were being herded into camps rather than exterminated, but allowed to live in safety. So we packed up, and here we are."

"But Sinead—Connor's mom—died anyway."

"That she did." The sadness of her death had never gone away. "But if we'd stayed in Ireland, we'd likely have lost Connor too. He came early and was so weak. He needed quiet and medical care. Here, me and Dad, Sean and Kenny, we were able to look after him without having to worry about fighting off villagers with pitchforks."

"Are you saying that you took the Collar to save him?"

"Pretty much."

"And then a feral Shifter killed Kenny." Kim's eyes flashed with rage. "Bastard."

Liam's heart warmed at her anger. She understood. "May hell rot all feral Shifters."

"Ferals are the ones who refused the Collar, right? Why do they kill other Shifters?"

Liam's deep anger stirred. "Because in their eyes, we betrayed them. Instead of waiting to get slaughtered or watching our children die, we chose to sacrifice our freedom and band together. What infuriates them most is that we now live with other species of Shifters—which, to ferals, is even worse than letting humans believe they tell us what to do."

"Safety in numbers?"

"And strength." Liam smiled. "When we buried our cross-species hatred, we got stronger. We helped each other instead of fighting. Shifters were scattered and dying out. Now we're growing in number again. And growing stronger."

"Are you telling me that Shiftertowns aren't so much places of captivity as they are fortresses? No matter what humans think they are?"

"I'd say sanctuaries, but you're not far from wrong." He lost his smile. "Do you understand now why Fergus doesn't want a human learning all our secrets?"

Kim glanced around, but still, no one had come to sit near them. The coffee shop was pretty much deserted, the lunch crowd not yet surging through Austin's streets. "Then why are you telling me?"

A nonchalant shrug. "You're my mate. I tell you everything."

"Sure you do. You're saying that you live in Shiftertowns for your own ends and that you don't care about the things humans keep you from having—like cable and new cars and high-paying jobs. I sort of understand that. But the Collars are still cruel."

"They are. Invented by a half-Fae with no love for Shifters. The truth is Shifters weren't all that violent in the wild. We used to hunt animals to eat—now we get our meat from the supermarket. But then, same with humans. We fight among ourselves for dominance or to protect the pride, but no indiscriminate slaughter."

"This from a man who killed a Shifter in my bedroom and was about to battle his clan leader yesterday morning."

He shrugged. "Extenuating circumstances."

"And you are supposed to hate other Shifter species?"

"We've learned to suppress our prejudices for the health of us all. Mostly. I count Ellison my friend, but I can still call him dog breath."

Kim's eyes sparkled. "What does he call you?"

"Cat shit."

She burst into nervous laughter. "I thought it would be 'Hairball.'"

"Glory calls us that sometimes. That or 'Cock-sucking Feline Irish bastards'."

Her brows rose. "And your father sleeps with this woman?"

The relationship between Glory and Dylan was unexplainable. "I'm glad to see him take an interest," Liam said. "I give him a break. He lost his mate."

"Your mom."

"Yes." Liam didn't fight his memories of his mother anymore. He had for a long time, not wanting to examine the hole in his heart. Dylan's taking off for a year had, in retrospect, been a good thing, even though at the time Liam had been furious with his father. But he realized now that Dylan had needed room to grieve, and Sean, Liam, and Kenny had needed to figure out how to live without a guiding hand.

"She was a fine woman," Liam said softly. "Beautiful, with green eyes and red hair. The wildcat she turned into was amazing—graceful and deadly—you didn't mess with her. She and Dad loved each other so much, it got embarrassing sometimes. You'd walk into a room, and they'd be kissing, with their hands all over each other. Imagine. At their age."

"I have a hard time thinking of your dad as old. Yes, I know you told me he's like two hundred. Do all Shifters age so well?"

"If they don't die young, yes."

"Do many die young?"

She was asking painful questions again. "They do. Or at least they did."

"Another reason you took the Collar."

Three people sat down in the booth behind them, humans, who must have been used to Shifters, because they didn't look too nervous. Liam changed the subject. "I should talk to Sandra on my own."

"Want me to drive you? Before I head back to my office?"

"Not now. After you get off work tonight." Liam pushed aside his coffee cup and stood, reaching to help her to her feet. "And after we stop by your house and get the things you want."

"You expect me to spend the night with you again?"

Kim said it a little too loudly. The diners in the next booth looked around, startled, curious, knowing.

"I meant at your house," Kim amended. "I don't need to stay there. I have my own house."

"But my nephew will be heartbroken if you don't come."

She gave him her annoyed look. "We'll talk about it later." She spun on her high heels and marched to the door, her sexy ass moving provocatively.

Liam took money from his pocket and dropped it on the table, thinking he could watch Kim's fine backside all day and never get tired of it. And after the day was done, he could lie next to her and her fine backside all night. He'd not get tired of that, either.

* * *

Kim decided she'd never have let Liam win the argument of her returning with him to Shiftertown that evening if she hadn't spied the shaved-headed Shifter from San Antonio sitting at a bus stop outside her house. He wore a turtleneck to cover his Collar—in this heat, what an idiot—but she recognized him and knew he wasn't waiting for any bus.

The thought of Liam leaving her alone in the house while Fergus's Thug Number One lurked outside made her cold with worry. Ironic, Kim thought as she drove through the city, heading back toward Shiftertown, that she felt safer in a house full of Shifters with a crazed woman next door than in her own neighborhood. Everything about her life since she'd met Liam was upside down.

Shiftertown was as lively as ever as she followed Liam on his bike through it. Kids were being called in from playing to have dinner. Kim smelled barbeques firing up and burgers on the grill. Men and women alike looked up as Kim's Mustang rolled past. Liam, ahead of her, sexy on his Harley, lifted his hand in greeting time and again.

Liam's yard was quiet, no barbeque going here. Kim wondered whose turn it was to cook and hoped the men inside hadn't decided it was hers. But something seemed wrong; the door was shut too tightly, the windows too dark.

Liam sensed it too, stepping silently in front of her as they went up the porch steps. He opened the door to reveal Dylan and Sean in the living room, facing each other in livid anger, their eyes feral white. Connor huddled in the kitchen, as far away from the other two as he could get and still be downstairs.

Liam's voice was very quiet as he asked, "What's the trouble, Sean?"

Sean swung from Dylan, his body so tight with rage Kim wondered that he didn't flow into his wildcat form. Claws extended from his fingers as he grabbed a paper from the table and shoved it in Liam's face.

"*That's* the trouble."

It was a printed e-mail. Kim rose on tiptoe to read it with Liam.

After the mate-bonding at the full moon, it has been decided by clan council that Dylan Morrissey shall step down as leader of the East Austin Shiftertown and another Feline of the council's choosing be put into his place. Authorized by Fergus Leary, leader of the South Texas Feline clan.

Chapter Sixteen

Kim had never seen Liam less than completely self-assured, never at a loss for words. Not her Irish Shifter with his gift of blarney.

Now Liam stared at the paper while his face flooded with color and his eyes changed to white-blue.

"I told Dad"—Sean's voice was strained—"that he needs to confront Fergus and get it over with. Dad refused."

Kim folded chilled fingers into her palms, deciding for once to keep silent. She remembered Liam telling her that he didn't know why Dylan never fought Fergus for dominance, but that he thought it was so the Shifters could live in peace.

"Son of a bitch," Liam said. "Dad, why?"

Dylan's voice was tight, his hands clenched. His fingers had changed to claws, and blood smeared his fists. "Leave it alone, Liam."

"I can't. Fergus wants you to step down? To put one of his lackeys in your place? Our lives won't be worth shite if that happens. He's undercutting your position in your own pride, not to mention the clan."

"I said, leave it alone!"

Liam didn't flinch. "Dad, this is a blatant smack in the face, an invitation to challenge him."

Dylan's eyes were red with rage, but Kim saw anguish behind the animal fury. "Don't you think I know that? But I won't. Not now."

"Why the hell not?"

"I have my fucking reasons!" Dylan roared.

If he'd directed that anger at Kim, she knew she'd run like hell. Liam stood his ground, his own hands showing claws. "If you think you're giving in for the good of Shiftertown, you're crazy. This will be his first step to drive us out of here. He'll make sure we end up in a Shiftertown far from here, where we're clanless and at the bottom of the pile. Kim will have to abandon Brian, and Brian will go down for the murder."

Kim noted Liam's big assumption—that if the Morrisseys had to go, she'd go with them—but she decided this was not the time to bring it up.

Dylan's eyes were bleak. "I know."

Liam's claws shredded the paper, which fell to the floor. "I can't go after Fergus myself. You know that."

"Yes," Dylan said quietly. "I do."

"Then why . . ."

His words trailed off as the back door banged open and hot wind flooded past them. Glory charged in, dressed in hot pink with silver sandals, her finger- and toenails painted in matching pink. "Dylan, what the hell is going on?"

Dylan gave her a weary look. "Glory. Not now."

"Fergus wants Grandda' to step down from leading Shiftertown," Connor babbled from the kitchen.

Glory's mouth opened in shock. "What? We won't stand for that. The asshole."

"You said it," Kim agreed.

The males in the room, except Connor, ignored both women. Sean met Dylan's gaze, his face quiet. "I'll do it. I'll fight Fergus."

A chorus of shouting drowned him out. Liam huffed a bitter laugh. "What, Sean, you'll kill me, then Dad, then go after Fergus?"

"No." Sean's face was white. "I'll just kill the gobshite. I can shoot him, can't I, and then stick him with the sword. Fergus is dust, no more problem."

"And then by Shifter law I'll have to take you out," Liam said in a hard voice. "Bad plan."

"What does it matter?" Sean asked.

The others fell silent, and Kim couldn't contain herself. "Are you all crazy? Why would you let Sean even think of that?"

"Stay out of this, Kim," Dylan said without looking at her.

"No, Kim has a point." Glory folded her arms, her perfect breasts straining against her pink shirt. "Sean, why should you sacrifice yourself?"

"To keep the peace," Sean said in a tired voice. "I would be the logical choice to be the assassin and pay the price. Because I'm mateless." Sean shot Liam a hard look, and Liam, surprisingly, dropped his gaze.

Glory said, "Listen to the human girl. If anyone should pay for this, it's Fergus himself. Let *him* be the sacrifice."

"Good idea," Connor echoed.

Dylan let his voice roar through. "There will be no argument. We do what Fergus says."

Kim opened her mouth to protest, and so did Glory, but suddenly Glory shut hers, as though she understood something. Dylan was staring hard at Liam, those nonverbal cues flying between them. Dylan's eyes were feral white, Liam's not much better.

Liam dropped his gaze and turned. Dylan gave him a look of almost disappointment, then swung away and slammed himself out the back door. Glory took a deep breath, but to Kim's surprise, she didn't follow Dylan.

"I really don't understand," Kim said into the silence. "Why would your dad stand back and let Fergus win?"

Liam shot her a quick look. He was worried. "I don't know."

"Because Dylan isn't ready to die," Glory said. "He's not that old, and he's completely virile. Besides, he has me."

Her smug statement broke the tension a little. Connor even gave a nervous laugh. "Sure, that would be worth living for," he said.

"You're a cub, youngling," Glory said. "You'll learn."

Liam remained silent, the smiling, damn-your-eyes man Kim had come to know fading into a bleak, angry Shifter. When he looked like this he was scary as hell, but Kim walked to him and ducked under his arm. The others had backed off, and for the first time since she'd met this group, they were giving another Shifter space.

Kim sensed that Liam didn't need space right now; he needed touch, reassurance. She melded to his side, and Liam finally looked down at her, the feral white-blue of his eyes darkening to human blue once again.

"We'll fix this somehow," Kim dared to say. "Without anyone dying or Sean shooting Fergus in the back. Although I wouldn't mind doing that—after I give him a piece of my mind."

"Don't you dare," Liam said, lips flat. "Or I'll chain you up in the basement."

"Are there spiders down there?"

"Possibly."

Kim lifted her hand. "All right, I'll try to be sensible. I see that I need to speed up my campaign to free Brian, and I have a few ideas about that."

Liam's gaze flickered, as though suspicious about her ideas, but his fangs and claws had retreated.

Glory snorted. "The little kitten has teeth, Liam. Watch that when she goes down on you."

Connor laughed out loud. Liam gave Kim a little smile. "I'm willing to risk it."

Glory stepped past them. "Excuse me. I think Dylan's had time to cool from killing rage to an even simmer. Time for me to go be a good little lapdog."

"I don't even want to know about that," Connor said in disgust, as Glory sashayed out.

Connor came to Kim and put his arms around her in a smothering hug. "I'm glad you're Liam's mate, Kim, and I'm glad you came home. The full-moon blessing tomorrow night is going to be some party. Me and Sean have invited everyone."

Kim remembered Liam saying something about his father pronouncing his blessing under the moon, but she hadn't paid much attention. "Party?"

"Mate blessings don't happen very often, so all of Shiftertown will want to see it," Liam said. "Don't worry, we dress casual."

"Oh, thanks." All of Shiftertown, coming to stare at her. Then again, it might be a good time to put some of her ideas in motion. If Silas was dying to learn about Shifters, she could give him a glimpse, and he could help Kim's cause at the same time. "Do you mind if I invite a friend?"

Liam's eyes narrowed. "Friend?"

"Someone I know who's helped me out in the past. Is this blessing something humans can witness?"

Liam gave her a nod. "Sure. It won't make Fergus happy, but screw him."

"That's what I keep saying." She smiled up at Liam. She knew she couldn't ease all his tension, but she could tell how far she'd made him relax. "I need to make a few phone calls. Mind?"

Liam released her. "Is this human all right about Shifters?"

"Yes, he likes them."

"He?"

Kim laughed at Liam's sudden, possessive stare. "Don't worry. He's just a friend. I've known him for a long time."

Liam's gaze softened a little, but Kim made a mental note to warn Silas not to touch her, not even casually.

"You make your calls," Liam said, his voice gentling. He'd climbed down a long way from the ready-to-kill Shifter, but he was still tense. "Myself, I'm going to go visit Sandra again. I'd like to figure out why Fergus is pulling out all the stops to keep Brian from going to trial."

Liam found Sandra in her backyard, alone. She'd wheeled her shallow charcoal-burning grill to the middle of the grass and started a fire in it. As Liam approached, he heard her chanting a prayer to the Earth goddess at the same time she tossed fragments of paper into the fire.

Liam approached silently. He meant to give her privacy to pray, but when he saw what she burned, he stepped forward and grabbed them out of her hands.

Sandra jerked around with a sharp intake of breath. Her wildcat fangs extended, her eyes going white.

Liam looked at the photos Sandra had been trying to burn. One showed Brian grinning at the camera with his arm around his mom, a bottle of beer dangling from his hand. Another showed Brian and his friends at a lake. Then Brian and a human girl, probably the murder victim, Michelle.

"It's not desperate enough for this yet," Liam said.

"Don't stop me. I need to make sure he gets to the Summerland."

"Brian's not going anywhere near the Summerland." Liam put his arm around Sandra's shoulder, trying to let his warmth comfort her. "That's why I've come, to ask for your help in springing him."

Sandra looked up at him with dead eyes. "There's nothing I can do."

"That's not true. Now come on, let's go in and have something cold to drink. It's too bloody hot out here to be doing any straight thinking."

Sandra let Liam take her into the house, where he fetched her a cold beer. He opened a bottle himself and sank down onto her couch to drink it. He'd sat here a couple days ago, he remembered, massaging Kim's feet. She had lovely feet, tiny in his big hands.

Liam tucked the photos of Brian into his pocket, knowing that if he let Sandra have them, she'd go back to burning them after he'd gone. An image of the loved one, sacrificed to fire, was the best way to make sure the loved one's passage into the afterlife was peaceful.

Sandra drank the beer but made no sign of enjoying it. "What do you want, Liam?"

"I want to know about this human girl, Michelle. Did Brian intend to make her his mate?"

Sandra regarded him in surprise. "I don't know."

"Because he would never have killed her if he did, and you know it. I hadn't thought of it before, because taking a human female for mate wasn't something I'd ever considered. But Kim, she's damn smart."

Sandra eyed him sharply. "I heard that you claimed her."

"That I did. Don't worry, it was sanctioned by Fergus himself. He insisted on it, actually, though I intended to make the bond anyway."

"Sun and moon?"

"Under the sun, so far. The moon is at its fullest tomorrow night, and Dad will bless us then. Come over. It will be a grand party."

"And Kim, she's fine with you claiming her?"

Liam thought of Kim's confusion, her outrage. He grinned. "Maybe 'fine' is going a bit far, but she'll get used to it. I'll make sure of that." He took a sip of beer and saw Sandra actually smile.

He got Sandra to let him have a look in Brian's room. Brian wasn't a cub anymore—he'd come of age and found his place in the hierarchy, but he had continued to live here to help out his mother. The custom of human kids moving out as soon as they turned eighteen had always struck Liam as odd. Shifters lived together in family groups for generations.

Sandra had lost her mate long before she and Brian had moved to Shiftertown. Only Brian and she lived in this house, and before Brian's arrest, Sandra had been hopeful that Brian would soon claim a mate and fill the house with little ones. Now her eyes were devoid of any hope as she led Liam upstairs.

Brian occupied two rooms on the second floor—he'd used one as a bedroom, the other as an office. An old computer stood on his desk, jury-rigged to a couple other boxes as though he was trying to set up a network. Liam wasn't a computer whiz by any means, though he could navigate the Internet fairly well. But he didn't know enough to understand whether Brian was trying to make his computer do something illegal or simply work better.

Sandra turned away after she let Liam in, as though she couldn't bear to enter Brian's rooms. That was fine with Liam. He went through Brian's desk thoroughly while he waited for the computer to boot up, but he didn't find anything useful. Old receipts for gas, cardboard coasters, souvenirs from various attractions around Austin, and old raffle-type tickets.

The computer, it turned out, didn't have the helpful

screen full of icons to click on. A list of files scrolled by when Liam hit the Enter key, and then the cursor sat at the bottom of the screen, blinking at him.

"Shite." He'd have to have Sean take a look. Sean knew far more about computers than Liam did, more than Shifters were allowed to know.

The rest of Brian's living room—his video and DVD collection, his books, his magazines—told Liam nothing except that, like Connor, Brian had an obsession with cars. Cars were a sickness among younger Shifters. Liam couldn't see the attraction; it wasn't as though they were Harleys.

Liam took a quick look through Brian's bedroom, but came up with even less. If Brian had secrets, he didn't hide them in the house he shared with his mother. Liam did find a few pictures of Michelle tossed carelessly into the drawer of the nightstand. She'd been a pretty girl, with honey-blonde hair and a sweet smile, her skin tanned from the Texas sun. Photos of her and Brian together told Liam she didn't mind at all that he was Shifter.

"Did you put these in here?" he called to Sandra.

"No," she said when she looked. "Brian kept them there. The police took away about half of them when they searched."

Liam was surprised they'd left any. But maybe they'd taken enough to show the jury what a pretty, helpless innocent Brian had corrupted.

"Can I have this one?" He held up a photo of Michelle with both arms around Brian.

"Sure."

She was trying to make herself stop caring. Liam recognized the signs, having seen them in both his father and Kenny when they lost their mates. Pretending that they'd let go, that their beloved's things were just things, of no importance.

"Will you ask Brian about her?" Liam asked as he pocketed the photos. "Find out whether he was going to claim her? It's important."

Sandra shook her head. "I'll not be visiting him again."

"Don't give up yet."

Vehemence entered her eyes, making her come alive. "I can't visit him. *He* won't let me."

"Who?" Liam's eyes narrowed. "Fergus?"

"Yes, Fergus. I've been told to stay away, to let Brian go."

Liam went to her and rubbed her shoulders. "Sandra, you can't do that. He's your son, your cub. He needs you now more than ever."

"Tell that to Fergus. I had orders."

"Well, here's me overriding those orders."

Sandra laughed, an unhealthy sound. "You can't."

"I'm using my prerogative of second in command of this Shiftertown." *For now*, he thought silently. "I say go see Brian, and let me deal with Fergus."

"I can't let you do that. He can kill you."

"He already wants to kill me for so very many reasons. You're the only one who can do this for us, love. Fergus won't let me near Brian, and he won't let Kim talk to him anymore, but stopping a mother from seeing her cub—that one he won't be able to justify. I'm betting he knows that."

Sandra looked tired. "I can't stand up to him, Liam."

"You won't have to. He's not here, and his lieutenants won't interfere with a mother's rights." Liam gave her an encouraging smile. "Even Fergus's thugs have mothers who wouldn't let them hear the end of it if they kept you from your cub."

Sandra relaxed a little. "You are full of shit, Liam."

"Try it. They won't hurt you, not around so many humans. You want to see Brian, don't you?"

"Will you come with me?"

"I can't." Liam rubbed her shoulders again, wishing he could tell her that everything would be fine and mean it. "They'll waffle about stopping you, but they won't let me anywhere near the jail. But you go on. Have a good talk with him, and tell me everything he says."

Kim hung up her cell phone as Liam walked in the back door. A strange sensation flashed through her, and it took her a minute to recognize it—she was glad to see him.

She hadn't been so happy to see someone enter a room in a long, long time, not since her parents had passed. Friends were fine, and Abel was— All right, so whenever Abel had walked in, her first reaction usually had been impatience and irritation.

Seeing Liam made her heart beat faster and not simply because of lust. She went warm as he smiled at her and leaned down to kiss her cheek.

"Where is everyone?" he asked.

"Your dad, still next door with Glory. Connor went out to hook up with some friends, he said. Ellison came over, and he and Sean took off."

"Oh, did he? Leaving you alone and unprotected?" He played with the hair at the back of her neck.

"Not with every single one of your neighbors outside staring at the house. Maybe you noticed them?"

"Wondering what I'm doing in here with the human woman." Liam massaged her neck, leaning down to nip the shell of her ear. "What would you like me to do?"

Kim's body grew pliant. "Liam, about this friend I want to invite . . ."

"What about him? He wasn't your lover, was he?"

"No. Really, he's just a friend. I've known him since college. I didn't want to say this in front of all the others, but Silas is a journalist. A very good one. He wants to do some pieces on Shifters and make a documentary. Kind of show how they're mistreated, that kind of angle."

Liam straightened up, eyes wary. "Let another human uncover Shifter secrets?"

"No, I mean show Shifter life in its reality—the kids playing in the yards, like that Michael in his pool I saw the first day I was here. He's cute, and he'd have great appeal. Humans can watch Shifter moms planting gardens, dads coming home from their working-class jobs. Teenagers like Connor playing soccer or holding hands with their girlfriends. Let people see how peaceful you are, how *normal*."

"Is that all? You know Fergus would never let that happen,"

"That's why I'm asking you." Kim smiled up at him, trying to look impossibly sweet.

Liam's gaze softened. "You're a crafty lass, Kim. You want these stories to switch public opinion to Brian's side, don't you now?"

"It couldn't hurt."

Liam laughed softly and kissed the top of her head. "And you know if I say yes, I won't tell Fergus."

"Something like that. Or your father?"

"Or my father, who would feel obligated to pass on the information. Bring this Silas to the party and let me meet him. No cameras, no notebooks. Strictly off the record until I get to know him."

"Of course. He's fair, Liam, which is why I thought of him."

"But if I don't like him . . ."

"I tell him no. Promise."

"All right then." Liam leaned down, resumed nibbling her earlobe. "But enough talking. I'm thinking about the fact that we're alone in this house."

"Having someone in the house didn't stop you yesterday," she pointed out in a shaky voice.

"That was mating frenzy. Today I want to take it slow. To give you everything I want, in my own time." Liam ran his fingers down her spine, trailing fire. "I want to see if you're wearing garters under that sexy skirt."

Kim leaned against the kitchen counter and slid her skirt up a few inches. "I am."

Liam's warm hands covered her thighs, his thumbs hooking into the tops of her stockings. "That's my girl."

Chapter Seventeen

Kim found herself seated on the counter with Liam standing between her legs. Liam's warm lips played on hers while he slid his hands to the insides of her thighs. "Could this be a thong?" he murmured, touching it. "The thing you said you couldn't be wearing?"

"Could be."

"Did you wear it for me, Kim?"

"Yes."

Liam nuzzled her cheek. "I like that." He licked where he nuzzled. "It's easy to move aside."

"That's the point of it."

"You're wet for me," he said.

"I am." Kim drew her hand along his zipper. "You're ready too, I see. Either that or you shoved a baseball bat down there."

"I'm thinking that would be painful."

"I'm thinking you're in pain now," Kim whispered in his ear. "I would be, if I had something that big in my pants."

"Want to find out what it's like?"

"I wouldn't mind."

She'd never done it leaning back on a counter, her skirt up, her panties shoved aside, and her lover letting his jeans drop around his ankles. But then, she'd never had a lover like Liam, a large, raw-muscled Irishman with beautiful eyes.

She found herself with her legs locked around him, his hands cradling her head while she felt the burn of them joining. His lips were all over her, face, throat, hair, mouth.

"You feel so good, Kim. You feel so fucking good."

Kim didn't answer. She sensed desperation in him, the need to bury himself in sex and forget the strange argument he'd had with his dad as well as Fergus's ultimatum. Liam seemed the most unnerved of all of them, even Dylan.

The untamed joy of what they did made Kim want to shout out loud, and so did the danger that someone could walk in and catch them. Her partners had always practiced safe sex—not only in the sense of using condoms, but in ensuring the lights were out, the doors locked, and the windows shaded, so no one would ever know what they were doing.

Liam wanted Kim and didn't care who knew. He'd broadcast the fact far and wide, proudly. Instead of being embarrassed, Kim's heart swelled with joy.

Another part of her did too. She rocked her hips, loving the sensation of him deep inside her.

"Liam," she groaned. "I want you to do dirty things to me."

"Happy to, love," he said, his face against hers. "You name them, I'll do them."

She moved faster, and he did, and she did again. "I'm loving *this* right now."

"I love what you make me feel," he whispered.

Kim tried to think of something sexy to say, but words fled her brain. "Just shut up and do me."

Liam laughed. He rocked into her swiftly, until they were both breathless with it. Liam held her tightly as he came, his seed scalding, his mouth hard on hers. His kisses were still unpracticed, but Kim didn't care. She caught his tongue, his lips, his teeth with hers, kissing him back with joyous abandon.

Liam smiled into her mouth, and Kim laughed with him. Sex didn't get better than this.

Her heart beat wildly when she thought that maybe it did—with Liam. The idea triggered her orgasm. She gyrated against him, unsure how much noise she was making and not really caring.

When she wound down, Liam backed out of her, still hard, pulled up his pants, and carried her to the sagging living room sofa. He collapsed onto it, Kim on top of him, both of them panting.

"Oh, man, that was good." Kim lay against his shoulder trying to get her breath. Laughter didn't help.

Liam ran his fingers through her hair. "Not what I had in mind, but not bad."

"What do you mean, not *bad?*"

Liam regarded her with half-closed predator's eyes. "I told you, I wanted to take it slow. Love you like you deserve. Not screwing you quick-time on a kitchen counter."

Kim kissed the tip of his nose. "I didn't mind. Not at all. Maybe you noticed?"

"I want to give you so much." Liam's hold tightened into a hard embrace. "So much, Kim. Everything I once had, everything I lost. I want it back—for you."

She heard Liam's heart beating rapidly beneath her ear, and her own heart squeezed. His declarations scared her. She could dismiss his words as those of a man happy he'd just gotten into a woman's pants, words that would evaporate as soon as he was sated. Except the throbbing of his heart was from more than physical exertion. His voice held uncertainty, a longing he feared he couldn't fulfill.

Kim ran her fingers along the hard plane of his chest. "You don't need to do anything for me."

"Don't be daft, woman. I take care of you now. I want to do everything for you."

She shook her head. "I take care of myself. I have a decent job and a nice house. That's more than a lot of people have."

"Before we took the Collar, a man took his mate home to his family and sequestered her. He did everything for her, hunted for her, kept her warm and fed and comfortable, pampered her in every way."

"Really? I guess you hadn't ever heard of women's rights."

"Not in the nineteenth century, love." Liam smiled. "Not *sequestered* as in kept in prison. Sequestered as in protected from all others. Female Shifters have always been in short supply, and we had to keep them from being stolen by other Shifters. The mate bond is sacrosanct, but when times were bad, other males stopped caring about sacrosanct." He cradled Kim closer. "So I have to fight my instincts not to lock you somewhere safe and beat off everyone from even looking at you."

Kim had never considered herself a precious object before. Certainly Abel had never treated her as more than a convenience, and men she'd dated earlier in life hadn't been much better. Her relationships had been the "friends with benefits" kind. No true, undying love, no *I want to take care of you and protect you for the rest of our lives.*

Kim had spent enough time taking care of herself that having someone want to relieve her of the burden felt strange, though nice. She wasn't going to let Liam do it, but the feeling was still nice.

Liam swung her into his arms and rolled to his feet at the same time. Kim found herself against his chest with her head on his shoulder, Liam striding toward the stairs.

"What are you doing?" she asked.

"Taking you upstairs where we belong. I'm tired of fighting my instincts."

A pleasant shiver went through her. "What does that mean?"

His eyes were white-blue when he looked down at her, his pupils changing. "I'm going to love you all night, my *mate*. On a bed. I'm going to love you until we can't stand up."

If Abel had said that, Kim would have rolled her eyes or thought about what unsatisfying work that would be. When Liam said it, her whole body came alive.

To tease him, she said, "I really should look at my case files."

The look Liam gave her was savage. "Screw your case files."

Kim laughed. Liam growled and sprinted up the last of the stairs, slammed into the bedroom and tossed her on the bed. As her clothes came off, then his, Kim gave in. For one night of her life, she was going to enjoy making wild, crazy love with a man who promised to make it unforgettable, no matter what might come in the morning.

It was Sean's turn to cook breakfast, and Liam grabbed a plateful of pancakes from him as the sun poured through the eastern windows. "Kim will be down in a minute."

Sean sent him an annoyed look with bloodshot eyes. "I'm thinking of soundproofing your room."

"The sounds of loving bother you that much, do they?" Liam asked him.

"It does when you're shouting all night."

Connor grinned from his place at the table. "I had to wear headphones with the music cranked up. It barely drowned you out."

"You gobshites are just jealous. Where's Dad?"

Sean slammed the spatula to the counter. "Where do you think?"

Next door. With Glory. Good. "Do you begrudge your old dad getting some?" Liam asked Sean in a light voice. "A grateful son you are."

"Sean's pissed because *he's* not getting any," Connor said. "I don't mind because I'm still too young and innocent to know what it all means."

"Bullshit," Sean growled.

Connor laughed at him. Liam clapped Sean on the shoulder and turned away with his breakfast. "You'll find a mate someday, Sean. Then we'll make fun of the noise from *your* room."

Sean gave him a dark look and went back to his batter. His bad mood was about more than Liam keeping him awake. Sean had been ready to lay down his life for them yesterday, and that hadn't been an easy thing for him to do.

Liam started to sit down, then felt the unmistakable presence of Kim coming down the stairs. Smelled her as well, all fresh from her shower. She wore a casual skirt and sleeveless shirt, her legs bare, feet in strappy, high-heeled sandals.

"Are those pancakes?" she asked. "I'm starving."

Liam drew her into his arms. He'd woken with her in his arms not an hour ago, and hadn't that been the best feeling in the world? Liam nuzzled her check, then kissed her lips.

Kim smiled up at him. "Pancakes are that good, are they?"

"Sean's almost as good a cook as me. Come and sit."

Connor got out of his chair as Kim approached, and Liam gave him a nod. Kim looked startled as Connor wrapped his lanky arms around her, ending his sloppy hug with a kiss on the cheek.

"Good morning, Kim," he said as he released her.

"Good morning to you too. I—" Her speech cut off as Sean stepped up and gave her a more practiced hug, tight squeeze, a rub on the back, a kiss to her hair.

"You like blueberry, Kim?" Sean asked, as he released her and turned back to the stove.

"Sure. Blueberry. Great."

Liam caressed the back of Kim's neck and led her to her place at the table. "Sleep well, did you?"

"No." Kim plopped down, reached for the pitcher of juice in the middle of the table. "But you know that. Sean, Connor, are you trying to comfort me for having to spend the night with Liam?"

Connor hooted with laughter. Even Sean broke out of his sour mood to grin. "Are you in need of comfort, Kim?" Sean asked. "Is he that bad?"

"Shut it," Liam growled, but he was too full of afterglow to care about their teasing. "They're acknowledging you as my mate, love. Welcoming you to the family."

"I forgot. Shifters like to hug. A lot."

Liam ran his hand up Kim's arm, her silken skin a joy beneath his fingertips. "Is there something wrong with that? Touching and hugging is a good thing."

"It's unusual," Kim said. "For humans, I mean."

"Touching is reassurance, keeping the bonds between family intact. It's more than love; it's necessary."

"Humans do it too," Sean said from the stove. "Except they get embarrassed. So they invent strange rituals, like giving flowers and candy to ladies. Human men punch each other when they like each other. I've seen them do it."

"Sean has made a study of humans and their behavior," Liam said. "It gives him something to do."

Kim gave Sean a look of respect. "Well, if you can

figure out human behavior, more power to you. Even humans can't figure it out."

"But I'm outside looking in," Sean said. "It's different."

"So are Shifters to humans." Kim accepted her plate of pancakes and dug in. "I know you all don't want to talk about this, but I don't want to hear any more discussion about you giving in to Fergus. He's just trying to sow dissention. I've been thinking it over, and I think what y'all really need is a good lawyer, and one just happens to be eating pancakes with you. I'm going to dig into Shifter law and see if Fergus really can tell your dad to step down, or try to find some loophole to keep him from succeeding. So I'll need to know what rules and customs or whatever aren't written down. I need to know *everything*."

With his mate so near, with her scent and his all over her, Liam didn't much care about Fergus, Brian, and the screwed-up mess they'd gotten the rest of Shiftertown into. "That's fine, Kim. I won't stop you trying. Just don't be getting your hopes up, love."

Kim finished the last of her pancakes and got to her feet. "It beats letting Fergus win."

"He won't," Liam said, watching her hips sway as she took her plate to the sink. "I won't let him."

Sean gave him a dark look. "I still think my way is best." He didn't mean it like he had yesterday, Liam could tell, because Sean's tension had eased a long way. But Sean was still angry.

"We need you as the Guardian, Sean," Liam said softly. "Connor's not yet ready to take up the sword."

"No-ho," Connor said, from deep in his car magazine. "Don't you dare die on me, Sean."

Kim looked confused again. Liam gestured her out to the back porch and followed her down the steps to the fenceless backyard and the Austin summer sunshine. It would be another hot one, but later tonight, the cool moon would cover the yard in silver light.

"I have to go to work," Kim said.

"I know."

"You'll try to come with me, won't you?"

"I will be coming with you. I'm not letting you out of my sight, not with Fergus's thugs wandering about and Fergus mad as hell at the Morrisseys. He's not above making an example of disobedient clan members."

"I'm going to fix this, Liam."

Liam just gave her a nod. "Even so—not out of my sight, love."

"What's with Sean?" she asked, glancing back at the house.

It took Kim a while to voice questions, Liam noticed. Must be the lawyer in her, thinking carefully before she pried out the information she wanted.

Liam rubbed his hair, not liking to think about it. "Sean has always blamed himself for Kenny's death. I blame myself, because I was stupidly obeying orders when I should have been protecting them both. But Sean was right there beside Kenny. Sean fought and survived, but he couldn't save Kenny. It eats at him, it does."

Kim gave him a skeptical look. "Oh, please. I know damn well Sean didn't simply stand aside and watch Kenny get killed. He must have fought."

"As the Guardian, his first duty is to the sword, and he couldn't risk letting the feral get it. Kenny knew that. He was fighting to protect the Guardian and the sword."

Kim gave him a wide-eyed stare. "You mean that piece of metal was more important than your brother?"

"No, that's not what I'm saying. But the Guardian has a huge responsibility to the whole clan. He has to survive to keep the sword free in case he needs to use it on one of us. Kenny knew what he was doing."

He could tell Kim didn't really understand, but her look softened. "That doesn't make it any easier, does it?"

"No."

Kim slid her arms around his waist. "Liam, I'm so sorry."

He felt her sorrow. Liam melted into her, tears tracking down his face for the brother he'd lost. Being a Shifter was all about sacrifice, and the fact that Kim understood that untwisted something inside him that had been knotted for a decade.

Kim worked through the day in her office, catching up on phone calls and paperwork, preparing for the court case she was determined to have for Brian. The private investigator she'd hired told Kim he'd discovered evidence that Michelle's ex-boyfriend had burned with plenty of resentment when Michelle had started seeing Brian. Threats had been made, and friends of the ex-boyfriend had been worried. Good. Kim told him to keep searching that angle.

Kim also pulled up every single piece of information she had on Shifter law and went over it again. She'd find something to stop Fergus trying to defeat the Morrisseys, no matter how long it took. The human government didn't usually interfere with Shifter hierarchy, mostly because they didn't understand it. But Kim would find some way to solve this, and Liam would figure out why Fergus wanted Brian executed.

Working with Liam stretched out on her office couch unnerved Kim, especially when he spent the whole time watching her. He didn't demand her attention or interrupt; he just . . . watched.

He reminded Kim of lions on the African veldt, sitting under the shade of whatever those trees were, watching herds of gazelles. Maybe the lions wouldn't be hungry right then, but they'd watch. Heads up, ears pricked, alert. Still. Waiting.

By five-thirty, the gazelle in her was ready to go home.

Kim didn't bother trying to go to her own house. She drove with Liam straight back to Shiftertown, feeling a strange kind of relief to do so.

When Kim and Liam arrived at the Morrissey house, Sean had a big charcoal-burning barbeque going in the backyard, and beer and ice overflowed from several coolers. A dozen Shifters lounged on the porch and through the yard, talking to Sean and Dylan. Connor kicked a soccer ball around with a few other young men his age, while two teenaged females stood back and assessed them.

Kim's journalist friend Silas pulled up shortly after. He was tall and very thin, with a prominent Adam's apple.

"What is this party for?" Silas asked when Kim presented him to Liam. Kim had warned Silas that only Liam knew what he was really doing there, and he promised to be discreet.

"It's a blessing under the moon, that it is," Liam answered him. He flashed his teeth in a grin. "It's after being a very interestin' ritual."

Kim rolled her eyes at the exaggerated Irish-isms, but at least he'd quit saying, "Top o' the morning."

"You sound like a cartoon leprechaun," she said to him, after they'd introduced Silas around and left him talking animatedly to Annie from the bar.

"Whist, it's my feelings you'll be hurting."

"Shut it, Liam."

His brows shot up, and he laughed. "You're learning, darling." His laughter was warm, reminding her of him loving her all night, and even now he gave her a look of undisguised hunger. "I haven't touched you in too long."

Pleasant shivers ran through her. She agreed. It had been too long since any intimate touching. Hours.

"I'm already wishing the ritual over and everyone gone home," Liam said in her ear.

"We should probably eat first. Be social."

"Aye." Liam slid his hands to her backside and scooped her against him for a kiss. "But I hope this doesn't take all night."

They strolled back to the barbeque as more Shifters joined the throng. Everyone Kim had met in Shifter-town was there—the wolf Ellison, Glory, Annie, Sandra, the women on the porches she'd passed the first day, little Michael who'd been proud of his plastic pool.

Kim stiffened when she saw Fergus's two thugs—the shaved-headed, tattooed guy and military guy with sunglasses. But Sean handed them plates of charred burger with buns, unsurprised.

"They aren't going to fight anyone, are they?" Kim asked as she took her burger from Sean. The two men had moved off to eat, and she noted the other Shifters gave them a wide berth. "Or bring out a cat-o'-nine-tails and start whaling on people?"

"They're here to observe the ritual," Sean told her. "Stand-ins for Fergus. And they'll be on their best behavior."

"I could have put Silas off if I'd known they'd be here."

Liam shook his head. "They won't disrupt the ritual. Fergus wants this mating done, and he wants to make sure Dad relinquishes power tomorrow."

Kim nodded glumly. She hadn't yet found a law that Fergus was bending by asking Dylan to vacate his post, but she would. She'd leave no stone unturned.

She chewed the burger Sean handed her, which was very good, especially with the gooey cheese melted on it. Her diet had gone to hell, but she couldn't bring herself to care.

Ellison came out of the crowd in his big black Stetson and cowboy boots. He high-fived Liam, and then the two men shared a tight bear hug.

"Kim!" Ellison boomed, his arms opened wide, and before Kim could duck away, Ellison swept off his hat and spun her off her feet. Liam rescued Kim's plate of half-eaten burger as Ellison swung Kim around. "Congratulations, woman." Ellison set Kim down and gave her abdomen a gentle pat. "When's it due?"

"What the hell are you talking about?"

Ellison looked shocked. "Liam, haven't you touched her yet? What's the matter with you? You're already sun-blessed. Are you waiting for Christmas?"

"We've done it, trust me." Liam handed Kim back her meal. "It will be soon."

Kim's face went hot. "Not that it's any of your business."

"Not my business? Hon, it's every Shifter's business whether a Shifter male can do the job. We have to be good at making babies, so we practice a lot." He balled his fists and thrust his hips in a parody of sex.

"Ignore him, Kim. Lupines are disgusting."

"Thank you," Glory said. She stepped past Ellison, tall and sleek in skintight black pants and silk top, every blonde hair in place. "Fucking Felines."

"Gobshite Lupines," Liam said cheerfully.

Dylan approached. "Kim."

Kim watched him in trepidation, but Dylan folded his arms around her and squeezed her in a very tight hug. She sensed something different in his hug than she had in the others'. Not happy exuberance—relief. Dylan held her close, and she smelled the damp cotton of his shirt and his shaving soap. But Dylan's hold wasn't in any way sexual. He held her as he'd cradle a child, as he might soothe Connor.

Dylan held Kim a long time, and his eyes were wet when he pulled away. He wiped them, unashamed, then turned and wrapped his arms around Liam.

Father and son stood still in the embrace, while Kim took her burger back from Ellison. To stem the tears that insisted on filling her eyes, she reflected that she needed to eat fast, before more people wanted to greet her with hugs.

Kim noticed that Glory didn't try to hug her—the woman sauntered away to get food with Dylan when Dylan finally released Liam. Kim wondered whether Glory was showing her disapproval for Liam taking a human mate, or whether the woman didn't feel like she was close enough to the family to join the hug-fest. Glory and Dylan might be hard at it, but sex did not necessarily mean intimacy, Kim knew from experience. The woman was a puzzle.

It took a while for the summer night to darken, but Liam and Dylan seemed in no hurry. Liam introduced Kim to all present, holding her hand or with his arm around her waist as they strolled from group to group. Kim met Lupines and other Felines, and bears.

The bear Shifters fascinated her, large-boned men and women who sported long manes of hair. Many of the bear-men were bearded, and both men and women obviously liked tattoos. They, too, welcomed Kim with hugs, though they were less intimate than the family's hugs. Not all of them looked happy that Liam was bringing a human into their midst, but they were cordial.

By the time Liam walked Kim back to the center of the yard, the night was dark and mercifully cooler. The moon rose rapidly, and as it reached its zenith, the crowd grew quiet.

Liam's neighbors silently formed two concentric circles, putting Liam, Kim, and Dylan in the middle of the inner one. The smaller, inner circle contained Liam's immediate family and friends, along with Fergus's two henchmen. The outer circle held the rest of Shiftertown.

Cool moonlight filtered through the trees, touching Kim's face as Liam turned her toward him. As he had when they'd stood before Fergus in the San Antonio Shiftertown, Liam held his left hand up, palm out, and pressed it to Kim's right one. He twined his fingers through hers and met her gaze with steady eyes.

Dylan closed both his hands around theirs and began chanting something in a language Kim didn't recognize. Irish—Gaelic? Or some kind of Shifter language? The circles of Shifters answered, chanting in slow rhythm. The Shifters began circling around them, the first circle moving clockwise, the second one counterclockwise. They stepped in deliberate, slow movements, an ancient-looking dance that was simple and powerful.

Dylan finally stopped chanting. "By the light of the moon," he said in a loud, grave voice, "I recognize this mating."

Ellison howled. Soon all the wolves joined in, followed by wildcat roars and the loud growling of the bears. Liam drew Kim against him and buried her in a kiss.

"Thank you, love," he grated. "Thank you."

In the San Antonio Shiftertown, the Shifters had gone nuts with beer and an impromptu party, but that had been nothing compared to the revelry that exploded here. Shifters grabbed one another, hugging, laughing, dancing around like maniacs. Beer flowed, kids ran around shrieking, couples kissed. More than one shed clothes and Shifted, and soon the yard was filled with wildcats, wolves, and bears.

Kim looked around for Silas, wondering what he'd make of all this. The tall man stood with Annie, a bottle of beer in his hand. Annie and he were the same height, and Annie had draped her arm around his shoulders.

"Great party, Kim." Silas grinned. He looked happy, not angry or scared. Good.

Glory approached, looking a little more relaxed. "Annie," she said. "Caught a human? Liam's starting a trend."

Annie pressed herself closer to Silas. "He's all right."

"He's my friend," Kim said. "I invited him."

"I know." Glory stepped away from Dylan and actually enfolded Kim in a well-perfumed hug. "They need you, honey. Be good to them."

Connor came hurtling toward her, followed closely by Sean, and Kim backed up against Liam. "More hugging? I'm going to be bruised all over."

"They're happy," Liam said in her ear. "We haven't had a joining in a long time. In our family, we thought we'd not have another for many years. If ever."

Kim's reply was cut off by first Connor, then Sean embracing her, then Connor again. "I have an aunt," Connor shouted. "I have an aunt, and I'll have a cousin soon."

"Something you want to tell me, Kim?" Silas said, grinning.

"Go along with it," Kim told him. "They like babies. They like even the possibility of babies, no matter how remote. They've had a hard time with infant mortality."

She'd piqued his interest. Again, good. Liam talked conversationally to Silas about the low ratio of females to males and the fact that it used to be sadly common for

Shifter women to die in childbirth. "But it's getting better," Liam finished. "That's one thing taking the Collar gave us, a bit of peace in which to take care of our families."

Silas looked curiously at Liam's Collar. "What are those made of? I heard that they have magic in them, but that's just a story, isn't it?"

Liam's eyes were clear and innocent. "Don't you believe in magic?"

"Shifters aren't magic," Silas said, smiling to acknowledge Liam's teasing. "You have some genetic quirk that allows you to shift to animal form, right? An ancient ancestor that we knew nothing about until Shifters were discovered."

"It's genetics partly, yes," Liam answered. "We were bred long ago to be playthings and hunters. Until our breeders discovered that hunters bite." He smiled, showing all his teeth.

"You were bred deliberately?" Silas asked. "I hadn't heard that."

"Aye. And our creators used magic to do it. What other explanation is there for us?"

"Genetic manipulation?" Silas shrugged. "Could ancient cultures do that?"

Kim wondered how much Liam would explain, but Liam kept talking. "The Fae could. That's the Fair Folk of Celtic and Gaelic legend, I'm meaning. Their magic made us, but our strength kept us alive when the Fae started disappearing from the world. Shifters were good at survival; Fae were good at running away. So which of us was stronger?"

The Shifters around them smiled and nodded.

Silas looked interested. "So the story that magic is in your Collars . . . ?"

"Is true," Liam answered. "Not that humans believe

it, but it doesn't matter, does it? All they know is that the Collars keep us tame. That's why you can stand so close to Annie without her eating you. Yet."

"The night's young," Annie purred.

Silas grinned. "Are you trying to terrify the human and make him run away?"

"Now, would we do that?" Annie asked him.

Liam's teeth were getting a little pointed. "How about a demonstration of what the Collars do? Would that put you at your ease?"

The Shifters looked uncomfortable. Kim knew Liam brought this up for Silas's benefit, the perfect opportunity to prove that the Collars worked, to show that Brian couldn't possibly have murdered a human. But the Shifters, including Dylan, started frowning.

"I read that the Collars send deep pain along the nervous system," Silas said, not noticing. "I couldn't ask you to show me that."

"But humans want to know everything about Shifters, don't they?" Liam continued, his voice silky. "The good, the bad, the underbelly."

A wolf loped up to them and threw himself on his back at Kim's feet, squirming happily.

"Underbelly," she repeated nervously. "Ha."

"Very funny, Ellison," Liam said. "Get on with you, now."

"That's Ellison?" Silas asked in surprise.

The wolf rolled to his feet, gave them a roguish look, and loped off again.

"In his glory." Liam turned back to Silas. "You're right, lad. The Collars are bloody painful. That's why none of us are violent, including the notorious Brian sitting in his jail cell. And no, none of us want to show you that."

"Speak for yourself, Liam." Glory put her hands on

her hips, her skintight outfit stretching in interesting ways. "The human isn't going to believe the Collars work until he sees it for himself. You want a demo, I'll give you one."

She fixed her gaze on Silas, her eyes going Shifter white. Her face didn't change, but the wild wolf she was shone out through the sex kitten she pretended to be. Annie and Liam moved to protect Silas, and as they did, Glory spun, caught Kim in a headlock, and started to strangle her.

Chapter Eighteen

So this was what it was like to die. No thought of martial arts, just Kim clawing at Glory's hands. She flashed back to the feral Shifter trying to kill her in her bedroom, her fear spiking.

Kim had no breath. Her vision went dark, her lungs burned, and her heart pumped frantically, desperate for oxygen. Dimly, she heard Liam roar.

Sparks flew out into the night, Glory's Collar going off. Air poured back into Kim's lungs, and she sat down hard as Glory flung her aside to face the wildcat leaping at them.

Liam.

Glory half changed, trying to meet the attack, but her Collar kept sparking, her body jerking with pain.

Dylan knocked into Liam's side, shifting as he went. Liam's clothes ripped as the wildcat burst out of them. Then the two were rolling over each other with savage intensity, snarling, raking claws, biting. Their Collars triggered, muscles and fur shuddering with the shocks, but they didn't stop.

"Mate," Glory rasped. Her hands were at her neck, the Collar stark black against her white throat. "Stupid. I attacked his mate. He couldn't help it. He had to defend . . ."

The rest of the Shifters moved back to give the fighting wildcats room. Sean watched, white-faced, looking poised to run back into the house.

"Stop them," Kim shouted at him.

He answered, tight-lipped. "I can't. I'm the Guardian."

"So *guard* something!"

Connor shrieked. Shifters jumped, turned his way. Connor balled his fists. "No," he yelled. "*No!*"

Sean grabbed for him, but Connor shook him off and leapt for the two snarling wildcats. He'd half changed to a gangly young wildcat when his Collar went off in mid-leap. His scream echoed through the clearing.

"Connor," Kim shouted.

Glory dragged herself up and ran to him. Still Sean hung back, watching, waiting.

Connor's Collar kept sparking, and he keened as he had when Fergus had done the Summoning. He shifted back to human, his clothes in shreds.

Glory pulled him into her arms. "Kim, help me," she called.

One of the wildcats rolled away from the other and landed against a tree. Its limbs distorted, and Liam emerged, naked, dirt and long, bloody scratches streaking his body. The other cat became Dylan, lying flat on his back in the mud, panting.

"Kim!" Glory yelled.

Glory was rocking Connor on her lap. Kim went to them and dropped to her knees behind Connor, feeling ineffectual.

"He needs your touch," Glory said. "You're family now."

Kim put her hands on Connor's bare back. "It's all right, Con."

"He needs more than that. Goddess, how do you humans survive?"

Because being human is all about personal space? Shifters' personal space was different. Kim had thought she understood—Shifters liked to touch, the same way cats rubbed against other cats they knew and liked.

But she realized now that there was more to it. The Shifters' need to touch wasn't simply for affection; it was comfort and reassurance. And maybe release from pain? Kim remembered how Sean and Liam had held Sandra between them to calm her the first day Kim had come to Shiftertown. Kim had thought that the three were being sexual, but she knew now that there hadn't been anything sexual about their group huddle.

Kim slid her arms around Connor and leaned onto his back. "It's all right, sweetie," she said. "They've stopped."

Glory had Connor's head on her shoulder, her arm around him. Connor had stopped his horrible keening, but he shivered violently.

He really was young, Kim had realized when he'd shifted. As a wildcat, Connor was underdeveloped, little more than a cub, never mind he was twenty in human years and attending college. The gulf between his world and Kim's gaped wide.

Gulf. Oh, hell, *Silas*.

Kim looked up. Silas remained with Annie, who'd taken a protective stance in front of him. Silas's eyes were wide, but the man had seen the worst areas of Iraq and Afghanistan. Two Shifter-cats battling it out shouldn't faze him. She hoped.

"Why didn't your Collars work?" he asked into the silence.

Dylan still lay on his back with his eyes closed, his face ashen. Liam answered, "They did. This is pain you're looking at, lad. Dad was teaching me a bit of a lesson, is all."

Liam's answer was evasive, but he wasn't lying about the pain. He looked awful, and so did Dylan.

Ellison had shifted back to human form but hadn't resumed his clothes. He went to Liam, helped him to his feet, put an arm around him. Sean stepped to Liam's other side, wrapped his arm around Liam's shoulder, nuzzled his cheek.

"Go to him, Kim," Glory said. "I've got Connor."

"What about Dylan?" Dylan lay alone, breathing hard, his body white and gleaming with sweat.

"Leave Dylan be. Liam's your mate. He needs you."

Kim gave Connor one last hug and unfolded to her feet. She never could decide whether Glory was a complete bitch or a complicated woman. Glory's tongue was sharp, but she looked up at Kim with such anguish in her eyes that Kim suddenly wanted to hug *her*.

She resisted and went to Liam.

Ellison relinquished his place at Liam's side to Kim. Kim kept her eyes averted from Ellison's very naked body, but Ellison didn't seem to notice or care.

"We need to get him to the house, away from everyone," Sean said from Liam's other side.

Kim nodded. She and Sean helped Liam walk, step by shaky step, to the back porch, and inside the quiet Morrissey house. It was dark, no one having been inside since sunset, but neither she nor Sean bothered to turn on the light.

"Get me to the couch," Liam said. "I'll be all right."

Kim and Sean lowered him gently. Kim took Liam's hand between hers, and Sean started to sit down next to him.

"Stop fussing like old biddies," Liam growled. "It's not that bad. You need to make sure Connor's all right."

"What about your dad?" Kim asked.

"Glory will see to him." Liam reached for her. "Poor Kim. We've given you a fright."

"Now you're patronizing *me*." Kim climbed to her feet and glared at both of them. "That was some serious shit out there, wasn't it?"

"It's over now."

"You can barely talk, Liam. So be quiet. And *you*." Kim pointed at Sean. "You just stood there. Like you did in San Antonio when Fergus went crazy with his whip. You stood there and let them fight each other, let Connor rush in and get hurt. I thought you were supposed to be the big Guardian of the clan. Doesn't that mean you're supposed to protect them?"

"Kim," Liam said. "Don't."

"It's all right, Liam," Sean answered. "She doesn't understand."

"So make me understand."

Sean looked at her a few moments, then lifted the sword from where it rested beside the couch. He drew it from its sheath and held the sword toward her in both hands, letting Kim see the interwoven Celtic designs etched into the hilt and blade. The workmanship was amazing, the lines featherlight, every single one part of the intricate pattern.

"It's Shifter forged and Fae spelled. Very old, not meant for fighting."

"For what, then?"

"The Guardian doesn't guard the clan," Sean said softly. "I'm the Guardian of the Gate. The Gate to the afterworld."

Kim dragged her gaze from the sword to look into Sean's quiet eyes. "You've lost me."

"It used to be that the Guardian was for his pride only. But now that we've taken the Collar, I'm responsible for every Shifter in this Shiftertown. When a Shifter dies or is without hope of survival, I bring the sword. The sword frees the soul, allowing it to enter the Summerland. The Guardian makes sure the souls aren't stranded, which makes them vulnerable to be enslaved again by the Fae. I save them from that."

Kim tried to understand, to make her very practical mind believe. "So, when you stand there, watching a fight . . ."

"I'm waiting to see if the sword is needed. If I join in, and I'm hurt or killed, there's no one else who can wield the sword. When I die, a new Guardian arises. Usually from the same family, but it's complicated."

"Are you telling me that if Dylan had hurt Liam enough tonight, you'd have stuck Liam with the sword? Turned him to dust like you did with that Shifter in my bedroom?"

"He would have, love," Liam said. "He'd have done what he needed to do."

"Aye, I'd have sent him to dust," Sean agreed. "Just like I did with our Kenny." Sean sheathed the sword, turned on his heel, and walked out of the house, clutching the sword in a tight hand.

"Oh," Kim said into the quiet. "Now I feel like a complete idiot. What a thing to remind him of. I'm sorry, I shouldn't have said anything. I was just so angry at him for not helping you."

"It's an old hurt. My fault for not explaining about it."

Liam looked exhausted, lines etched into his tired face. Kim sat down next him, kissed his hand. "You're not all right. You told me how strong your dad was, and the Collar really punished you out there."

"It's not so bad," Liam said, his voice nearly a whisper. "Yet. Can you help me up to bed, Kim? I'm thinking I'll be spending the rest of my mate-bonding night there. Not what I really had in mind, but eventually, I'm going to feel better." He smiled. "And I'll want you next to me."

He tried to speak lightly, but Kim saw the pain in his eyes, remembered how it had clouded him the night he'd saved her from the feral Shifter. She kissed his lips, softly, trying not to hurt him, then put her arm around him and helped him to his feet.

Dylan had never screwed like *this* before. The sofa springs dug into Glory's back, and Dylan's weight pinned her wonderfully. He drove into her hard, harder, never mind the angry scratches and bruises that covered his body. His face was set, his eyes almost feral.

She'd feared that he'd be enraged with her, and he *was* angry, but it was anger Glory didn't understand. Instead of berating her when he stormed in her back door, he'd grabbed her and started sexing her before they even reached the sofa. His clothes had already been gone, and she helped him tear off her own clothes before clasping him in her arms. Now Dylan pumped into her until Glory screamed with joy, not caring if everyone in Shiftertown was still outside to hear.

She was under no illusion that Dylan loved her. Dylan still loved his mate and resented himself for what he did with Glory. Dylan tried to be kind, but Glory knew that he considered himself betraying the woman who'd borne his children. His need for Glory angered him. Whenever the anger finally overrode his desires, he'd refuse to see Glory for months.

Glory held on to him, feeling him slip away from her again. Damn it, why couldn't he make up his mind? He was tearing her apart.

She felt his seed as he groaned with it, and she hoped against hope that *this* time, she'd conceive. Dylan might consider taking her as mate if she had a cub. It was more difficult to produce a baby cross-species, but it could be done, and Glory would love bearing Dylan's child.

Glory squeezed him inside her and held him close. Dylan collapsed on her, breath ragged.

The sounds of the revelry outside filtered into the

house. The Shifters were enjoying themselves again. The fight was over, nothing had changed, and there was a mating ritual to celebrate. Perfect excuse to party all night.

Dylan disentangled himself from Glory and sat up, breathing hard. He ran his hands through his sweaty hair.

She loved his hair. He kept it fairly short, and it was going gray at the temples, which complemented the fine lines around his eyes. If this man could be hers . . .

"I won't ask if you're all right," Glory said. Her lips were swollen, and she winced as her tongue found a cut. "You wouldn't be here if you weren't."

Dylan didn't answer. He sat back, still catching his breath. Glory got up and went to the kitchen, gratified that when she came back with a wet towel his gaze was fixed on her naked body.

She sat next to him and started dabbing blood from his face.

"Thank you," Dylan said. "Are *you* all right?"

Now she worried. Dylan never reverted to politeness unless things were truly bad. "My Collar gave me only one burst. It went away fast." A lie, but Glory knew that Dylan's hurting when it came would be far greater than hers. Staving off the consequences of the Collar brought worse hurt than going along with it.

"I'm sorry, Dylan," she said. "I didn't realize Liam would react so strongly. I thought my Collar would stop me, and he'd laugh at me for being foolish."

Dylan looked away. "I didn't think he'd react like that, either."

"And then you leapt in to save me. My hero."

Dylan shot her a look. Glory went back to dabbing his wounds. "It's over now," she said. "You wrestled, you stopped the fight. I'm sorry about Connor."

"Connor needs to learn to back off until he's fully grown." Dylan paused. "And I didn't stop the fight. Liam did."

"Liam backed down. I saw him."

"No." Dylan's words were flat. "Liam stopped the fight, because he was winning it."

Glory froze, and the cloth dripped water on her bare thighs. "Goddess, are you sure?"

"Very sure, love. Liam stopped before he could hurt me. If this had happened before the Collar, he'd have killed me." Dylan closed his eyes and rested his head on the back of the sofa.

"What are you going to do to him?"

Dylan gave a mirthless laugh. "I'm not going to do anything to him. I can't. He's my son, and he's mated now. It's up to him." He opened his eyes. "If you say anything, tell *anyone*, I'll . . ."

She liked that he didn't finish the sentence. When a Shifter said, "I'll kill you," he meant it. Dylan wouldn't say it casually. "Like I would. I keep your secrets, Dylan."

Dylan's look softened, and he closed his eyes again. "Thank you. I know you do. The Collar's going to pay me back now. You might want to go out to the party. This won't be pretty."

"I'm not leaving you."

Dylan reached out and took her hand. Glory twined her fingers through his, her heart thumping. Dylan's body shuddered as the pain started to flow. A tear slid from his tightly closed eyes.

"Thank you," he whispered.

"It's bad," Liam said. As though all the agony in the world was twisting his body to one fine point.

"What can I do?" Kim knelt on his bed next to him.

"You being here with me is good." Liam broke off as a spasm rocked him. *"Damn."*

Kim put her arms around him. Liam loved that she instinctively knew he needed her warmth and closeness. Nothing else would get him through this.

"That was one hell of a fight," Kim said. "Why did you have it?"

"Glory attacked my mate. The beast inside me had to stop her." He grimaced as another wave rocketed through him.

"Her Collar activated right away. She knew she wouldn't be able to hurt me."

"Sure, my brain reasons that now. But at the time, the feral Shifter in me wanted nothing more than to protect you."

"And your father tried to protect Glory. Is that it?"

"That's it in one, love." Liam tried to smile, though the muscles of his mouth didn't want to move. "The big liar. I knew Dad cared about her more than he let on."

"That's a good thing, isn't it? Even though you two had to tear each other up to learn it?"

Liam looked into her honest eyes and felt something break inside him. He knew what had happened in the fight, something far more significant than learning that his father liked Glory more than he admitted.

Dylan had felt it too. Liam had seen what was in his father's eyes when they pulled apart.

Defeat.

The wildcat inside Liam wanted to roar his triumph. The pride was *his*. Liam was mated, powerful, and he'd just bested the only one in Shiftertown stronger than himself.

"Crap," he whispered. "Goddess help me."

Kim kneaded his shoulders. "Does it hurt?"

She thought he meant the Collar. The Collar was nothing compared to the grief that now twisted him, warring with the fierce joy of his victory. It was nothing to the heartbreak of what he'd seen in his father.

Fear. Dylan feared him.

"Kim. I've just screwed everything all to hell." Liam pulled her down on top of him, held her close, and explained in a low, rapid voice what had happened.

Liam's descent to breakfast the next morning was difficult for three reasons. First because he was sore as hell—from the fight with his father and the Collar's payback, then from sex with Kim, as gentle as it had been. Second, because Kim lay snuggled and cute in his bed, sound asleep. Third, because he'd have to face Dylan.

In the space of a few seconds last night, Liam's entire life had changed. He didn't know what to do about it, or even how he felt about it. The turmoil of emotions and thoughts nauseated him.

He descended the stairs, scrubbing his hand through his wet hair. He'd showered twice, once last night with Kim while she washed his cuts, which had led to water all over the bathroom floor. There was something about bathrooms and Kim. The second time was this morning after he'd left the bed.

Dylan leaned on his elbows on the breakfast bar, drinking coffee and reading a newspaper. Morning sunlight winked on his Collar.

"Did Fergus oust you yet?" Liam asked, as he headed for the coffeepot. They didn't have a coffeemaker, not because it was forbidden to Shifters, but because they'd never taken to anything but coffee brewed right in the pot.

"Haven't heard from him. I'm sure he'll be along."

Liam poured coffee. "Where have Sean and Connor got to?"

"I sent them off."

"Why?"

"So we could talk."

Liam took a sip and grimaced. "Sean must have made this." Sean, terrific at the griddle, lousy at the brew-up.

"Fergus has to know."

"That Sean made the damned coffee?"

"Liam."

"Shit."

Both men fell silent. Liam cradled his cup while Dylan pretended to read the newspaper. Liam had never heard Dylan come in last night; Glory must have been comforting him the way Kim had comforted Liam.

"Do you want me to leave?" Dylan asked without looking up.

"No, you're fine. I don't mind you reading the paper." Liam stopped pretending. "You mean for good, don't you? Why should you?"

"My own father died before we found out whether I could best him. Defeated males had two choices back then—be killed or cast out."

"I know."

Dylan turned a page. "I knew in my heart it would happen to me sooner or later. I didn't think it would be last night."

"We never finished the fight."

"Good thing." Dylan finally looked up at him. The man was much too calm. His eyes were watchful, but other than that, he rested against the counter, the cuts on his face already healing. "If it had been obvious that you'd bested me, Fergus would be up here demanding to fight you, to establish his dominance."

"Did you tell anyone?"

"Glory."

"You trust her then?"

Dylan gave him a thin smile. "I might have to move in with the woman. I thought it only fair that she knew why."

"Damn it, Dad. You don't have to move out. We're not feral anymore. We don't have to disembowel each other to make a point."

"No, we're too civilized for disemboweling," Dylan said in a dry voice. "The choice is yours, Liam. I don't mind going."

"No." Liam slammed his cup to the counter and it broke. Hot coffee spilled on his hands and spattered on his thighs. "I don't want you going. Why the hell should you? You belong here."

Dylan left his newspaper, caught Liam's shoulders in his big hands. "It's natural, son. It happens."

"Screw that."

Dylan pulled him close. Liam resisted the hug, wanting to push him away. All his life he'd felt protected and confident because Dylan and his strength was there. Even when Dylan had disappeared to grieve, his protection had permeated the walls of their castle, and Liam had known Dylan would return. He'd never doubted.

When they'd come to America, a land they'd never seen, and during the torture of taking the Collar, Dylan had been there. Dylan was the anchor in the madness of Liam's life, in the chaos of the world.

Last night, the moment Liam's wildcat had known he could destroy Dylan anytime he wanted to, that world had changed. Gone was the ground beneath Liam's feet, the tie to sanity. The abyss howled at him, and now he'd have to face it alone.

Liam jerked away. He and Dylan were the same height; he could look his father straight in the eye. "Don't tell Fergus. Not yet. I don't want him coming after you."

Dylan nodded, and Liam tamped down his anger with difficulty. Primal rage made him want Fergus in front of him, right now. Liam would make the man eat his fucking whip.

"Is this the true reason you never would fight Fergus?" Liam asked. "Because you knew once you'd bested him, I'd be compelled to best you?"

Dylan waited a silent moment, then nodded.

The enormity of the knowledge was enough to make Liam sick. He had always thought Dylan held back from challenging Fergus to keep the peace in Shiftertown, because living life and raising the children were more important than fights for dominance. Liam had agreed, believed it with all his heart. Now Dylan was confessing that part of the reason he'd kept himself from fighting Fergus was simple fear.

When a clan leader died, usually the second in line stepped into his place without fuss, unless a Shifter close to the second knew that he could vie for leadership. Other Shifters down the line might fight among themselves to move up a place or two, and a series of fights could happen until the pecking order settled again. Typically the hierarchy didn't change, but sometimes a young Shifter grew more dominant or an older Shifter weakened and moved down. Dylan had realized that Liam's natural dominance would emerge the instant Fergus was gone, that Liam wouldn't have been able to stop himself from challenging his father.

"Shite, Dad."

"Fergus will have to know sometime," Dylan said.

"We wait. We'll tell him on our own terms, when *we're* ready."

Dylan nodded once. "Agreed."

Liam loved his father so damn much, and now his instincts were telling him to push Dylan out, take over his power. The Collars might keep Shifters from being violent, but they didn't take away the fiery urge to dominate.

Dylan knew it too. His instincts must have been telling him to cut and run, get out while the going was good. By the white lines around his mouth, Liam knew he was resisting the urge with difficulty.

"Damn it," Liam said. "Why didn't you warn me this was coming?"

"I hoped it wouldn't happen for a few more years, that we'd both have time to prepare. But claiming a mate triggered something in you. You're the oldest son. Don't tell me you didn't know that one day you'd take over the family."

"I didn't think it would be now, and I didn't think it would hurt so much."

Dylan smiled. "Your mother would be proud of you for showing compassion. For not throwing me out with your bare hands."

"Mum was too damn good for us."

"I know that."

Liam met his gaze and said something that would have gotten him knocked across the room before today. "She'd want you to be with Glory. She'd want you to be happy."

"Don't push it, Liam."

Liam wanted to laugh, but he was wound up too tight. His dad might have switched places with him in the hierarchy, but that didn't mean the man was a wimp.

Liam grabbed Dylan in a bear hug, then released him abruptly and left the house.

Even in the embrace, Liam's instincts had kicked in,

urging him to remind his father who now ran the pride. Liam needed some distance from his father to get used to his new position, to learn to control himself.

He looked back and saw Kim peering down at him from his bedroom window, but even that couldn't make him stay.

Chapter Nineteen

Kim found Liam in a sorry excuse for a park on the far side of Shiftertown. He sat on a low brick wall next to the only trees in the somewhat bare strip of land, hands braced on the top of the wall.

The park had one swing set for kids, no picnic tables, and bald patches where grass should grow. The city had tacked the park onto Shiftertown as an afterthought, then forgotten about it. The Shifters didn't use it much, from what she'd seen, seeming to prefer the common greens behind their houses.

Kim approached Liam slowly but determinedly, wondering if he'd stand up and walk away. He didn't. Liam didn't look at her, either, as she sat down next to him and stretched out her bare legs. The summer warmth felt good on them, though she knew the day soon would turn excruciatingly hot.

"Is this your place?" she asked him.

He glanced at her. "Mmm?"

"The place you go when you want to think. My place is a coffeehouse on the river that sits right on the water. You can suck down a latte and watch the river go by. It's soothing."

Liam looked into the distance. "I'm thinking they wouldn't be letting Shifters in."

"Maybe not. But this is your place, isn't it?"

"No, it was a convenient spot to sit my sorry ass down."

Kim let it go. She wasn't sure she should have followed Liam, but what she'd overheard of his conversation with Dylan confused and bothered her. She didn't understand fully what Liam had explained about him knowing he was now dominant to Dylan, but she sensed the tension, the violence simmering below the surface. A person didn't have to be a Shifter to feel it.

She argued with herself that maybe Liam wanted to be alone, but something inside told her she shouldn't leave him by himself. His shoulders were tight, arms knotted, his mouth a rigid line. As usual, Liam kept his words light, almost careless, but the darkness in his eyes spoke volumes.

Kim sat in silence with him. Birds chattered in the trees, but otherwise, the park was quiet. No kids came to swing, and no cars turned down the quiet street beyond it. She heard faint sounds of the city on the other side of the derelict block beyond Shiftertown, Austinites heading to the city to make money or play politics. Here in Shiftertown, power that humans didn't understand ebbed and flowed in ways they'd never realize.

"Are you all right?" she ventured. "I mean from having your Collar go off and . . . well, everything."

"You're referring to the exuberant and athletic sex we had later?" A ghost of a smile touched Liam's mouth. "That's why I had to sit down."

Kim covered his hand, feeling the tension in it. "Liam, last night was my fault. I was the one who wanted to bring Silas here. There never would have been a Collar demonstration if I hadn't."

Liam touched her fingers to his lips. "Don't fret yourself, sweetheart. I agreed to invite Silas. It's my fault for encouraging his questions about the Collars. I didn't anticipate Glory jumping in, damn the lass, or that Conner would get hurt or that anything very dramatic would happen. My thought was that I'd grab for Silas, let my Collar spark, and have everyone laugh at me."

"Laugh at you in pain?"

"I've been in pain before, and I've gotten over it."

"Liam . . ."

"What's between me and Dad would have happened sooner or later, love, and maybe it was best the fight occurred with you and Connor and your journalist watching so avidly. You all gave me the strength to break it off. If me and Dad had been alone, it might have turned deadly before I could shut down my instincts." He smiled, a little shaky. "So maybe I should be thanking you instead."

Kim caressed his fingers with her thumb. "Don't make me feel worse, damn it." She sighed. "And on top of it all, I have to go to work."

"I know."

"Come with me?"

"No fear I'd let you go alone, darling. Not with you flagrantly disobeying Fergus every second."

"I thought you wanted me to keep helping Brian."

"I do. I was referring to your lack of stealth. I know why you're such a good defender. You're so honest it glows from you. When you say the man didn't do it, everyone wants to believe he didn't do it."

"I wish it were that simple. Every *i* has to be dotted and every *t* crossed. You miss one, the case goes the other way."

"Sandra is visiting Brian this morning, and she's going to ask if he was ready to take Michelle as mate. Sandra's grateful to you for believing in him."

"Really?" Kim asked. "Her looks of hatred are false impressions, are they?"

"She's afraid. Fergus has put fear into her, and she

doesn't know why. All she knows is that she's been told to sacrifice her son." He shook his head. "For a mother to lose her child—I can only imagine how it feels. If it's anything like losing a brother . . ."

"Then it's pretty shitty."

Liam ran a hand through Kim's hair. "It would be like losing you."

Her pulse sped. "Not the same thing at all. We barely know each other."

"We know a lot about each other. I know you have a little mole on the inside of your right thigh."

"I wasn't talking about sex."

"Neither was I." Liam turned and straddled the wall, pulling her between his thighs. "*Mating* doesn't mean going at it until we have a litter of cubs. It means a bond that no one breaks. Ever."

"It's not a marriage humans would recognize or sanction," Kim pointed out.

"Damn, woman, will you stop shoving everything into your legal terms? I'm not talking about the bits of paper humans love so much. It's a bond inside us, stretching between us. Nothing can sever it, not human law or my family, or bloody Fergus. Are you telling me you don't feel it?"

His eyes held anger, fear, hope, and something raw—all fighting inside him.

Did Kim feel the bond? Of course she did. This man was compelling and mesmerizing, with his blue eyes and lilting voice, not to mention his hot body. But it was more than his sexiness and his strength.

Liam dominated any room he walked into without saying a word. Every Shifter Kim met was drawn to Liam, every Shifter hero-worshipped him, even if they might not admit it. Anyone who had troubles went to him. Even the kids did, like little Michael in his pool.

Michael had called out to Liam, had been excited to tell Liam of his achievements. He'd wanted Liam's approval.

Kim remembered Liam's words to the boy—"you look after your brother, now." Kim realized now he'd not been making an offhand remark. Liam, who had lost a brother, knew the importance of taking care of those you loved.

Liam took care of everyone in Shiftertown, even more than Dylan did. Kim had always sensed that, and she knew that Dylan had too, and had let it happen. Not because Dylan feared losing to Liam, but because Dylan loved him.

"I wish I'd never come here," she said.

Liam stroked her bare leg, his fingers sliding beneath the hem of her skirt. "Why is that, love? Me, I'm glad you walked into my bar."

"Because you've messed up my mind. I was independent, didn't worry about anyone but myself. When I went home at the end of the day, I could do whatever I wanted. Hang out with friends, watch TV, be alone, whatever. And now I'm worried about you—and Sean, and Connor, and your father, and Brian and Sandra, and every other Shifter in this damned Shiftertown. Even Glory." She glared at him. "Stop making me care. It's annoying."

Liam's fingers moved farther under the skirt. "Then you do care?" His eyes held heat. "I'm not dreaming that?"

"Of course I care. Who could help caring about you? But we're still not married."

"No," he said softly. "Not in the marriage license kind of way. You're my *mate*, Kim. I have you and no other." Liam rubbed the small of her back, his body warmer than the Texas sunshine. "Will you have me, and no other?"

Kim's heart pounded. *Forsaking all others, as long as you both shall live.* "There is no other for me."

"Maybe not now. But what if some human male, some high-powered lawyer in your firm, decides to make you his wife? His prize? So you can flash your beautiful legs at his parties and draw people to his side?"

Kim shook with nervous laughter. "His *prize?* Thanks a lot. Besides, I don't like high-powered lawyers. They take credit for cases I win."

"Good."

"I liked you when I met you, Liam, but what I feel now, it's gone far beyond like." Kim leaned against his chest as his seeking fingers found the elastic of her underwear. "But you're asking me for commitment."

"I don't need to ask. The mate-bond does it for us."

"Maybe it does for Shifters. Not for humans."

"Shifter-human pairings happen sometimes. We'd never have survived all these centuries if the gene pool had remained pure. Inbreeding makes for weakness. Mongrels survive."

"*Mongrels.* You sweet talker."

"I think we're doing too much of the talking."

The leg band of her panties moved aside, and strong fingers touched the moisture between her legs.

Kim glanced around. "We're outside."

"Are we?" He sounded amazed.

Kim didn't object to sex, and in college she'd once done it in a car, but that had been late at night in a deserted parking lot. This was broad daylight in the middle of thriving Shiftertown.

Liam leaned down and pressed an openmouthed kiss to her throat, making Kim's body hotter. She was wet, she was naughty, and she loved it.

Liam drew his tongue up her chin and kissed her mouth. His kissing skills had certainly progressed. He knew how to part her lips, how to stroke his tongue inside her, how to make her mouth tingle.

"This is bad," she whispered.

"No. It's good."

"I want to unbutton your pants right here on the street," she said. "I'd call that bad."

"Our notions of bad and good are the exact opposite, then."

Kim gave in and popped the button of his jeans. His cock was hard behind his underwear, the tip reaching past the waistband. Kim slid her fingers inside the elastic and grasped the full shaft.

Liam groaned. "You've got the touch, love."

Kim slid her thumb over the crown, and Liam's fingers moved between her legs. She'd never thought she could get turned on sitting on a wall, but Liam also had the touch. More than the touch. She found herself rocking back, closing her eyes.

"Liam."

"I'm right here, baby."

He was, all eleven inches of him. Not that she'd measured, but she could guess. She ran her hand along Liam's penis, gripping it all the way down. He moved his hips, face softening in pleasure.

"Love, you don't know what you do to me."

"I have a pretty good idea. I make you stiff and hard, and when I touch you, you want to screw me."

His eyes were slits. "You're close."

"You mean you *don't* want to screw me?"

"I mean I want to screw you all the time, whether you're touching me or not. I want to lift your pretty skirt and do you right now."

Excitement spiked through her. "Right here on the wall?" she asked in an innocent voice.

"Right here on the wall."

Liam half stood, and she lost her hold of him. The next thing she knew, his jeans were around his thighs, her underwear was gone, he was sitting on the wall again, and he'd pulled her down to straddle him. Her skirt hid their mutual bareness, but only just.

She opened her mouth to admonish him, but he kissed her. The wicked look in his eyes both excited her and made her want to laugh.

She'd never gone out with a man as in-your-face as Liam. He was a Shifter, restricted and shunned, but he was better at doing whatever he damn well pleased than anyone she'd ever met.

Right now, he was doing her on a wall in the middle of a park. In broad daylight. As he went deep, he pulled her close and kissed her.

Words flew through Kim's mind, then dissolved. This wasn't about words. It was feeling, pure, basic, raw feeling.

Liam was opening her like he never had before. The sun on her thighs excited her as much as his hardness inside her, a hardness that stretched and widened her. This was free and wild and strange. Sweat rolled in a bead between her breasts, and he leaned forward and licked it away.

His breath came fast, and so did hers. Liam's fingers were hard points on her thighs, then her back, her buttocks, her face. He pressed into her, fast, faster, his mouth twisting in pleasure.

Kim's head dropped back. She bit back her scream, not wanting people to come rushing out to see what was going on. Liam licked between her breasts again, his breath scalding. "I'm coming," he whispered into her skin.

So was she. White-hot waves of excitement poured

through her, blotting out everything but the feeling of Liam joined to her.

He took her face between his hands. His eyes had gone Shifter, the predator wanting her. Then he gave a strangled groan and shot everything he had into her.

Shaking and sweaty, Kim clasped him to her breasts and kissed his hair. *I love you, Liam*, she wanted to whisper, but she kissed his hair again and rested her cheek on his head.

Liam insisted on accompanying her to work, and Kim was fine with that today. Having him next to her in her car, though, his dark sunglasses trained at the world going by, distracted her.

Kim's body felt warm and supple, aching slightly from having to spread so far for him. Liam caught Kim looking at him, and he reached over and laid his hand on her thigh. He didn't have to say a word. Kim felt the connection between them, the warmth that wouldn't go away.

Kim earned a few stares when they walked in. She was: one, late; two, not in a suit; and three, shadowed by her tall Shifter with menacing eyes.

She was starting to dress like a Shifter woman, she realized as she sat down and sorted through her messages. She never came to work outside of a skirt suit, stockings, and black pumps. She'd changed out of the clothes she'd made love in, but had put on another loose skirt and blouse and high-heeled sandals. Clothing easy to remove.

She sensed that the last thing Liam had wanted to do this morning was leave Shiftertown, but he'd been adamant about not letting her go to work alone. Last night he and his father had switched places in Shifter hierarchy, which meant he could go one-on-one with Fergus now—a fight that might end in Liam's death.

The entire balance of Shifter power in South Texas was at stake. Liam showed how torn he was about this by stretching out on her sofa and catching up on the latest issue of *Angler Today*.

"Will you stop that?" she asked in irritation.

"Stop what? Reading's good for you. You learn things."

"Sitting there like nothing's wrong. I might have made a breakthrough in the case. Your dad might have to leave Shiftertown. Fergus might try to kick your ass into the next county. And you read about fishing. Do Shifters fish?"

"Kim, sweetheart, if I didn't absorb myself in fishing lures, I'd either tear down the building or come over there and screw you senseless on your desk. Maybe both. Is that what you want? I can oblige."

Kim scrubbed her hand through her hair. "Never mind. You have me on edge. I guess the Shifter pheromone thing really works."

Liam was off the couch and on his feet, the magazine falling to the floor. "And yours are pouring over me, enticing me to come and slide my hands up your skirt."

"You've already done that."

"That was two hours ago. I want to do it again. And again. All day and all night. It burns like fury."

Kim's blood heated. "I can't say I'm turned off by that."

"You're lucky you're not Shifter. You can't feel the mating frenzy like I do. If you were Shifter, we'd have been doing it constantly since San Antonio. To hell with work or family, or eating and sleeping." Tension rippled through his big body.

"You've been feeling that since San Antonio?"

"Hell yes. I want to be inside you every second. Fergus and his demands, your case, and even my father can go to hell."

"Oh." Kim moved closer to him. She was in her office, her very formal, law-firm office in its nice building in downtown Austin, and she wanted nothing more than for Liam to throw everything off the desk and lay her back on it. Or maybe sit her on the edge. Or against the wall. She wasn't particular.

Liam's smile was feral. "Don't play with fire, Kim."

"I think I have a little of this mating frenzy too." Kim pressed her hands to his chest to feel his heart pounding beneath her fingertips. "I want to touch you all the time, have you kiss me, have you *be* with me. I didn't say that, because I was afraid you'd think I was clingy."

"My love, what gobshite wouldn't want you clinging to him?"

"Pretty much everything male."

Liam drew her against him. "Bloody fools can't see what's in front of their own noses. It means you're all mine."

Kim rose to meet his kiss, not caring that her secretary could pop in any moment, not to mention all the lawyers in the building. But what the hell? She'd already done it outside on a wall, and her colleagues probably thought she was shagging the Shifter in here anyway.

The kiss turned deep. Kim tasted his need, the frenzy inside him, and his conflicted emotions. Likely his heartbreak was fueling his sexual needs, and Kim would be the one fulfilling those needs. She somehow couldn't be sorry about that.

Liam's cell phone buzzed. He kept kissing her a few seconds, then reluctantly reached for the phone. "Damn it." He flipped it open. "What?"

His expression changed, and he turned away, shutting Kim out. She thought the voice she could barely hear was Sean's, and from the stiffening of Liam's body, something had happened.

Her heart froze. Dylan? Or Connor?

Liam snapped the phone shut and turned to her with a grim look. "Michael's mum says he's missing. She can't find him anywhere."

Kim blinked. "Michael? The little kid with the pool?"

"Yes. Dad and Sean are organizing a search."

Kim's blood went cold. "Fergus?"

Liam shook his head. "I don't think so, and neither does Dad. Fergus's head would come off if he tried to hurt a cub, or even use him as a diversion. Fergus has power, but cubs are sacrosanct."

Kim wasn't sure she took Liam's word for it. "Call the police," she said quickly. "They'll do one of those alerts . . ."

Liam shook his head. "Shifters can find him a hell of a lot faster than your police can. We know his scent." Liam slid his phone back into his belt. "I have to be there. His mum and dad . . ."

"Will need you." Kim thought of the way Liam and Sean had done everything to calm Sandra, how the woman had relaxed somewhat under their mutual touch. The parents would be terrified, need reassurance. "Go then. I'll be fine."

More conflict. Liam looked uncertain, and Kim had never seen him uncertain. "Really," she said. "I have a hell of a lot to do here. You know, Brian's butt to save. I'll be fine."

Liam came to her, his hard body against hers the best thing in the world. "You stay in this office, all right? Have someone bring you lunch; don't go out. And after work get into your car and drive straight to my house. No stopping, no lingering. All right?"

Uneasiness stole through her. "Fine. I can do that."

Liam pulled her into an embrace. A Shifter embrace, tight, long, warm, comforting and drawing comfort at the same time. "I hate to leave you."

Kim hated for him to leave her too. When did she get so needy? "I'm fine. Go."

Liam kissed her again, lips lingering on hers. "You call me," he said. "Every hour if you have to."

"It will be all right, Liam."

Liam gave her a hint of a smile. "I wish I could believe that, love." And then he was gone.

Kim tried to concentrate on work but found her attention wandering to Shiftertown. She had much to catch up on, phone calls to return, reports from her investigator on Michelle's ex to go through, letters to compose. But she worried about Michael—had he merely wandered off or had something more sinister happened? Was he exploring some place exciting to small Shifter boys; was there another feral Shifter on the loose?

Liam hadn't been gone an hour before she was on the phone to him. He told her, his voice warm as ever, that he had nothing to report. Apparently, Michael's mother had stepped inside for a minute, when his little brother had come running to the front porch to tell her that Michael was gone. Early searches had turned up nothing. All Shiftertown was now about to start a serious one.

Kim heard the worry in Liam's voice. This happening, on top of his fight with his father and Fergus's threats, couldn't be easy on him.

When had she started caring so much? Her fascination with Shifters, her first attraction to Liam, her growing physical need for him had blossomed into something much deeper. It was more than the mating frenzy Liam kept talking about. There was something about Liam that made her want to be near him, to hold him when he hurt, to laugh with him when he was happy.

She squeezed her eyes shut. *Damn it all, I've fallen in love with him. When did I get so stupid?*

Kim tried to return to work. She couldn't bother Liam; he'd have his hands full. But she couldn't help calling him back as she ate lunch at her desk. Nothing, Liam reported.

He sounded even grimmer. Kim assured him that she was all right—no need to worry about her. He told her to take care, warmth in every word. When Liam said the trite phrase, he really meant it.

Kim called Liam back at two, but he didn't answer.

Leave him alone, she told herself. *He's busy doing his job.*

To think she'd once assumed his job was managing a bar.

By three, Kim couldn't take it anymore. She packed her briefcase and told Jeanne, her secretary, that she'd work the rest of the day at home.

Kim hurried out into the parking lot to nearly run into Abel, who was returning from a day in court. "Kim," he said.

"Hey, Abel. I gotta go. See you tomorrow."

Abel stepped in front of her. He was perspiring, his face red and shiny above his tight suit coat. He looked furious, which meant he must have lost his case.

"I heard that you dumped me for a Shifter."

The boy wonder had finally caught on. "That's none of your business. I have to go."

He stepped in front of her again. "Where to? Your Shifter? That stinking animal you dragged in here?

You're screwing him, aren't you? You're screwing an animal."

Kim rolled her eyes. "You were always so clueless."

"I'll have you fired. I'll get you disbarred."

"It's not against the law to go out with a Shifter. Or even to go to bed with one. Grow up, Abel."

Kim tried to go around him again, and again, Abel barred her way. After meeting Fergus, Abel frightened Kim about as much as a gnat, but she wondered what he was going to do. Deck her in the parking lot? Great PR for the law firm.

"Would you get out of the way?"

"Were you doing him while you were going out with me? Tell me the truth. You were already screwing him then, weren't you? You were double-dipping."

"Obviously you want me to say yes."

"Shifter-whore," Abel said. "I'll tell everyone I know that you're nothing but a Shifter-whore."

"Abel, you moron . . ."

She broke off as two Shifters materialized on either side of Abel. Fergus's thugs—bald Tattoo Guy and Military Man. Their Collars glinted in the hot sunlight. Military Man wore sunglasses and looked like the Terminator.

"Everything all right, Ms. Fraser?" Tattoo Guy asked.

"Everything's fine. I'm heading to my car."

"We'll walk you there."

Kim's heart started to pound. "No need, I can make it."

Military Man stepped to block Abel, while Tattoo Guy motioned for Kim to go. "Want us to teach him some manners?" Tattoo Guy asked her.

"No, leave him alone," Kim said. "He's just a dickhead."

Tattoo Guy shrugged as if he didn't care one way or

another. Abel beat a retreat into the building, and Kim started for her car, which was only a few feet away. The two of them fell into step beside her.

"When Shifters don't wear Collars," Tattoo Guy said, "assholes like that will be wetting themselves to be nice to us."

Sure. Kim quickened her pace, but she reached the car without incident. The two men didn't try to grab her or drag her off; in fact, they acted more as though they were protecting her. Whose side were they on? Military Man opened her car door for her, shutting it again once she was settled. "Drive carefully, now."

"Right," Kim said as she started up.

"Hey, no one messes with our females," Military Man said. "You're Liam's now."

She wasn't sure whether to be reassured or irritated. "Thank you, gentlemen," she said. "I appreciate your help."

She firmly rolled up the windows and backed out of her parking space. The two followed her to Shiftertown on their motorcycles, keeping pace with her, again, protectively.

Kim was halfway to Shiftertown when Tattoo Guy's words struck her. *When Shifters don't wear Collars.* What the hell did that mean? He'd said the words as though it was a real time to come, not wishful thinking.

Kim gripped the steering wheel and kept driving. She'd have to ask Liam whether the man was simply blowing off steam—if Liam would ever answer his damn phone.

Chapter Twenty

Liam walked around the next block of derelict and empty buildings. The brick walls were battered and worn, and rotted boards covered broken-out windows.

A place like this might attract a curious kid who'd decided to head out on his own. Liam remembered how he, Sean, and Kenny had liked to explore the ruins of castles—Ireland was full of them—crumbling stones barely held together of some long-forgotten keep. Did they care that it was dangerous, that they could get trapped, buried, crushed by unexpected rock fall?

Not really. They were Shifters. Tough, dangerous, bold.

"Bloody stupid," Liam said under his breath. No wonder their mum had raised hell with them.

He turned a corner between buildings and heard Michael crying.

The sound came from the warehouse beside him, the wide door covered with planks of old wood. Liam kicked apart the wood, mildewed and rotted, and it broke easily.

The warehouse inside was dim, the concrete floor pitted and covered with dust. A metal door made of new, shining, solid steel, gleamed in the wall to his right. Its handle was wrapped in chains and padlocked. Banging came from behind it, along with two voices—Michael's high-pitched wail and the shouts of a man he didn't recognize.

Liam's nostrils widened as he took the scent of the

air. Nothing but terror from Michael and the man behind this door, overlaid by the decay of the building. Even if this was a trick to trap Liam for some reason, it was certain that the prisoners hadn't padlocked themselves into the room from the outside.

Liam wrapped the hem of his shirt around the padlock, let his hand shift to strong Shifter claws, and broke the lock. He swung the door open, backing up quickly when a wave of fetid air poured from the tiny room beyond.

A man rushed out and collapsed on the floor outside his makeshift cell, breathing hard. His hair was tangled and matted, and his clothes were rank. A Lupine, by his eyes and smell, but Liam didn't know him. Michael rushed out behind him, his hands manacled, and Liam gathered the boy up in his arms. Michael clung to him, soaking up all the comfort he could.

"How did you get locked in there?" he asked Michael.

"The bad man brought me."

"What bad man, sweetie?"

"A Feline captured *me*." The man on the floor glared up at him with bloodshot eyes. "Like you."

"Which Feline? Fergus?"

"No. That wasn't his name." The stranger pushed himself to his feet, screwing up his eyes against even the dim light. "Oh, yeah, Brian. That was it."

Liam's blood froze. "Brian."

"That's what he said. Then this morning, some other Feline opens up the door and throws this little guy in with me. I'm glad you came when you did. I was getting hungry, and the Feline said I wasn't allowed to eat."

The Shifter's gaze moved to Michael. The boy wasn't timid, but when those bloodshot Lupine eyes landed on him, he backed away fast until he crouched into a dusty corner. "Something's wrong with him, Liam," Michael whimpered.

The Lupine moved out into the light, and Liam saw clearly that instead of a Collar, a line of blood-blackened bare skin ran around his neck. His Collar had been removed.

"Michael," Liam said. "Run!"

Eyes round with terror, the boy scuttled away. Liam grabbed the Lupine by the shoulder, spinning him around. The Lupine snarled and leapt, and Liam met the attack.

The two fell to the ground, Liam's hands becoming claws. They fought, Liam trying to sever the feral's spine. The feral reared up and brought down a most unlikely weapon—a hypodermic needle. Before Liam could roll aside, the feral plunged the needle into his shoulder.

Liam fought a few more seconds, and then his muscles went slack and he couldn't move at all. He didn't black out, but he prayed hard in the next hours for unconsciousness to come.

At first glance Shiftertown seemed to be in chaos. Shifters roamed everywhere in parties of two and three, calling Michael's name. Shifters on motorcycles and in ratty cars cruised the streets both inside and on the outskirts of Shiftertown, moving slowly and peering into the shadows of every building.

When Kim entered the Morrissey house, she realized that the searching had been organized in almost military fashion. Dylan stood alone in the kitchen, a map of Shiftertown and its environs spread across the table. A careful grid had been drawn on the map. Dylan's cell phone was at his ear, and he marked off squares in the grid as he talked to the person on the other end.

Dylan spotted Kim. "Kim's here," he said into the phone. "And Nate and Spike. Come back to the house and pick up Kim. Nate and Spike will make up another team."

Nate and Spike? Tattoo Guy and Military Man were dismounting their motorcycles at the front curb. Kim briefly wondered which was which.

Dylan hung up his phone, came to Kim, and enfolded her in his arms. *Shifter greeting. They're tense; I bet they need a lot of reassurance right now.*

Kim returned the hug, squeezing Dylan hard before releasing him. "Were you talking to Liam? Where is he?"

Dylan shook his head. "Sean. Liam hasn't checked in."

"He doesn't answer his cell phone, either."

"Cell phone service isn't the most reliable around here. He'll find a way to call when he has something to report. Sean's on his way."

"I want to help."

"You will." Dylan turned back to his map. "I want you and Sean to make up a team. Sean's the strongest, next to Liam, and I don't want to worry about you on top of everything else."

"Liam told me what happened," she said in a low voice. "About you and him, and the fight."

Dylan turned from the map again. He didn't look conquered. He was as tall and formidable as ever, only the touch of gray at his temples betraying that he was older than his sons. He radiated strength, competence, and decisiveness—everything you'd want in a general.

"It's irrelevant right now," Dylan said.

Meaning they'd talk about it once Michael was found. "I just wondered what was going to happen."

"That's up to Liam." Dylan looked past her, and she realized that Nate and Spike were approaching the front door.

Kim shut up, and Dylan invited the two inside. The hostility they'd exhibited to Dylan in San Antonio was absent as the three bent over the map. Nate turned out to be the military guy, and the shaved-headed, tattooed man was Spike.

The two Shifters left with their orders, and Dylan took another phone call. Sean approached through the backyard, and Kim went out to meet him.

"Where's Connor?" she asked.

"Searching with Glory and Ellison. Dad's putting you with me."

Sean looked grim, flat black sunglasses hiding his eyes, his sword hilt protruding over his shoulder. Kim knew without being told that his greatest fear was that he'd have to use the sword on Michael when and if they found him.

"Have you heard from Liam?" she asked him.

"No."

"That doesn't worry you?"

"It does. But Liam's one of the strongest in the clan, and if he's out of communication, it's for a good reason."

His words made sense, and so had Dylan's. But Kim shivered, some feeling in her gut bothering her. "We should find him."

"We should find Michael."

Kim nodded. Michael's mother must be going through hell. Kim remembered how her own mother had sobbed uncontrollably when she'd been told that Mark was dead. Mark had lingered in the hospital all night, giving them hope he'd survive, but in the end, he hadn't. Michael's mother must be living through that same hell of hope.

Kim nodded. Find Michael. That was top priority.

"It's easy," the feral Shifter said. "Go with it."

Liam gritted his teeth against profound pain. "Easy for who? Who the hell are you, anyway?"

"I was called Justin."

"Yeah? What are you called now?"

"Human names have no meaning for us anymore."

"Oh, for the gods' sake." Liam lay flat on his back on the cement floor, his limbs on fire. He felt the beast in him snarling and raging, but his body hurt so much it could snarl and rage all it wanted to. Lying still was a good thing.

Heat pressed on the warehouse, and Liam felt the tingle of an approaching storm. He sensed clouds building, the electricity that fused the air miles away.

"Where is the boy?" Liam asked

"Still here." The Lupine smiled. "I'm saving him for you, like I was told."

Liam then sensed Michael in the alley outside. The Lupine must have chased after him and tethered him. Liam tasted the boy's fear on the wind, arousing both Liam's protective nature and his innate instinct that the male offspring of another male had to be eliminated. The two feelings warred in him, escalating his confusion.

"And why haven't you rid yourself of me as I lay here helpless?" Liam asked.

"I know my place in the hierarchy. You will lead us to greatness."

"You've lost it, mate."

"You're the leader. I smell it on you. You defeated the

only one greater than you, and now no Shifter can best you. I'm weak, but you will make me strong."

"Shite." Liam's neck felt like fire and at the same time, strangely light. Justin peeling away Liam's Collar had been the worst agony Liam had ever felt in his life. He'd screamed as the metal had unfused from his skin, his mind clouding with nothing but pain. When the fog cleared he'd found himself flat on his back, unable to move.

"The pain will go away," Justin said. "And then you'll be free."

"Terrific."

"Shifters are strong, my master. Stronger than any human will ever be. Why should we be slaves to them? When they put Collars on us, they only made us stronger."

Liam felt weak as a flea. "How did you figure that?"

"You feel it, don't you? The instincts you suppressed for so long, the strength you lost when the Collar was put on you. I bet at first you didn't have the strength to make it through a day without vomiting. We've learned how to live even with the oppression of the Collars. So when they come off, the instincts pour back, your strength comes back—twenty years worth of it in one go."

"Bloody hell."

Liam knew Justin was right, as crazy as the man sounded. His strength was slowly returning to his limbs, whatever drug he'd been given starting to wear off. Liam's sense of smell and hearing seemed sharper than ever, and the growing storm pounded at his brain.

The heightened scent ability was a little unfortunate, since Justin hadn't bathed in a long, long time. Justin didn't seem to mind, but then ferals had different ideas about cleanliness. To hell with that. Even if Liam were now feral, he was still taking showers.

Liam worked to mask his raw fear, and raw fear covered the killing instinct rising inside him. All his protectiveness was quickly ebbing. Michael was not his offspring. He should kill the cub while he could. Liam fought the urge with difficulty.

I am so screwed.

Liam thought of Kim, how terrified she'd be if she could know the thoughts that whirled through his brain.

Mate. Mine.

Liam wanted her—on her back, on her hands and knees, he didn't care. He wanted her here so he could bury himself inside her. Over and over again until she and her sassy mouth knew who had mastered her.

No, I'd never hurt her.

Kim would give him children, his brain ground on remorselessly. As many as Liam wanted. Birth control be damned. He'd find some way to counteract it and never allow her to take it again. He'd lock her in the attic room of his house until she obeyed. It was big up there— Connor could take Liam's room. And Liam would move into the master suite after he killed Dylan.

Oh, father god, help me.

Dylan should die. He was defeated, Liam now leader of the pride. Justin had known that without being told. Dylan should be driven out where he'd face death alone—or he could be given the dignity of letting Liam break his neck.

Glory would mourn him. But Glory was a be-damned Lupine, and who cared how much she howled? If she loved Dylan so much, she could join him.

Liam rolled over and pressed his face to the floor. *This isn't me. These aren't my thoughts.*

It's inside you. It's what's right. Give in to it.

"No!" he shouted.

Justin laughed. "I went through that too. It's much more fun to go with it."

Liam hated Justin's laugh. He hated the male for doing this to him. Liam's Collar lay on the floor about ten feet away. It was nothing but a piece of silver and black chain with a Celtic knot on it, a harmless bit of metal. Without it, Liam was free.

Liam climbed to his feet. Pain still gripped him, but it was starting to recede. He fixed his gaze on Justin.

Justin grinned. "You see? You're getting stronger. I'll show you how the Collars work, and we can go back to Shiftertown and start freeing Shifters. You're stronger than this Fergus, now. I can feel it. It won't take you long to kill him."

Liam growled. Justin backed up some more and let out a growl of his own.

Weak, mewling bastard who's made me want to kill my own father and make a slave of my mate.

Justin growled again, this one defensive. A growl of fear.

Wherever he'd come from, Justin must have been fairly far down in his hierarchy. He smelled wrong, weak, evil.

Liam followed Justin's advice and let the feral beast come. All the thoughts that had been spinning in his head focused into one specific thought, and Justin was its target.

Liam leapt, and Justin started to scream.

Chapter Twenty-one

Sean took Kim to the east side of Shiftertown, speaking little but tight with tension. Dylan remained behind, saying it was his job to keep coordinating the search.

"These streets are a maze," Kim said anxiously as they turned down yet another block.

"We can't search as well in a car."

"No kidding."

The roads were narrow and potholed, and blind alleys ran behind buildings like a maze without end. This part of Austin had been more or less abandoned when the Shifters moved in nearby. Kim had been a kid at the time, but she remembered her father saying that thriving businesses had moved out of the area and left it to Shifters and the homeless.

Not many homeless were around, which was odd. It was true that in the summer, vagrants left southern cities, like migrating birds, to find the cooler climes of the north. Even so, many stayed, panhandling from prosperous businessmen and politicians in downtown Austin. None lingered out here. Was that because they thought the pickings wouldn't be good or because they feared Shifters?

Whatever menace they felt, Kim picked it up as well. The humid air bristled with electricity, a prelude to a storm. She glanced at the horizon and saw that dark clouds were indeed building, thunderheads ominous. Austin didn't get many tornadoes, but some came through on occasion, and those clouds looked ready to play. All the more reason they needed to find Liam and Michael.

"I hope we find Michael before Nate and Spike do," Kim said. "I know they're helping, but I don't trust them. And I can't believe his name is Spike."

"He was a *Buffy* fan."

Kim had a surreal vision of Tattoo Guy eating popcorn and cheering on Buffy and her pals, and wanted to laugh in nervous hysteria.

Sean, Shifter-fashion, would not let Kim walk ahead of him. He turned down yet another alley, shadows gathering in it from the storm and the coming night, and stopped so abruptly that Kim ran into his back.

"What?" she demanded.

"Call Dad."

"Mind telling me why?" Kim pulled out her cell phone as she tried to peer around him.

"We've found Michael." Sean walked slowly into the alley.

Kim's phone read "no service." Damn wireless providers. Perfect when you were in the middle of a teeming city where there were plenty of other ways to communicate, useless out where you needed them the most.

She *could* walk back down the long alleys behind the crumbling buildings until she found a good spot. Alone. Without Sean and his mean sword to protect her.

Kim ducked into the alley behind Sean. If they'd found Michael, they could grab him and hightail it out of here.

Sean slipped his sword out of its sheath without breaking stride. *Oh, no. Please, no.*

Kim raced after him, her sandals pattering on the

broken asphalt. She reached the small body stretched out on the pavement the same time Sean did and went down on her knees beside him.

"Michael." Kim lifted him, breathing a sigh of relief to find him warm, his small heart beating. "Oh, thank God."

Michael whimpered, and Kim held him close. The boy's eyes were tightly closed, as though he'd withdrawn far into himself. Kim cradled him, rocked him, pressed her cheek to his hair. One of his hands was manacled, the chain stretching to a ring in the brick wall.

"You're all right, sweetheart," she said. "I have you. Sean, can you get the chain off him?"

Sean didn't sheathe the sword. "Something's dead."

"What?"

Sean's nostrils flared, and his eyes went white. Gripping his sword, he kicked the rest of the rotten boards free from the open doorway and ducked into the shadows of the building. A second later, Kim heard him exclaim violently.

Kim stood up. Michael clung to her, whispering, "The bad man. The bad man."

"What bad man, Michael?"

He didn't answer. The tether let her carry him just inside the shaded doorway. A wide warehouse floor opened out in front of her, an empty room a couple of stories high. Texas dust coated the floor and hung in the air.

Sean stood over a body sprawled in the middle of the floor. The man was large and naked, with shreds of clothes around him. Kim couldn't see his face, and fear stabbed through her.

"Liam?" she asked, heart in her throat. *Please, please, no.*

"No," Sean said. "I've never seen him before. But he's Shifter, and he's dead."

Sean solemnly raised the sword, point down, the hilt between both hands. He whispered words Kim couldn't catch as he brought the blade down into the Shifter's chest. Air around the fallen man seemed to shimmer. Then, as had the Shifter who'd attacked Kim in her bedroom, its body crumbled to dust.

"He was feral." Liam's rich voice rolled out of the shadows. Sean straightened and turned, and Liam himself walked toward them from the back of the warehouse. Kim went slack with relief. "He told me Fergus and Brian were experimenting on him," Liam went on. "They found a way to remove his Collar. That's what Brian was doing the night his girlfriend was killed, and that's why he couldn't tell anyone where he'd really been."

Kim put Michael down on the cool pavement, smoothed his hair, and reassured him she'd be right back. The boy lay down and curled into a ball, and Kim hurried inside. "Liam."

Sean put a large hand on Kim's shoulder and yanked her back. Kim collided with Sean's chest, and his hard hand kept her pinned.

"What are you doing? Let go of me."

Sean didn't release her. Liam kept walking toward them. He was shirtless, and angry scratches bled across his chest. But he didn't move as if he was hurt; he walked slowly, like a lion stalking its prey, every step deliberate, focused.

"Don't touch her," Liam said clearly to Sean.

Kim tried to start forward again, but Sean's iron grip held her back. "No," he said in her ear.

Liam stopped. "I said, *get your fucking hands off her.*"

Kim went ice-cold. Sean let go of Kim's shoulder, but he didn't step away. "Let her take Michael home."

"Better idea. You run like hell and leave Kim and the boy to me."

Kim's heart pounded. "Liam, what is the matter with you?"

Liam walked into the light. His eyes were fixed, glittering, wrong. Around his throat was an angry red line where his Collar had been.

"He's feral," Sean said grimly.

"Oh, God."

Kim's heart pounded. No wonder Fergus wanted Brian dead; no wonder he'd told Brian to plead guilty and face the consequences. Fergus couldn't risk that Brian wouldn't tell a courtroom about their experiments on the Collars. *Shit*.

The Liam who stood before them was nothing like the Liam Kim knew. His warm smile, his loving blue eyes, the compassion that usually radiated from him— all had been wiped away. This man had hatred in his eyes, primal rage, the need to kill. He'd killed the feral in there and left Michael chained.

"Liam," she whispered.

The Lupine who'd invaded Kim's bedroom had terrified her. Having Liam's white-blue gaze trained on her now was ten times scarier. No other Shifter was powerful enough to stop him, and Liam knew it.

"Run away, Sean Morrissey," he said. "Or I'll kill you too."

"I have to stay. I'm the Guardian." Sean went on in a low voice, "I already sent one of my brother's souls to eternity, Liam. Please, please don't make me have to do it to you."

"You stood back and let him die."

Kim gasped. "Liam."

Sean flushed. "How the hell would you know, Liam? You weren't even there."

"I know you, Sean."

Sean's rage crackled, and the storm outside answered with a rumble. "Fuck you, Liam. Kenny died while you played good little deputy to a man you loathe."

"And Fergus will pay for that."

"Stop it!" Kim put herself between the two Shifters—not a reassuring place to be. "I know you're not thinking clearly right now, Liam, but fighting Sean isn't going to help. Kenny died, and I'm sorry, but you two killing each other won't bring him back. Do you think that's what he would have wanted, you remembering him by blaming each other?"

Liam's gaze swiveled to her. Being pinned with that stare had to be one of most frightening things that had ever happened to her.

She'd had scx with this man, watched him while he slept, held him when he hurt. Somewhere inside that walking menace was the Liam who mourned his dead brother, who teased Kim and worried about the missing Michael, who grieved that he'd hurt his father.

Please don't let that all be a sham. Please let that man still be in there.

Please let me reach him.

"Don't leave me," she said to him. "I love you."

Liam didn't move, didn't betray any emotion. "It's not love. You're my mate. We have the mate bond."

She put her hands on her hips. "I'm not a Shifter, thank you very much. I have emotions, not instincts, not mate-bonds. If I say I love you, that's what I mean. At least, I love Liam."

"Emotions are instincts. You dress them up and write songs about them, but that's what they are."

"Oh, way to romance a girl. I liked you better with the Collar."

"Of course you did. Because you could control me."

"Like anyone could ever control *you*, Liam Morrissey. The man who does whatever he pleases, Collar be damned."

Sean leaned down to her. "Do me a favor and run like hell instead of provoking him."

Liam roared. "I *said*, don't touch her!"

Michael started crying. Sean backed off. Kim headed for Michael, and found Liam blocking her way. She hadn't seen him move, but suddenly there he was, right in front of her.

"Michael's hurt and scared," Kim said to him. *Right there with you*, kid. "Let me take him home. His mother is worried."

"Sean, get the boy out of here. Before I give in to my instincts and kill him, and you."

Kim folded her arms, trying a glare. "What, you mean you haven't given in to your instincts already?"

"No. Sean, *do it*."

Kim sent Sean a shaky look. "I agree with him. Please get Michael out of here."

"And leave you here with *him?* Are you insane?"

"Liam is right about the mate-bond thing," Kim said. "I don't think he'll hurt me."

"You don't *think* so?" Sean asked. "Not very convincing."

"Stop arguing. Michael has a mother worried sick about him, and he needs to go home. I'll be fine." She glanced at Liam. "I'm pretty sure."

"Kim, I've never seen him like this. He wasn't like this before we took the Collar. This is—something else."

"The instincts are enhanced," said a new voice.

Fergus pushed himself from the wide door frame where he'd been leaning and strolled inside. His own Collar was still intact, thank goodness, but he moved confidently, as though he knew he'd done something clever.

"See, this is why you shouldn't argue," Kim said to Sean. "You lose your window of opportunity to get away."

"Says the woman who never shuts up," Fergus said.

Kim turned what she hoped was a fearless gaze on Fergus. "Just what I need. Another asshole to make my day complete."

"Your mate has a mouth," Fergus said to Liam. "You need to teach her manners. If you don't, I will."

Liam pivoted to face Fergus, his boot heel turning on the gritty cement floor. Fergus stopped, his body coming alert.

"Then again," Kim said. "I might enjoy this."

The world had gone to hell. The smell of death clogged Liam's nostrils, despite Sean already sending the feral's body to dust. He smelled fear as well. Watery terror from the cub. Fear from his own brother. Fear from Kim, his lover, his pride mate.

Fergus's fear was the strongest of all.

The whole place stank of terror, enough to gag him. If Liam killed all of them, except Kim, he could get rid of the smell.

A little corner of his brain tapped him. *What the hell is the matter with you?* Sean was right—it hadn't been like this before the Collar. They'd lived freely, hunting when they wanted to, going hungry when there was no food to be had. They'd huddled together—three brothers, father, and mother—warming one another, playing together in the good times, sticking together in the bad. Loving each other.

Now Liam hated every Shifter in this room, Fergus especially. He didn't hate Kim, but she drove him the most crazy. He wanted to get her away from the others, to keep her safe. They wanted her—Shifters needed mates, and Sean had never claimed a mate. Sean was a danger.

The cub was a tiny thing, no threat, but it was the offspring of another Shifter. *Kill it*, Liam's senses whispered.

Fergus wanted Liam to kill the cub, then kill Sean. Liam knew it, and he didn't know how he knew it.

Fergus wanted power, Fergus wanted Kim, and most of all, he was afraid of Liam.

Ergo, Fergus should die first.

"The Collars were programmed to suppress everything that makes us who we are," Fergus was saying. "The Fae who made them hated Shifters. And understood them. Removing the Collars will remove that suppression and make us powerful. Unstoppable."

"And crazy as hell," Kim said. "Look at him."

Fergus couldn't look at Liam. His gaze slid sideways, back to Kim. "He senses his mate. He wants to fuck."

"Wipe that disgusting look off your face," Kim said. "I don't even want you *thinking* about us like that."

"Shut up, human. You'll be his slave, and that's all you'll be. He'll screw you until you die pushing out his cubs, and then he'll find another female to give him more. It's what we do."

"I'm sure your mates would be happy to hear that."

"My mates know their place."

"I see," Kim said. "Is this how you plan to take over the world? Repulsive imagery and insults?"

"We're far stronger than humans. Without the Collars, we'll quickly suppress those who suppressed us."

"If your plan is so terrific, why is *your* Collar still on?" Kim asked him.

Fergus gave her a deprecating look. "The leader of

the clan couldn't be risked. We first needed to know that removing the Collars wouldn't simply kill us."

"How many did it kill?" Sean asked. The storm outside was building, the pressing humidity cut by an icy breeze.

"One or two."

"Did it make one victim so crazy he went out and killed a Shifter woman and her cubs?" Sean went on.

Fergus's eyes flicked sideways. "There were complications. You took care of him."

"Sure," Kim put in. "After he attacked me in my house."

"He wouldn't have if you hadn't smeared your scent all over Liam," Fergus said in disgust. "It smelled a rival's mate."

That's why the thing was so fast and so good at tracking, Liam thought. *It was a Collared Shifter, made crazy by having its Collar ripped off.*

"I didn't know that feral," Sean was saying. "Or this one. Where did they come from?"

"New Orleans. I offered them something better than hiding out in the bayous."

"Great offer," Kim said. "'Come to Austin. First we'll make you insane, then we'll kill you.'"

"No," Sean said, voice tight with fury. "He no doubt offered them mates, their pick. Maybe the chance to move up in the hierarchy. My guess is they were low in their packs in the first place. And they were Lupines. If something went wrong—death or madness—they were only bloody Lupines."

"I offered them freedom," Fergus growled.

"Free to be hunted like you were in the past?" Kim asked.

Fergus's face darkened. "Free as we were before humans rounded us up like animals. We had the run of the land. We feared no one. Humans took that away from us. All I'm doing is taking it back."

"We were hungry," Sean said, his voice quiet. "Remember? Winters with no food, watching family die, watching cubs not make it until spring?"

"And if we had humans feeding us, being our slaves, not the other way around, that wouldn't happen."

"Dream on," Kim broke in. "Shifters are strong and hard to kill, but not impossible. I'm sure machine guns would do the trick. Is that what you want to see happen? Your pride mates mowed down by a SWAT team?"

"It won't happen if you're the slaves, you stupid woman. Liam, you might want to consider a different mate. Or at least use her up quick and get rid of her. I knew she was a pain in the ass the minute I laid eyes on her."

"You touch Kim, you die," Liam said clearly.

Everyone stopped talking. Liam walked toward Fergus, his boots loud on the stone floor. Fergus wanted to run—Liam saw that in the man's eyes, his stance, every inch of his body.

Liam wouldn't let him run. Fergus was his inferior; he had to obey Liam, and Fergus knew it, no matter how much he blustered. The instincts Fergus boasted about would force him to acknowledge his own weakness.

Kim had a power that Shifters lacked: the power to see all sides of a situation clearly, no matter how scared she was or how angry. She could argue with conviction, she could find a flaw in the other person's obsession and tap it until he opened his mind and saw what she saw.

Fergus would never see anything clearly. But Liam did. At least, Liam had before Justin had ripped off his Collar and made his brain scramble.

Liam's emotion and instinct warred with his reason, and none of them won. The wind outside grew colder, a bad storm for certain. Liam smelled the icy hail in the clouds, electricity that would fork down on the city at any moment.

One thought stood out from the others: Fergus had to be stopped. If Liam let Fergus go today, he would continue to push to "free" the Shifters, continue his awful experiments, making his victims crazed and violent while he honed the process. Fergus couldn't control his ferals yet, and, Fergus-like, he was trying to make other people clean up his mess. For him, the end always justified the means.

"Kim is right," Liam said, surprised his voice was so calm. "You are an asshole. You'll set Shifter against Shifter. We'll kill each other long before the humans even know there's trouble. We'll each want *our* families to survive, and ours alone. Our gene pool, our pride. The Shiftertowns, the living with other species—you're right, that's artificial."

"Exactly my point," Fergus said. "We get Sean's Collar off him, we get the Guardian—who can stop us?"

"I can." Liam came to a halt in front of Fergus.

He saw Fergus's pupils change to slits, his nostrils widen, his body emanate fear. He was not far shy of wetting himself. He tried to cover it by puffing out his chest with false bravado. "You can't touch me. I'm your clan leader."

"You are weak." Liam's voice was completely flat.

"I outrank you," Fergus said abruptly. "It's me first, then Dylan, then you. You can't beat me."

"Liam fought Dylan and won," Kim said. "Last night."

"What?" Sean stared.

Fergus's face whitened until it was almost green. "You don't know what you're talking about, girl. No one can best Dylan. Only me."

Kim went on. "You've been out of the loop. Liam defeated his dad. Liam isn't happy about it, but he did."

"Shit," Sean whispered.

"That doesn't matter," Fergus tried. "I am still clan leader."

"You are nothing." Liam sounded strange, even to himself. "I have no ties to anyone outside my family. Michael would be easiest to kill. But I think it's more important to kill you."

"Crap." Sean braved Liam's wrath to grab Kim and pull her well out of the way of Liam and Fergus.

Liam fought the urge to take Kim back and rake his claws across Sean's face. He forced himself to let Sean go; Sean was protecting Liam's mate from the enemy. Fergus would use Kim to distract Liam, and Sean was right to get her out of the way. Liam's bloodlust still wanted him to throw Sean down for touching her, the need burning through him.

Deep down, his love for Sean, his brother, boiled up, wanting his attention. It showed him visions of himself and Sean and Kenny, playing together as cubs, wrestling until they fell asleep in a pile in exhaustion. When they were older, talking about the world and speculating on females and what it would be like to be with one. Celebrating when Kenny took a mate, and again when Sinead became pregnant. Sean and Liam holding each other the day Kenny had died, weeping profusely.

Memories of love, frustration, joy, and family were being erased by the adrenaline, the need to fight. Fergus wanted to do this to all Shifters everywhere. He'd destroy them.

Liam fixed on Fergus again. He toed off his boots and peeled away his T-shirt. Fergus watched with a sneer, then smiled and began yanking off his own clothes.

Fergus attacked while Liam was still shifting. Liam

rolled out of the way, his limbs crackling and stretching, muscles moving into new positions. Fergus leapt again, and this time, Liam spun out of reach and came to his feet as his wild Fae-cat.

Liam couldn't stop his roar. It came from deep within, the beast finally free. It proclaimed that this place was *his,* not only the warehouse or Shiftertown, but everything for miles: the city, Hill Country, as far as Liam could roam. He was clan leader, and Fergus was nothing. As it should be.

The roar shook the building. Beams shifted, and loose bricks and plaster rained to the floor. Michael started screaming, his screams becoming yowls as he shifted into Feline form. Sean dragged Kim outside, straight into a pouring rain.

Liam closed his mouth, shook out his body, and leapt on the terrified Fergus.

Chapter Twenty-two

"Can you get him free?" Kim yelled at Sean, over the frenzy of violence inside the warehouse.

"If he'll hold still." Sean grabbed the chain that had been linked to the wall. Michael continued to snarl and thrash, the manacle cutting into his paw.

"Michael." Kim knelt next to him and reached for him but got scratched for her pains. "Michael, sweetie. It's all right."

Michael knew damn well it wasn't all right. Inside, two enormous wildcats fought for dominance, and they wouldn't stop until one was dead. Their snarls sounded over the thunder that boomed through the alley. The building heaved when the two battling Shifters smashed into a wall.

If Fergus wins, he'll kill the rest of us. Or maybe Fergus would keep Kim alive to be his sex toy, which was not something she wanted to think about. Still less did she want to think about Liam losing, dying, Sean having to send him to dust.

Sean yanked the chain, hook and all, from the wall. Michael yowled, then took off down the alley, the chain dragging behind him.

"He'll run home," Sean said. "You go too, Kim."

"I'm not leaving Liam."

"Kim, damn it, I don't know what's going to happen in there."

"Why don't *you* go? Round up Dylan and everybody to come and stop Fergus."

"With Liam like that? Too dangerous."

"At least you'd be safe. Fergus won't let you live, and Liam keeps thinking you want me for yourself for some reason. He might kill you in his frenzy."

"Oh, and you'll be safe from him, will you? I'm staying, Kim. I'm the Guardian."

He meant he'd have to dispatch the loser with his magic sword, sending his soul into the next world. From Sean's grim look, he feared it would be Liam.

"Then I'm staying too," Kim said. Inside, the two Shifters fought like crazy, foam and blood flying. "I love him."

"Fine then. We'll die together."

Sean marched back into the warehouse. The rain changed to a pelting of pea-sized hail, bouncing on the alley floor.

"Perfect," Kim muttered.

The hail came down so fast it piled on the pavement before it could melt. Kim ducked into the shelter of the building, afraid and angry.

The two Shifters rolled over and over, and Sean stood back like a referee, his sword ready. Weeks ago, Kim wouldn't have been able to tell the fighting wildcats apart, but she knew Liam now. He and Fergus were matched in size, but Liam's cat was thicker with muscle, his coat darker, his eyes a deeper gold. Right now his eyes glittered with hatred, and his teeth were fully extended as he snapped them at Fergus's neck.

Fergus scrambled out of the way, half shifting back to human to do so. Liam followed him, pinning him again. The wildcats clawed and bit. This was worse than the fight between Liam and Dylan, because there'd never been love lost between these two. Rage and hatred burned in the thickly humid air.

Thunder boomed outside, and then a bolt of lightning struck the roof. Kim screamed as bricks came down around her.

She saw Liam turn to her, drawn from the fight. In that moment, Fergus, his hide nothing but bloody strips of skin, pounced on Liam's back. His mouth was open wide, jaws ready to snap Liam's spine in two.

Sean shouted. Kim couldn't hear him over the thunder; she just saw his mouth open. Liam whirled in time, closing his teeth on Fergus's throat. He ripped, and blood sprayed across the floor.

Fergus went down in a heap. Liam stepped back, his fur red with Fergus's blood, and roared his victory. His eyes held fire, joy, and triumph.

Sean walked forward with his sword. Liam stopped him, rising into his human form as he moved, his body covered in scratches and angry bruises. He went to Fergus and nudged him with his foot. The wildcat's body flopped against the floor, blood spilling from a pool beneath it.

Liam turned away, contempt for his fallen enemy in every movement. As soon as his back was turned, Fergus whipped to his feet, bellowing in dying rage as he launched himself at Liam. Kim shrieked.

But Sean was there. He stepped between Fergus and his brother, and caught Fergus's leap on the Guardian's sword.

Fergus's wildcat eyes widened as the sword went through his chest. He'd been dying already, and the blade completed it. The body fell to the ground, silent and still. Chanting in a language Kim didn't know, Sean slowly withdrew the blade. The big cat shimmered, then crumbled to dust.

"You weren't supposed to do that," Liam snarled at Sean. "His final breath should have been mine."

"Yeah, well, I've done it." Sean's stance was defiant. He'd have done anything, the tiny rational part of Liam realized, to keep from having to send a second brother to the Summerland.

Again his love for Sean and the wildcat's jealousy warred within him. "Go," Liam said. "If you don't, I might kill you, and I don't want to lose you too."

"Kim," Sean said.

Liam's white-hot rage rose. "Kim stays with me."

Sean strode for the door, moving fast. "Kim," he said again.

"It's all right. I'll stay."

Her voice was quiet, a cool note amid the heat. Sean gave Kim one last look, then made himself sheathe the sword and duck out into the deluge.

Liam was across the floor, pulling Kim against him before Sean's footsteps faded.

"Kim." He loved saying her name.

"Are you hurt?"

"I don't know, and I don't care." Liam pressed Kim against the brick wall.

He wanted her with an intensity he'd never felt before. She was his mate, his, forever. A dim part of Liam's mind kicked him. *You love her. Don't hurt her.*

"You should get away from me," he said.

"What?"

Liam focused on her eyes. They were beautiful, wide and blue. Like an Irish lake, he'd thought once. He hadn't changed his mind.

"Don't let me hurt you."

Kim touched his face. He flinched, then made himself accept her touch. "I don't want to go," she said. "Besides, it's frigging hailing out there."

"I can't go slow. I can't be *nice*."

She smiled and laced her arms around his neck.

She was shaking, but her eyes were soft. "Sounds like fun."

"Kim."

"Liam." She kissed the tip of his nose. "I don't want to go slow. I need you."

He kissed her. The bricks scraped his arms as he shielded her from the wall. She wrapped her legs around his hips, her skirt riding up her thighs. It was easy to shove aside the elastic of her thong, to find her opening with his cock. She sucked in a breath, eyes widening, as he slid firmly into her.

How could he have ever thought that sex in human form was boring? He was content never to do it as a wildcat again. Kim was hot and wet, so easy to enter. She arched against him, her nipples rubbing him through her thin shirt. Liam shielded her from the wall with his arms, the bricks abrading his already bloody skin.

His adrenaline hadn't cooled from the fight. He *needed* this mating. Liam's heart rocketed, his blood hot.

Kim's sheath clenched him, her body and his fitting together perfectly. His mind went blank. All he felt was Kim, all he smelled was her body and her sex, her breath, her hair. He licked her face. He tasted her neck. He thrust into her, his blood pumping. Outside, lightning crackled, blinding flashes followed by booms of thunder. The hail fell like bullets on the roof, balls of ice bouncing in through the wide door.

"Liam. *Yes.*"

Liam squeezed his eyes shut and leaned his forehead on the wall. He shoved himself into her as though he wanted to crawl inside her and be part of her. His shoulders bunched; his breath burned in his lungs.

Kim shuddered in climax, her feet around his buttocks. The heels of her sandals grated his skin, and he didn't care.

Still holding her with one arm between her and the wall, Liam pounded his fist into the brick. Another lightning strike lit the world, and Liam came.

Sweat poured from him, his body on fire. Kim was screaming, and Liam heard his own voice ring through the warehouse. He was falling. Kim, he had to catch her.

He landed flat on his back, Kim's soft body on top of his. The movement slid him out of her hot sheath, and he groaned with loss.

Kim smiled down at him. "Holy shit. That was . . . *good*."

Liam wanted to answer her, tell her it was the best he'd ever had, that he loved her. He could only gasp for breath. The pain of his fight, the bewilderment of his flooding instincts, robbed him of his voice.

Kim closed her hand on him, and he groaned again.

"You're still hard. I thought you came."

Liam nodded. "I did." Gritting his teeth, he turned her over to put her beneath him and entered her once more.

Sex had never been like this before. Not free-for-all, no-holding-back, wet and messy sex. Kim laughed with it.

Not to mention having it on a bare cement floor with a naked, half-crazed, hard-bodied Shifter on top of her while a hailstorm raged outside. Another lightning bolt could strike the building and bring it down on top of them, and Kim didn't care.

"I love you, Liam," she shouted.

He opened his eyes. Once beautiful blue, they were now Shifter gray-white.

Kim would be afraid later. Right now, she was as crazed as he was. Was this what he meant by *mating frenzy*?

Liam pumped into her for a few more minutes, then dragged in a breath and filled her with his hot seed. Liam collapsed on top of her, breathing hard, his body roasting. He lingered on her, kissing her face and hair, then rolled off onto his back, still breathing as though he'd just finished a ten-mile run.

They lay still for a long time, Liam's breathing hoarse, Kim too tired to move. Gradually the hailstorm slackened, the time between lightning strikes increasing. Thunder rumbled in the distance, the storm drifting away, following the river.

Liam didn't move, and Kim wondered if he'd dropped off to sleep. She propped her aching body on one arm. "Are you all right?" she asked.

Liam lay face up, eyes open, his breathing rapid. "I don't know."

"The storm's letting up. It's what my mother liked to call a 'wham-bam, thank you, ma'am' storm."

Liam didn't answer, didn't laugh.

"You know what the storm dying off means," Kim continued. "It means that Sean and your dad are going to come looking for us. I bet Connor and Glory will too. And Ellison. He was real worried about you when I saw him earlier. In fact, every Shifter curious about what happened to you will be showing up pretty quick."

Liam raked his sweating hair from his face. "They shouldn't."

"Like that's going to stop them."

"Kim." Liam's face twisted, and he wrapped his arms around his chest. "I need to find my Collar before they get here."

"Is that what you really want?" she asked in a quiet voice.

"Fergus was crazy. He'd have destroyed us."

Kim noticed he hadn't answered the question. "You

don't think Shifters can adapt to going without the Collar again?"

"Not like this." Liam's chest expanded with an agonized breath. "We'll kill each other. Gods, Kim, I wanted to kill Michael. I *needed* to. Even Sean. My own brother. And the feelings haven't gone away. If they come to get us, I'll fight. I'll kill until someone kills me."

"And me?"

He reached for her. "No. You, I just want to fuck."

"I should be flattered, but I have the feeling I wouldn't last very long. You have stamina."

"I'd hurt you. I've already hurt you." He touched her bruised lip.

"You didn't. Don't you get it, Liam? You could have, but you didn't."

"That's no guarantee, love. I want you so damn bad." He kissed her swollen lips and drew back, eyes flicking from white to blue to white again.

Kim touched the red line on his neck. Liam flinched but didn't stop her.

"Or you could go," she said softly. "Run away back to Ireland or something. Live free."

Liam closed his eyes, blotting out the awful look in them. "Not without you. I don't want to live without you." He bowed his head, resting on Kim's shoulder. "But Fergus was right. I'd use you until there was nothing left of you. I'd not be able to stop myself." He raised his head, expression anguished. "Don't you understand? If I'm this way, I can't have you."

Kim rubbed his arms, wishing she could tell him that everything would be all right. *You'll be fine, you'll get used to it, you'll learn to control your instincts.* But she had no idea whether it would be all right. The Lupine who'd attacked her in her bedroom had been the victim of Fergus's experiments, ready to slaughter Kim to torture Liam. She'd seen the way Liam had looked at innocent Michael and at his own brother, as though they were enemies he needed to destroy. She had no idea what kind of crazed being Liam would become.

"I can't tell you to put yourself into captivity again for me," she said. "I don't want you to."

"I hate the Collar. Kim, I hate it so much. It hurts us when we so much as think about the way we used to be. One surge of adrenaline and it's giving us pain. You can't know what that's like. Always living in fear of the pain."

"You're right. I don't know."

"Being free of it . . ." Liam slid his fingers and thumb around the mark where the Collar had been, his wild smile emerging. "It's a joyous thing, love. I can do anything I want, and no one can stop me."

"Not even me?"

"No. That's the trouble."

"Sean said you weren't like this before—before you all took the Collar, I mean."

"Not this out of control. Not with twenty years of need falling on me at once. But it *was* like this too. We were strong and free, and those few who knew about us were in awe of us. Even the Fae acknowledged our strength, that we no longer served their whims. That's what rankles most—the Fae helped to bind us. They've always wanted to bind us." Anger danced in his eyes, lines pulling the sides of his mouth. "We hate them for it."

"What about humans?" Kim made herself ask.

"Human beings are weak, short-lived. No threat." Liam's eyes eased back to the blue she'd fallen in love with. "The one I'm lying on now is so beautiful. And I love her."

"I'll help you escape, Liam. I want you to be free. Don't find the Collar. Please."

Liam closed his eyes again, tight. He shuddered, lips shaking, as though wave after wave of panic ripped through him.

After a long time, he opened his eyes again, and something in them had been defeated. "No, love. They need me here. And I never, ever want to wake up in the morning knowing that I hurt you."

Kim touched his face. The anguish in his voice a moment ago when he'd said he hated the Collar had been real. He hadn't mentioned his loathing before this, but Shifters were strong and could resign themselves to pain, and he'd probably seen no use in voicing his rage to Kim. Having the Collar off, feeling the pain evaporate for the first time in twenty years, must be incredible for him. She wasn't sure how he could even contemplate putting it back on.

"No one would blame you if you went," she said. "Dylan would take over again, like before, and Sean would still be Guardian. They'll look after Connor and everyone else. You know that."

"I'd blame me."

"But free, you could start working on how to liberate the rest of your kind."

Liam kissed her forehead. "No, love. Free I'd be thinking of only myself and how good it felt to be away from all this. I'd start despising them for being weak, find myself a pride of ferals and try to take over. A wonderful Shifter-man I'd be."

"You can't know that. Like you said, all these urges are built up. Maybe in time—"

"And maybe not." His voice went hard, and he rolled off Kim and to his feet. "We find the Collar."

Kim remained on the floor, staring up at his hard

body. He was beautiful—firm muscle, broad shoulders, chest dusted with dark hair, now damp with sweat. His skin was covered with scratches from the fight, but they were healing, even the deepest ones only angry red lines. The worst wound was around his neck, where his Collar had been.

As he forced himself to turn from Kim to look for the Collar, Kim knew that Fergus had never understood just how strong Liam was. He'd made the choice to give up his freedom to stay with his family and help them in their captivity. Fergus had sacrificed others in his cause; Liam was sacrificing himself, just as he had when he'd stepped forward and taken the whipping to spare Connor pain.

Kim got reluctantly to her feet, trying to brush off the worst of the dirt she'd rolled in. Liam was already looking, quick gaze darting everywhere as he skirted the dust in the corner that had been Fergus. He didn't show much remorse about killing his clan leader, but Fergus had been nuts. Also, she knew the man wouldn't have gone meekly home, promising to stop his experiments: *I'm sorry, Liam, you're right. I've been a bad Shifter.*

Kim thought about Fergus's mates, and the offspring Fergus had mentioned. Would they mourn him? Would they try to exact revenge on Liam or move on with their lives? What would Liam, as clan leader, do to them? Would all of those Shifters down in San Antonio accept him without rancor? This would be interesting to watch—*interesting* being a euphemism for *scary.*

Behind her, Liam said, "Here it is."

She swung back to find Liam holding the thin silver and black chain as if it was a poisonous snake. Kim chewed her lip as he gripped the ends, one plain, one with the Celtic knot, in his white-knuckled fists.

"Will it work?" she asked. "It's not broken?"

"Once it's on me again, it should. Justin said that Brian's experiments let him figure out how to unfuse the Collars from us, not disable the chips inside. He hadn't got that far, yet." Liam took a long breath. "This will hurt me, Kim. You should go."

"I'm not going anywhere."

"Maybe I just don't want you seeing me weak and pathetic, love. A Shifter's got his pride."

"Liam, I've seen you strong, crazed, violent, angry, happy, sad, and far gone in passion. I love every single one of those, especially the last one. Did you know your pupils widen when you come? It's like you want to take all of me in, forever. It's very sexy."

"Is it, now? Well, this won't be. It wasn't pretty the first time I put on a Collar, and I don't imagine this will be much better."

Kim folded her arms. "I'm not leaving. I'm your *mate*, remember? In the traditional human wedding ceremony, we promise to stick together for better or worse. That means not just when everything's pretty, but when it's bad, very bad."

"I'm thinking there's no line in there about watching your Shifter mate take his Collar."

"Not last time I checked, but the idea is the same."

Liam looked down at the Collar, chest rising sharply. "I can't lie to you, Kim. It's a bit easier knowing you're near me." He looked up, his eyes clear, dark blue, full of fear and full of love. "Wish me luck."

"I love you," Kim said.

A hint of his warm, wicked smile touched his mouth. "Love you too, sweetheart."

He studied the Collar a long moment, then took another sharp breath and lifted the chain to his throat.

Liam's muscles tightened as the Collar settled against his neck. Kim had no idea how the thing fastened, but as he touched the bare end to the Celtic knot, she heard a loud click, and then Liam screamed.

Cords stood out on his neck, and his entire body arched backward. He balled his fists and clenched his teeth, fighting the agony.

Kim rushed to him. Shifters comforted and helped each other with touch—maybe she could ease him a little bit if she could hold him. Liam thrashed as spasms racked his body, his screams becoming hoarse cries.

She reached for him. "Liam."

Liam focused on her, his eyes white-blue. "No, Kim. Stay back."

"You need me." Kim grabbed his wrists, but he snapped them away from her.

"I said *stay back*."

"And I said, you *need* me."

Kim darted between his hands and slid her arms around his sweating waist. His skin was ice-cold. She rubbed his back, trying to warm him.

"Kim, no."

"You need me," she repeated firmly.

Liam drew breath after shuddering breath. He stood stiffly, body shaking at the same time. Then with a cry of agony, he wrapped his arms around her and buried his face in her neck.

Chapter Twenty-three

How long they stood like that—arms locked around each other, Liam rocking in pain—Kim didn't know. She held him while his hot tears dropped to her shoulder, while he kissed her neck and held her as if he'd never let her go.

Kim heard shouting outside. She lifted her head to see that the warehouse had grown darker, the rain still pelting but more softly now, the storm over. Flashlights cut through the gloom, and then the tall forms of Sean and Dylan emerged out of the darkness. Others trailed behind them—Glory, Ellison, Connor, Nate, and Spike.

Dylan played his flashlight on the two of them in the middle of the warehouse, Liam filthy and naked, Kim in rumpled clothes and probably just as filthy.

She called to them, "He put the Collar back on and the pain is tearing him up."

Dylan approached, but the others hung back. Liam managed to lift his head, his eyes filled with incredible pain. "Dad."

Dylan stopped just shy of Liam, eyes troubled. "Do you want me, son?"

"Of course he wants you," Kim said. "You're his dad."

"He's clan leader now," Dylan said. "And pride leader. He can reject me if he wants."

"He won't." Kim shook her head. "He told me once that he wouldn't fight you because he loves you."

"That was before," Dylan said.

"Doesn't matter. People's status might change, but love stays the same."

Dylan opened his mouth to argue, but Connor jerked away from Ellison, who was trying to hold him back. The lanky boy charged past Dylan and threw his arms around both Liam and Kim. "Damn it, we thought Fergus would kill you," he sobbed.

The others tensed, Dylan taking a step back.

Liam looked up at Connor, his eyes wet. Connor held him tighter, and Liam's eyes flicked from feral white to beautiful blue. He wrapped an arm around Connor and pulled him close.

Like water released from a dam, the others flowed to them. Dylan clamped his arms around Liam and Connor, gathering them in. Sean laid down his sword and joined the group hug, followed by Glory, Ellison, and to Kim's astonishment, both of Fergus's thugs.

Kim's eyes filled as Sean leaned his head into Liam's neck. Kim could feel the warmth, the caring, in the huddle, heard the soothing words they whispered to each other. She was squished between Dylan and Liam, Ellison and Connor. She started to giggle. "A Kim sandwich."

Ellison laughed his big, booming Texas laughter. "Sounds good. Let's eat."

"You are so disgusting," Glory said to him. She had her arms firmly around Dylan's waist.

Ellison gave Glory a big kiss on the cheek. "You love it, darling. I say we all blow this place and go get shit-faced drunk."

"Damn straight," Spike said.

Liam's immediate family remained silent. Kim felt the energy flowing between them, love that had kept them alive and together all these years. And now they wanted her to be part of it.

"Drunk," Liam rasped. "You don't know how good that sounds."

The group began to part, slowly, smiling the unembarrassed smiles of people who'd shared a happy experience. Sean rubbed Liam lightly on the back and moved to pick up first his sword and then Liam's clothes.

Connor gave Liam one last squeeze, then backed off, wiping his eyes. Dylan was the last to leave. He held Liam's arms and looked straight into his eyes.

"Are you all right, Liam?"

"I will be."

"I know you will. You've been moving toward this moment all your life. It's yours now."

Liam put his hands on his father's shoulders. "With you at my back, Dad, there's nothing we can't do."

Dylan relaxed, as though he'd still been waiting for Liam's acceptance. "I'll be there." He pulled Liam down to him and pressed a kiss to Liam's forehead. He finally turned away, eyes full.

Liam reached for Kim's hand. "Are you all right? Did I hurt you, love?"

"I'm resilient." Kim kissed his lips, and Liam crushed her to him in a long, satisfying hug. "Let's go home," she whispered.

"Are you up to the walk?" Sean asked, handing Liam his clothes.

Liam hugged his T-shirt and jeans to his chest and looked around at the assembly, a hint of the old glint in his eye. "Are you telling me that none of you thought to bring wheels?"

"No," Connor said. "As soon as the storm let up, we ran out here."

"What, you were thinking you'd trundle me back in a wheelbarrow, all hurt and bloody? This is the planning of my friends and family."

"I'll run and get my car," Kim said. "There isn't room for everyone, but that's all right. I can take Liam home, at least."

Liam gripped her wrist. "No. Don't go yet."

His eyes were desperate. Kim gave him a reassuring smile and a little hug. "I won't leave you."

Glory swayed forward. She was wearing sturdy boots for once, though they had three-inch heels. "I'll get it." She plucked the keys out of Kim's fingers and gave Kim a big tooth-filled smile. "I'll take good care of it. Promise."

Liam lay in his bed in heavy sleep next to Kim for about four hours after they got home. Then he woke up, threw back the covers, and declared he needed to go to the bar.

"What for?" Kim demanded, not liking the absence of his warmth in the small bed.

"I've taken too many days off. The paperwork in the office must be a mess."

"*Liam.*"

Liam stopped in the act of leaning over for his pants, his delectable backside in full view. "I'm all right, love. Shifters heal fast."

Maybe their bodies did. "Why do you work at the bar at all? You don't seem to live paycheck to paycheck. And how did Fergus afford all that artwork in his basement? How did he even afford that huge basement?"

Liam sat back down, his eyes a mystery. "Shifters live a long time. We accumulate things."

"Like money and Old Masters paintings?"

"Like money and Old Masters paintings. Which Dad thinks should be sold to a museum."

"How are you going to explain where you got them?"

"We won't." Liam reached for his jeans again and pulled them up. "There are dealers who will work with us discreetly."

Kim sat cross-legged against the headboard. "Before I came down here the first time, I thought I knew every little thing about Shifters. I didn't know jack, did I?"

"No." Liam's smile flashed in the harsh lamplight. "I thought I knew all about humans. You taught me so much." He stopped. "I'm going to miss you, love."

Kim's heart skipped a beat, then gave a hard bang. "What do you mean, 'miss me'?"

Liam sank to the bed again, one blue-jeaned leg folded under him. The red gashes on his torso had closed, the heavy bruising already fading. A dark swirl of hair covered his chest and pointed to his navel, the indentation into which she'd slid her finger the night he'd first brought her up to his room.

"I want you to go home," he said. "Go back to living your own life."

She stared. "Hold on. For days you insist I stay here, whether I like it or not. Tonight, after all that's happened, not to mention the incredible sex, you're telling me to *go?*"

"Fergus is dead. His followers have gone home. His threat is removed. No one will be taking off any more Shifter Collars."

"You sound very sure."

"I am sure. I lead the clan now, which means our pride is now first. No other Shifter will dare harm you, whether they approve of you or not. My protection is on you, and no other Shifter can override that."

Kim slid out of bed. She wasn't wearing anything, but at the moment, it didn't seem important. "What about this mate thing? That's all gone now too?"

Liam smiled. "That will never be gone. We've been mated under the sun and moon, the mating recognized by the clan. We'll always be mated."

"So what does that mean?"

"For Shifters, it means I take no other mate. For humans, it means—nothing. A Shifter mating isn't valid in the human world; it's not marriage. I remember you telling me that."

"I meant, what does it mean to *you?*"

Liam looked away. "It means everything to me."

"Then why are you telling me to leave?"

Liam got to his feet, looked across the bed at her. "Because you can't stay. You've tried to pound it into my brain all this time why you can't. I'm a *Shifter.* I can love you with everything I've got, but I'll ruin you, and you know it. You'll lose your job, your friends, your respectability. I'm from the wrong side of the tracks, darling. Not from your world."

"It's not that simple—Shifters bad, humans good. I know that."

"*You* do. But the rest of the world doesn't. Not yet. Maybe in another twenty years, when people are used to us. Right now, I love you enough not to keep you here."

Suddenly cold, Kim reached for a long T-shirt and dragged it over her head. It was one of Liam's, too big for her and carrying his scent.

"Don't come over all altruistic on me, Liam Morrissey. Like you haven't put me through enough hell already. You made me love you, damn it. *Really* love you. Now you're saying, 'Thanks, Kim, go away'?"

"Do you think this is easy for me?" Liam asked. "When my Collar was off, I wanted nothing more than to lock you away upstairs and never let you go. No matter how much you screamed or begged or told me off, which is more likely what you'd do. I wanted to imprison you here with me. Mine. Forever."

"Your Collar is back on, now," Kim said.

"And that fact cancels everything out? It doesn't. I'm still feral. I always have been, always will be." Liam tapped the Collar around his bruised neck. "This keeps it down so I don't destroy myself, my people, and everyone I love. All Shifters are like me. Wild beasts in captivity. Not domesticated. There's a difference."

Kim folded her arms. "I'm not afraid of you."

"Then you're foolish. You saw me. I was ready to kill a child, my own brother, my father."

"But you didn't."

"Only because Fergus distracted me, love. Thank the Goddess he did, because he drew my fury. If he hadn't been there for me to fight, I would have destroyed everyone I loved."

"So you won't take your Collar off again," Kim said. "End of worry."

"But Fergus was right. We need to be free of the Collars someday. He was in too much of a hurry, but he wasn't wrong."

Kim balled her fists. "Make up your mind. Do you want the Collar on or off?"

"Shifters are getting stronger, love. We were dying off before, which is why we needed to capitulate with the humans and take the Collars. To let us live again, regroup, regain our strength. When we're powerful enough again, we'll rid ourselves of our chains, and be who we are supposed to be."

"And you think I have no place in that world?"

"No." Liam stood with his hands on his hips, his body still, eyes dark.

"You're lying to me," Kim said.

"I'm not."

"I'm not as good as you are at reading body language, but even I can tell you're coming up with excuses for sending me away. You think it's for my own good."

Liam whirled suddenly and punched the headboard. It cracked, wood splintering. "You're maddening, Kim, did you know that? Of course it's for your own good. You have your career, your life, your pretty house, your friends. I want you to have that. Find yourself a normal man, not one who might go crazy on you, not one who has to pretend to be a bar manager while he runs Shiftertown. Go home and be human."

"Just like that?"

"Yes. Go, Kim. Please."

"Doesn't it matter that I love you?" she asked, throat hurting.

"Yes, that matters. It matters a lot." Liam reached across the bed and touched the bruise on her lip. "And it's all the more reason I want you gone. I need to know I can't hurt you, ever again."

Kim stood still under his touch, her heart constricting. She'd broken up with men before, had sometimes done the breaking herself. She recognized Liam's look, the implacable expression of someone who'd made the painful decision to walk away and wouldn't be talked out of it.

"I don't want to go," she said. Kim knew how pathetic she sounded, but she couldn't stop herself.

"It makes me glad that you don't want to." Liam touched her lip once more, then took up his shirt and boots from the floor. "But it's all the more reason you need to."

He gave her another long look, as though he were memorizing her, then turned and walked out. He shut the door behind him, and a few minutes later, the front door's banging shook the house. Kim heard his motorcycle rev, heard its throb as he drove off down the street, the noise dying into the distance.

Kim stood by the bed for a long time, staring at the closed door. Tears choked her throat, but her burning eyes wouldn't shed any.

She heard the others downstairs, talking, their voices inquiring. Wondering where Liam was off to? Or had he told them he was sending Kim home?

Suddenly she wanted nothing more than to get out of there. Kim dressed with numb fingers, packed what things she'd brought here, and carried them down to her Mustang.

The last thing she saw as she backed out of the Morrissey driveway was Connor standing under the glow of the front porch light, his arms folded, a look of vast sadness on his face.

Kim arrived at her office early the next morning, dressed in a conservative gray suit.

"No Shifters today?" her secretary asked innocently.

"No, Jeanne." Kim's voice had gone cold and hard, the take-no-shit defense lawyer returning. "No more Shifters in the office. Sorry."

Jeanne, used to years of Kim's ups and downs, smiled at her. "Too bad. He sure was hot."

Kim had to admit that yes, he sure was. Her gut was so churned up that she didn't know what she was feeling. Loss, pain, sorrow, anger. Liam had thrown her out. That hurt. But hadn't Kim told Liam repeatedly that she couldn't stay? She wasn't certain who provoked the most anger, herself or Liam.

Once at her desk, Kim immediately dove into Brian's case. Arguing with the prosecutor's office helped keep her thoughts from Liam—from the traumatic fight in the warehouse, from the amazing sex afterward.

She worked all day, her businesslike suit and panty hose more confining by the hour. She'd gotten used to loose skirts and sandals far too quickly.

The next day wasn't any better, though the monotony was interrupted by a call from Silas.

"I talked to Liam," Silas told her. "He's agreed to let me interview him for the documentary, and for the feature stories for the newspaper. He's going to show me around Shiftertown himself."

"That's great." It really was great. Trust Liam to begin his rule of Shiftertown by doing what Fergus would have loathed. But Liam wanted the world to stop fearing Shifters, to move toward freedom. Showing the world what Shifters truly were was a first step.

A few weeks later, Kim's hard work and persistence finally paid off. With her tip on the jealous ex-boyfriend angle, her investigator had found out Michelle's ex had been boasting that he'd brought the Shifters to their knees and about his obsessive behavior toward Michelle before her death. He'd started calling her "the fucking Shifter-whore who'd got what she deserved." That was enough for police to reopen the case and bring the guy in again for further questioning. He'd been reluctant to talk about Michelle at all, until the detective revealed evidence of photos on the young man's digital camera of Michelle lying strangled on the floor. A vitriolic confession came pouring out. Michelle had betrayed him— with a *Shifter*. Michelle should die, and the Shifter should be ripped apart. If there were any justice in the world, he'd be given a medal for ridding the world of filth.

After that, it wasn't too difficult for Kim to get the

prosecutors to dismiss the case against Brian, who was released to a surge of publicity. Kim walked with him, under the scrutiny of black camera lenses the day he was freed, to where Sandra waited in her old car. Mother and son had a tearful reunion, but Kim could see Brian's grief over Michelle. Sandra had confirmed that Brian had been prepared to take Michelle as his mate, and her loss was hard for him. He'd truly loved her.

After seeing Brian off, Kim returned to her office and went to see her boss.

The head of the firm was a large man with graying hair and pictures of his wife and four children on his desk. "Good work, Kim," he said, a man who rarely praised. "But I doubt we'll be getting any more Shifter cases. People wanted Shifter blood, and we just made the prosecutor's office look stupid."

Kim shrugged, not caring about the damned prosecutor's office right now. "It doesn't matter. I came to tender my resignation."

"What?" His thick brows shot up. "Why? You've just won the biggest case of the year."

"I'm contemplating a business venture of my own. Human advocate and legal liaison to Shifters in the Austin–San Antonio area. Want in?"

Her boss sat there with his mouth open, then moved his nameplate from one side of his desk to the other, which he did when he got nervous. "Are you crazy, Kim? You're a good attorney. One of my best. You're on your way to a terrific career. You throw in with Shifters and you'll be finished."

"Shifter-human law needs to be reevaluated and changed," Kim said. "It will be a challenge, something to live for. You could make your mark as a champion of Shifter rights. You love defending people's rights."

He glanced at the photos on his desk. "But Shifterhaters can be dangerous, and I wouldn't be risking just myself."

Kim nodded, understanding. "Well, I don't have anyone but myself to risk. I'm tired of living an empty life, so I'm going to fill it doing something crazy like helping Shifters wade through the morass of law. Jeanne's agreed to go with me. She's training as a paralegal, and she's excited about getting a chance for more experience."

"She's as crazy as you are."

"Maybe," Kim conceded. "But that's what we want to do. Thanks for taking me on when I was a green law-school graduate."

"No problem," her boss said faintly. "Good luck."

Kim dragged in a breath as she left her boss's office, the words *Good luck* ringing in her head. She knew she'd need it.

Kim spent the next weeks cleaning out her office and finding space to rent for her new office, a tiny one with enough room for herself and Jeanne. The others in the firm agreed with the head, that Kim was crazy. Some admired her; some openly castigated her, Abel in particular.

Kim ignored them and bought office furniture. Jeanne was an enthusiastic partner and even helped take Kim's mind off her sorrows for five minutes now and again.

The first day Kim spent at her new office, Silas e-mailed her some video files for the Shifter documentary he was working on, asking for her feedback.

Kim played the files, her heart aching. There was a lot of footage of Liam smiling his warm smile and speaking in his deep Irish lilt, telling Silas what he wanted the world to know about Shifters. Dylan spoke too, giving the same details but in a different enough way that it didn't sound as though they'd worked it out beforehand. Kim knew they had. She also knew exactly what they had decided to leave out.

There was footage of how the Shifters lived from day to day, shots of Michael playing in his front yard. Michael was photogenic, and his cuteness radiated from the screen. Silas also showed Connor and his friends kicking a soccer ball around the backyards, Connor talking about his love of "football" and what a fan he was of the Irish national team.

Silas didn't show only sparkles and smiles, however. He talked to Shifters about the darker side of their lives—the high death rate of Shifter children, which had started to come down only in the last decade, the low fecundity of the females. He talked about how the different Shifter species didn't get along "in the wild" but had made concessions to live together in harmony. Ellison was particularly eloquent in that segment, looking handsome with his big cowboy hat and wide smile.

A group of Shifters did a Collar "demonstration," which proved that Collars worked well, and Silas showed a meditation by some Shifter parents for children they'd lost.

Kim viewed the files again and again, pausing on Liam's smile, his blue eyes assuring the viewers that Shifters were little different from humans.

She watched the recording far too often. And far too often, she opened her cell phone and looked at Liam's number, wondering if she should tell him all the things she'd decided.

"Call me anytime, love," he'd said, when he'd programmed the number into it weeks ago.

Damn Shifters.

In the cool of late September, Kim came home from her new office on a Friday and spent the weekend packing.

Sunday afternoon, she put everything in her car that she could fit. She'd get help with the rest. She closed the trunk, started the car, and drove back to Shiftertown.

Chapter Twenty-four

Liam knew the car was Kim's without looking up. He crouched in the driveway beside his motorcycle, wrench in hand, completing a few tweaks to his bike.

He'd ridden this motorcycle to the posh neighborhood north of the river every night for the last two months, cutting the engine before he reached the hill above Kim's house. He'd sit there for a long time, the bike silent between his legs, watching her lighted bedroom window. When the light went out, Liam would kiss his fingertips to it, then coast back down the hill and ride home.

The hole in his heart wanted to close in hope as she stopped the Mustang and climbed out. She wore the high-heeled sandals he liked, ones that made her bare legs sexy as hell.

He watched the legs out of the corner of his eye as she strode up the driveway, letting her scent flow over him as she walked past him.

Walked past him?

Liam looked around to see Kim shove a cardboard box at Connor, who'd bounded out of the house.

"Will you carry that in for me?" Kim asked Connor sweetly. "Put it anywhere. I have a couple more in the trunk."

Kim returned to the car, again moving past Liam without speaking to him. She reached through the open passenger window, giving him a view of her nice ass, and pulled out an overnight bag.

"Hello, Sean." Kim smiled as Sean came out of the house behind Connor. "Can you grab the suitcases in my backseat? They're heavy."

She waltzed up the driveway, a determined smile on her face, bag slung over her shoulder.

Liam wiped his hands, stood, and planted himself in her path. "And what would you be doing here?"

"Moving in. Don't worry, I'll pay for my share of the groceries."

Kim started to go around him, and Liam stepped in front of her again. "Why?"

"Don't argue with her, Liam," Connor said, carrying the second box from the trunk. He rubbed Kim's shoulder as he went past her, like a cat to a litter mate. "She's back to stay, where she belongs."

"She belongs with her own kind," Liam said sternly.

"Not anymore," Connor said. "We need her, Liam, you especially. You've been pissed off for weeks. Don't mess this up."

Sean, Liam's dear supportive brother, didn't offer any comment. He silently removed Kim's suitcases from the backseat and carried them inside.

Liam's breath hurt. Gods, Kim was beautiful. Her dark hair looked shinier than ever, her eyes a deeper blue, her full breasts making his hands itch to cup them. If he did that right now, he'd leave greasy handprints on her pretty white shirt, and wouldn't everyone laugh?

"Why, love?" he asked. "Why are you back to tear out my heart?"

She smiled. "It's got nothing to do with you. I want our kid to know its father, and when it first changes into a wildcat, he or she will need someone who knows what to do standing by."

Liam stopped. "Kid?"

"A little half-Shifter boy or girl. I don't know which; haven't had an ultrasound yet."

"Ultrasound . . ."

Kim laughed in true mirth. "You knocked me up, Liam Morrissey. Now you have to live with the consequences."

Connor came running out of the house, whooped, and punched the air. "Kim's pregnant! Woo-hoo!" He hurtled toward Kim, caught her in a hug and swung her off her feet. "I'm going to be a cousin!"

Connor's shouting drew people outside. Glory emerged first, sauntering down her porch stairs, her tight leopard-print pants startling. Dylan strolled out behind her. He'd moved in with Glory the day after Kim left, further emptying the house.

"Did I hear that right?" Glory called. "You're up the spout?"

Kim drew a breath once Connor finally put her down. "Confirmed by my gynecologist last week."

Liam kept wiping his hands on the rag. "I thought you took contraceptives."

"I was coming up on the end of my dose, and we had a lot of sex, Liam, if you recall. And maybe Shifter sperm are livelier than human's."

"Shite," Liam said around the lump in his throat.

More neighbors emerged onto front porches, and Ellison came around from his backyard, shirtless, his jeans covered with dirt and grass stains. When Ellison understood what was going on, he put his hands on his hips, threw back his head, and howled. Answering howls came from up and down the street.

Great. How long before the news reached the other side of Shiftertown? Five minutes? Two?

"I'm staying, Liam," Kim said. "Whether you like it or not."

"*Gods.*" Liam threw down the oily rag and caught Kim in his arms, damn the stains. He crushed Kim against him, lips finding her hair, her face, her mouth. "I love you, Kim. Don't ever leave me."

"That's the idea."

"I need you."

She rubbed his cheek. "I know."

Liam had driven her away to keep her safe, most of all from himself. But having her in his arms again, smelling her, tasting her, hearing her voice—it broke him, defeated the beast inside him. The feral in him crumpled as surely as Fergus had crumpled under the Guardian's sword.

Liam held her tighter. "You're all mine."

"You betcha."

Liam touched his forehead to hers. "I love you so damn much."

Kim grinned at him. "And I adore you."

Liam gave her a long, heartfelt kiss. She got into it, sliding her arms around him to cup his butt, snaking her fingers into his back pockets. She was a loving, warm, sexy woman. How'd he get so damn lucky?

Liam eased back from the kiss, licking the light bruise he'd already put on her lip. He'd learn how to be gentle with her, tender. And then he'd be wild. The sparkle in her eyes told him she wanted it both ways.

As soon as he raised his head, they were hit by the family. First Connor, still shouting, throwing his arms around both Liam and Kim. Then Sean, laughing, catching Liam in a bear hug, rubbing Kim's shoulders and kissing her cheek.

Dylan, his eyes full, holding Liam hard, then Kim. Kim gasped when Glory flung her arms around her, squeezing her.

"You did good, kid," she said.

And then Ellison, whooping and howling like the Lupine he was, jerking Liam off his feet in a rough embrace. "You virile shit, you. Taking the best woman for yourself."

"Watch it," Glory said.

Ellison draped his arms around Connor and Sean. "This calls for a beer." He started with them for the house, his way of leaving Liam and Kim tactfully alone. Glory followed, after a look at Dylan.

"Seamus," Connor was saying. "Patrick, maybe?"

"What are you talking about?" Ellison asked him.

"Names for the wee one. Eoghan, maybe?"

"Give the kid a break. Who the hell could spell that?"

The house swallowed them. Dylan put his hands on Kim's and Liam's shoulders. "The Goddess bless you both." He kissed Kim's forehead. "Thank you, Kim."

He smiled and walked away. Liam watched him, his heart full.

"Is he thanking me for getting pregnant?" Kim asked. "It wasn't difficult, with all the sex we kept having. You did as much as I did."

Liam pulled her against him again. She belonged there, felt so right fitted to him. "He meant for coming back to us. For keeping us a family."

"That wasn't difficult, either." She gave him a smile. "You're wrong about where I belong, Liam. This is the kind of family I had before my brother died, one of warmth and laughter, of knowing the house was full every night. It's what I've been looking for in the last decade or so, even when I didn't know it." Kim looked up at him, her blue eyes full of love. "I belong right here. With you."

She'd break his heart all right. Or maybe she'd finally heal it. Liam pulled her close, his lips meeting hers.

Damn, kissing the human way was good. How could he have never liked it before?

Because he'd never done it with Kim before.

Kim caught his lower lip between her teeth, and Liam felt the front of his jeans get unbearably tight. He murmured in her ear, "Do you think we can make it upstairs?"

"I'm all for trying." Her gaze turned sultry. "Besides, they're shouting so much, they'll cover up all the noise I plan to make."

Liam squeezed her, growling. "I love you, woman."

"Good to know."

They did make it past the mob and up the stairs. Dylan saw them go, but he only smiled quietly and turned away.

The door closed, the lock locked. Clothes came off, and Liam had Kim naked against him. His heart was whole, his brain clear, and his body melting with desire. Kim's smile put him over the top.

"Love you, Liam," she whispered.

"Always," Liam said brokenly. "I'll love you forever."

They had strong, bed-shaking, wet, and sweaty sex that drowned out even the revelry downstairs.

Liam's brother, nephew, friends, and every member of his clan never let them hear the end of it.

THE
BATTLE
SYLPH

Welcome to his world.

(CHECK OUT A SAMPLE:
www.ljmcdonald.ca/Battle_preview.html.com)

INTERACT WITH DORCHESTER ONLINE!

Want to learn more about your favorite books and authors?
Want to talk with other readers that like to read the same books as you?
Want to see up-to-the-minute Dorchester news?

VISIT DORCHESTER AT:
DorchesterPub.com
Twitter.com/DorchesterPub
Facebook.com (Search Pages)

DISCUSS DORCHESTER'S NOVELS AT:
Dorchester Forums at DorchesterPub.com
GoodReads.com
LibraryThing.com
Myspace.com/books
Shelfari.com
WeRead.com

New York Times Bestselling Author

ANGIE FOX

"Fabulously fun." —*Chicago Tribune*

A Tale of Two Demon Slayers

Last month, I was a single preschool teacher whose greatest thrill consisted of color-coding my lesson plans. That was before I learned I was a slayer. Now, it's up to me to face curse-hurling imps, vengeful demons, and any other supernatural uglies that crop up. And, to top it off, a hunk of a shape-shifting griffin has invited me to Greece to meet his family.

But it's not all sun, sand, and ouzo. Someone has created a dark-magic version of me with my powers and my knowledge—and it wants to kill me and everyone I know. Of course, this evil twin doesn't have Grandma's gang of biker witches, a talking Jack Russell terrier, or an eccentric necromancer on her side. In the ultimate showdown for survival, may the best demon slayer win.

"This rollicking paranormal comedy will appeal to fans of Dakota Cassidy, MaryJanice Davidson, and Tate Hallaway."
—*Booklist*

ISBN 13: 978-0-505-52827-8

✂ ☐ **YES!**

Sign me up for the Love Spell Book Club and send my
FREE BOOKS! If I choose to stay in the club, I will pay
only $8.50* each month, a savings of $6.48!

NAME: _____

ADDRESS: _____

TELEPHONE: _____

EMAIL: _____

☐ I want to pay by credit card.

☐ **VISA**   ☐ **MasterCard**   ☐ **DISCOVER**

ACCOUNT #: _____

EXPIRATION DATE: _____

SIGNATURE: _____

Mail this page along with $2.00 shipping and handling to:
Love Spell Book Club
PO Box 6640
Wayne, PA 19087
Or fax (must include credit card information) to:
610-995-9274

You can also sign up online at **www.dorchesterpub.com**.

*Plus $2.00 for shipping. Offer open to residents of the U.S. and Canada only.
Canadian residents please call 1-800-481-9191 for pricing information.
If under 18, a parent or guardian must sign. Terms, prices and conditions subject to
change. Subscription subject to acceptance. Dorchester Publishing reserves the right
to reject any order or cancel any subscription.